Praise for the Zoe C

"I loved *Bridges Burned*. The action starts on the first page never lets up. Zoe's on the case, and she's a heroine you'll root for through the mystery's twists and turns—strong and bold, but vulnerable and relatable. I adore her, and you will, too."

— Lisa Scottoline,
New York Times Bestselling Author of *Betrayed*

"New York has McBain, Boston has Parker, now Vance Township, PA ("pop. 5000. Please Drive Carefully.") has Annette Dashofy, and her rural world is just as vivid and compelling as their city noir."

— John Lawton,
Author of the Inspector Troy Series

"I've been awestruck by Annette Dashofy's storytelling for years. Look out world, you're going to love Zoe Chambers."

— Donnell Ann Bell,
Bestselling Author of *Deadly Recall*

"An easy, intriguing read, partially because the townfolks' lives are so scandalously intertwined, but also because author Dashofy has taken pains to create a palette of unforgettable characters."

— *Mystery Scene Magazine*

"Dashofy has done it again. *Bridges Burned* opens with a home erupting in flames. The explosion inflames simmering animosities and ignites a smoldering love that has been held in check too long. A thoroughly engaging read that will take you away."

— Deborah Coonts,
Author of *Lucky Catch*

"Dashofy takes small town politics and long simmering feuds, adds colorful characters, and brings it to a boil in a welcome new series."

— Hallie Ephron,
Author of *There Was an Old Woman*

"A vivid country setting, characters so real you'd know them if they walked through your door, and a long-buried secret that bursts from its grave to wreak havoc in a small community—*Lost Legacy* has it all."

— Sandra Parshall,
Author of the Agatha Award-Winning Rachel Goddard Mysteries

"A big-time talent spins a wonderful small-town mystery! Annette Dashofy skillfully weaves secrets from the past into a surprising, engaging, and entertaining page turner."

— Hank Phillippi Ryan,
Mary Higgins Clark, Agatha and Anthony Award-Winning Author

"Discerning mystery readers will appreciate Dashofy's expert details and gripping storytelling. Zoe Chambers is an authentic character who will entertain us for a long time."

— Nancy Martin,
Author of the Blackbird Sister Mysteries

"A terrific first mystery, with just the right blend of action, emotion and edge. I couldn't put it down. The characters are well drawn and believable...It's all great news for readers.

— Mary Jane Maffini,
Author of *The Dead Don't Get Out Much*

"Intriguing, with as many twists and turns as the Pennsylvania countryside it's set in."

— CJ Lyons,
New York Times Bestselling Author of *Last Light*

"Dashofy has created a charmer of a protagonist in Zoe Chambers. She's smart, she's sexy, she's vulnerably romantic, and she's one hell of a paramedic on the job."

— Kathleen George,
Edgar-Nominated Author of the Richard Christie Series

WITH A
VENGEANCE

Books in the Zoe Chambers Mystery Series
by Annette Dashofy

WITH A VENGEANCE

A ZOE CHAMBERS MYSTERY

ANNETTE DASHOFY

To Judy
Thanks for reading!

Annette Dashofy

HENERY PRESS

Copyright

WITH A VENGEANCE
A Zoe Chambers Mystery
Part of the Henery Press Mystery Collection

First Edition | May 2016

Henery Press
www.henerypress.com

All rights reserved. No part of this book may be used or reproduced in any manner whatsoever, including Internet usage, without written permission from Henery Press, except in the case of brief quotations embodied in critical articles and reviews.

Copyright © 2016 by Annette Dashofy
Cover art by Stephanie Chontos

This is a work of fiction. Any references to historical events, real people, or real locales are used fictitiously. Other names, characters, places, and incidents are the product of the author's imagination, and any resemblance to actual events or locales or persons, living or dead, is entirely coincidental.

Trade Paperback ISBN-13: 978-1-63511-017-3
Digital epub ISBN-13: 978-1-63511-018-0
Kindle ISBN-13: 978-1-63511-019-7
Hardcover Paperback ISBN-13: 978-1-63511-020-3

Printed in the United States of America

To all the selfless men and women in law enforcement, EMS, and fire/rescue, who put their lives on the line every day.

ACKNOWLEDGMENTS

As always, without my wonderful team of experts, this book would not exist.

Thank you to my law enforcement friends, Bernie LaRue, Terry Dawley, and Kevin Burns for guiding me through the techniques used in these kinds of circumstances and for giving me ideas I'd never have thought of on my own. Thanks to Chris Herndon for answering my ghoulish autopsy questions, to Diana Stavroulakis for helping keep my characters legal and above board, and to my dear friend Jessi Pizzurro for catching my mistakes in the hospital scenes. Also a special thank you to another dear friend, Stephanie Szramowski, for sharing her exploding airbags experience with me so I didn't have to go out and wreck my car in the name of research!

Any mistakes in this book are entirely my own fault, not theirs.

I have a fabulous support team in my Pittsburgh Sisters in Crime and Pennwriters. I wouldn't be here without you! Thank you to Ramona Long for creating the morning sprint group without which I'd never get any pages written, and to Heather Desuta for your graphic art brilliance.

Words can't express how much I adore my critique group who pick my pages apart and then lovingly brainstorm them into something far better. Jeff Boarts, Tamara Girardi, and Mary Sutton, you're the best! Thank you. And thank you to Ann Slates for being my extra set of proofreading eyes.

Huge hugs and many thanks to the team at Henery Press: my editors,

Kendel Lynn, Erin George, Rachel Jackson, and Anna Davis; my wonderful cover artist, Stephanie Chontos; and the man behind the curtain, Art Molinares.

And last, but not least, much love and thanks to my husband Ray for all his support and his willingness to get out of my way (translation: go fishing) so I could get some work done in peace and quiet.

ONE

Adrenaline kicked Zoe's pulse into high gear. The black Glock clutched in her hands weighed more than she'd imagined. She wished she'd had a chance to test the weapon on a firing range at a bullseye target. Instead of here.

A shooter had reportedly been seen in this school bus parking lot. Zoe advanced although her feet felt rooted to the ground. She eased around the fender of one empty bus. Ahead of her, voices. Shouting.

There. Inside the next bus. A large man with a gun. Worse, he held Zoe's partner, a female police officer, in a chokehold, the weapon aimed at the cop's head.

"Shoot him," her partner yelled. "*Shoot him.*"

The man appeared crazed. "Get away," he bellowed at Zoe.

"Drop the weapon," she ordered.

"Shoot him," the female officer demanded.

Zoe's hands held steady. But with the shooter using her partner as a human shield, her target was small. His head. And her partner's head was right there too. If Zoe's aim was off the least bit...

"*Shoot him!*"

The man's finger was poised on the trigger. Zoe aimed. And squeezed. The gunshot popped. And the scene in front of her froze.

The lights of the classroom came up. The Meggitt firearms projection screen in front of her took up most of one wall and showed a red dot on the shooter's head by his ear. Nearly a miss. But good enough.

The other Citizen's Police Academy students burst into applause. One of them, a retired Marine, said, "Oo-*rah.*"

Zoe Chambers laughed, relieved the exercise had ended without her making a fool of herself. Even more relieved it was only a simulation. As a paramedic, she was accustomed to saving lives. Not taking them.

With the Glock—a very real handgun made incapable of live fire—hanging at her side, she turned to see the instructor grinning at her.

Pete Adams had taken time from his job as Vance Township's police chief to run the simulator for the Monongahela County's CPA. "Not too shabby, Chambers."

Zoe's cheeks warmed. She gingerly set the Glock on the desk next to Pete. "I can't believe how scared I was." She pressed a hand to her chest. "I knew it wasn't real, but no one told my heart."

County Detective Wayne Baronick rocked back in his chair next to Pete's. "That was good shooting," he told the class. "But I'm not sure in a real-life situation, it would have been the wisest choice."

Deflated, Zoe battled to keep from glaring at the detective. She was here to learn and experience. Not bask in false glory.

Wayne tipped his head toward the still frozen image on the screen. "You should have ordered the assailant to drop his weapon."

"I did."

"Not loud enough." The detective demonstrated, barking out, "Drop the weapon!" in a voice that reverberated inside the small classroom.

Zoe had to admit, she would have dropped her gun if ordered to do so in that booming voice.

"And if you had waited a little longer, he was going to surrender as the scenario progressed."

But I didn't know that. Zoe kept her thoughts to herself. The purpose of the exercise for the non-law-enforcement students was to gain insight into what police officers faced every day in the streets. The danger. The split-second decisions.

Pete's cell phone rang. "Take over, Detective." He rose from his chair at the Meggitt control. "You done good," he whispered to Zoe as he turned toward the back of the room.

She contained a smile and returned to her desk.

Baronick called, "Next."

Another student, one of the regulars, moved to take his turn at a new scenario. Zoe was there for only the one class. When Pete accepted Baronick's invitation to lead the Firearms Training module, he'd invited her along for the ride, claiming it might help in her struggle to decide about her career path in the County Coroner's Office. She had no clue what a shoot-or-don't-shoot exercise had to do with whether or not she wanted to perform autopsies, but she wasn't going to argue the point. It was an evening out with Pete. Not quite a date. They still sucked at those.

Pete drifted toward the back of the classroom, his phone pressed to one ear, his fingers pressed to the other. Zoe couldn't see his face, but his shoulders tensed. The room lights dimmed, and another interactive scenario played out across the screen. Zoe, however, watched Pete with the same trepidation she'd experienced a few moments earlier when faced with a hostage situation.

Gunshots rang out. The lights came up. The room erupted into laughter. The student had emptied his virtual magazine without one clean hit.

Pete pocketed his phone and turned, his gaze locking on Zoe's. "I'm sorry, Detective Baronick. Something's come up back in Vance Township. I'm afraid I have to leave."

Baronick raised an eyebrow, and Pete whispered something to him. The detective's jaw tightened and he gave Pete a quick nod. "I can give Zoe a lift home."

"No. She's with me." Pete crooked a finger in her direction.

Ordinarily the domineering gesture might have irked her. But the grim pallor of Pete's face told her now was not the time for smartass quips. She snatched her purse from the back of the chair and scurried after him, catching him in the hall. "Pete?"

He didn't slow his long stride. "There's been a shooting. An ambush."

She jogged to keep up. "Ambush? Where? Who?"

"One of your medic units responded to a call. I don't have all the details, but two paramedics were shot."

Zoe stumbled, her knees suddenly weak. Pete kept going. She regained her balance—and her wits—and caught him once again. "Shot? Who? How bad?"

"I don't know the victims' names yet." They reached the heavy metal front doors, and Pete punched through. "One medic is being Life Flighted to Pittsburgh."

The cool evening air of early September chilled Zoe. "What about the other?"

Pete stopped so fast, she almost slammed into him. He turned to face her, his dour expression telling her the awful truth. The second paramedic—one of her colleagues—was dead.

The fifteen-mile trip between the county seat and Vance Township usually took a half hour. Zoe had made it in twenty minutes when driving the ambulance, lights and sirens. With Pete behind the wheel of the police department's Explorer, odds were good they'd beat her old record by at least five minutes.

Pete's radio, tuned to a non-public channel, crackled with a steady stream of police chatter as every department within a twenty-five-mile radius responded to the scene. The unknown shooter was still at large. State Police manned roadblocks, and county law enforcement had set up a command center near the shooting. Vance Township Officer Kevin Piacenza, who'd been first on the scene, had the lead, with Pete giving orders over the mic.

The one detail they weren't broadcasting was the names of the ambulance crew.

Zoe's partner, Earl Kolter, wasn't supposed to be on duty. She prayed he hadn't been called in for some reason.

While Pete drove and took charge of the crime scene remotely, Zoe pulled up Earl's number on her phone. He answered, his voice tight.

Her relief was short-lived. "Earl, have you heard?"

"Hell yes, I heard. Where are you?"

"On my way back from Brunswick with Pete. What happened?"

"Barry and Curtis responded to a call of an ATV accident out in the cuts behind Dillard. They called in that they were on the scene, but nothing more."

"Barry and Curtis?"

"Yeah." The line went quiet for a moment. "I thought you knew."

"They haven't given any names over the police radio." Barry Dickson and Curtis Knox. Two men Zoe had known for years. She'd graduated high school with Barry, and she'd gone through paramedic training with Curtis. She'd worked with both on dozens of calls. "I—I heard one of them is..." She couldn't choke out the word.

Apparently Earl couldn't either. If it weren't for the background noise, she'd have thought they'd been disconnected.

When he responded, his voice had dropped. "Barry didn't make it. They're Life Flighting Curtis to Allegheny General, but we haven't had an update on his condition. From what the guys said, it didn't look good. He lost a lot of blood."

Ahead, a string of red taillights sliced through the night and indicated they were approaching one of the police roadblocks. Pete swung the SUV into the other lane, roaring past the line of cars. On the left, the small parking lot of a squat, single-story brick building housing a medical clinic had been transformed into news media central. Already, a pair of satellite trucks were setting up for remote broadcasts of the incident.

"Any word on whether they've caught the guy?" Earl asked.

"Not yet."

"Let me know if you hear anything."

"I will. You do the same, okay?"

Zoe ended the call as Pete eased past the Pennsylvania State Trooper manning the roadblock.

Pete raised a hand, acknowledging the trooper, before once again mashing the gas pedal to the floor. "You got names?"

"Dickson and Knox. Curtis is still alive. For now."

Pete's face tensed in the glare from the dashboard lights. "Good men."

The next two miles rushed past in a blur. The radio blared reports of new roadblocks.

The police had cordoned off a five-mile radius. No one in. No one out. State Police were responding with a helicopter with thermal imaging. Yet so far the elusive shooter remained at large.

Pete slowed as they entered Dillard. Five police vehicles from various jurisdictions idled at each corner of the usually quiet coal-mining town. Officers attired in Kevlar patrolled the streets.

After jouncing over a half mile of deep ruts, Zoe spotted the milky gray glow of rescue lighting on the horizon marking their destination. They topped one last rise, and the crime scene lay before them.

Halogen lights attached to rumbling generators turned the darkness into artificially vivid daylight. Law enforcement vehicles from a variety of jurisdictions parked around the periphery of a manmade canyon, the result of decades-old strip mining. A trio of firetrucks formed a barricade of sorts at one end.

At the center of the chaos, one Monongahela County ambulance. Zoe recognized the unit she and Earl usually drove on their shift, now a lonely witness to the unthinkable. Several yards in front of it rested an overturned all-terrain vehicle. On the ground next to the ambulance, a body.

Pete cruised the perimeter to park between a boxy truck with Monongahela County Police Department Mobile Command Center emblazoned across the side and a white van bearing the county coroner's insignia. Franklin Marshall had beaten them there.

Pete opened his door. "Stay close to me. The scene isn't secured. We don't know the shooter's location." He glanced toward the ambulance. "And Dickson isn't going anywhere."

The gravity of the situation settled even heavier over her. Barry was dead. Curtis was gravely wounded. And there was a very real possibility that others, including her and Pete, could still be in danger. She shivered. In the distance, hounds barked. Multiple helicopters *thwap-thwap-thwapped* overhead in a cloudless star-filled sky. "News choppers?" Zoe asked.

"Some. Plus the State Police." Pete took her arm, guiding her toward the box truck. "They're using night vision to search for our shooter from the air."

Coroner Franklin Marshall and Officer Kevin Piacenza stood inside the mobile command center truck. The cases Zoe worked had never brought her in contact with it before, and she gave the inside of the high-tech beast a curious perusal. A pair of county police officers wearing headsets manned computer keyboards. Radios broadcast an array of police transmissions.

"Update?" Pete asked Kevin.

"No shots have been fired since I arrived on the scene. The K-9 unit arrived about ten minutes ago and is doing their thing. The search helo's been circling and hasn't located anything suspicious. Roadblocks are in place."

"So we have nothing."

"If he's still out there, he's hunkered down."

Franklin clamped a hand on Zoe's shoulder. "It sounds safe enough for us to retrieve the body."

Pete turned to her. The intensity of his pale blue eyes might have made her blush under different circumstances. Tonight, though, his concern chilled her. Franklin was taking her into a potential active shooting zone, and it was up to Pete to give the green light.

Kevin looked back and forth at them. "From the position of the victims, we believe the shot came from that wooded area to the west. I had the fire department park their trucks on that side. Circling the wagons."

Pete shot a look at the young officer.

Kevin shrugged. "My granddad makes me watch cowboy shows with him when I go to visit." He grew serious again. "Anyway, they should be safe."

"Provided our sniper hasn't relocated," Pete said.

Zoe's chill deepened into her bones.

The coroner, his hand still gripping her shoulder, must have felt her shudder. "You don't have to go in," he said, his voice soft, understanding.

Zoe recalled the time she and Barry had responded to a barroom brawl. The police were tied up with a traffic accident. Rather than wait, Barry put himself in harm's way to shield her and their patient, bringing them both out unscathed.

She steeled herself against her fear. "I'm ready. Let's go."

Franklin clapped her on the back before heading for the door.

She followed, pausing to meet Pete's eyes. His jaw was clenched so hard, she half expected to hear his teeth crack. An unspoken order—*be careful*—passed between them.

As she stepped out into the night air, his command over the police radio trailed after her. "The coroner and deputy coroner are coming out. *Cover them.*"

Pete hated everything about this incident. Two men he knew and respected, emergency responders, who put their lives on the line every day, had been gunned down by a coward. One wouldn't be going home again. The other? Too soon to call. And now Zoe was walking smack into the middle of ground zero.

Pete stepped closer to a bank of monitors showing different angles of the scene. One was trained on the body, and into that frame appeared the coroner's wagon. Franklin parked close, using the vehicle as an additional barricade from whoever may or may not still lurk in the darkness. The coroner and Zoe climbed out and moved to the rear of the van, removing a gurney. A camera hung around Zoe's neck.

"Anything?" Pete asked.

One of the county techs looked up from his computer. "The State Police helo reports no sign of any heat signatures outside the perimeter. Roadblocks are negative as well."

The second tech touched his earpiece. "The K-9 unit is still searching. Nothing yet."

"He's probably long gone," Kevin said.

"You willing to bet your life on that?" Pete snapped.

"No, sir."

Neither was Pete. And he sure as hell wasn't willing to bet Zoe's. "Take me through it from the top." His focus stayed glued on the monitors, watching for movement where there shouldn't be any. Watching Zoe and Franklin process Dickson's body.

"According to the county EOC dispatcher, at nineteen forty-six a call came in for an injured ATV rider giving this location. Dickson and Knox responded from the Phillipsburg garage. They radioed they were on the scene at nineteen fifty-two."

So the shooter set up his victims shortly before eight p.m. Just after sunset. "If he was up on the hillside to the west as we suspect, the sun would have been low and to his back."

"Even without the cover of the trees, they could've looked right at him and not been able to see him."

"What happened next?"

"Nothing. That was their last radio transmission. When dispatch couldn't raise them, she called and asked me to check on them."

On the monitor, Zoe was taking photos. "Go on," Pete said.

Kevin's voice grew heavy. "I arrived at twenty twenty-one." He motioned toward the monitor Pete was watching. "And I found the overturned quad, but the only victims were Dickson and Knox. Dickson was already deceased. Knox was unresponsive, but had a pulse. There was a blood trail indicating he'd tried to drag himself over to his partner, but couldn't make it."

Pete's jaw ached. "Where are you, you son of a bitch?" Other questions remained unvoiced. "Where's the crime scene unit?"

"On their way," one of the techs said. "ETA five minutes."

Not that it mattered. The bulk of the work would have to wait for daylight.

"Do you think he's still out there?" Kevin asked in a hushed voice.

No sightings on the infrared. No movement. No gunshots. For Zoe's sake and the sakes of all the law enforcement officers lying low, waiting and watching, Pete hoped he was long gone. "Oh, he's out there. Somewhere. And we will get him."

TWO

"Thanks for the lift." Zoe had hitched rides in ambulances, police cars, and once on a firetruck. This was the first time she'd been dropped at her door by the coroner's wagon.

"No problem," Franklin said. "Look, if you don't want to attend this autopsy, I'll let you off the hook."

She hated autopsies and avoided them whenever possible. She'd made a deal with Franklin last summer to assist at six, though, and still owed him two.

His offer of a reprieve was tempting. "No," she said after some consideration. "I think I need to be there for this one."

"Suit yourself." Franklin gazed past her out the passenger window. "Did you leave lights on?"

"Yeah, I—" She did a double take at the house where she'd been living for the last two months. Yes, she'd left the porch and kitchen lights on, but now every window blazed. "What the hell?"

"Should I call the police?"

"They're all at the crime scene. Besides, burglars don't generally put *all* the lights on. Do they?"

Franklin shrugged. "How should I know?"

"But teenagers do." Zoe opened the passenger door and stepped out. "I'll see you in the morning."

"Eight o'clock. Sharp."

Eight o'clock? "Oh, crap."

"What's wrong?"

"My truck's at the garage in Phillipsburg. Pete was supposed to take me to pick it up first thing tomorrow."

Franklin shook his head. "Pete's going to be a little busy for the foreseeable future."

She glanced at the house with its lights blazing and had a feeling she might have another ride available. "Yeah. Never mind. I'll be there at eight."

"Sharp."

She headed toward the house, aware of the van still idling behind her. Ever the gentleman, Franklin would make sure she made it inside safely before pulling away. Meanwhile, the neighbors were probably peering through their curtains, curious and nervous about the presence of a coroner's wagon on their quiet street.

The door flew open before she got the key to the lock. Rose Bassi, Zoe's absentee best friend, pulled her inside and into her arms. "Thank God." Rose's voice wavered. "When I kept hearing sirens, I turned on the news and heard one of our ambulance crews had been attacked. I was afraid you might have been..."

Zoe returned the crushing embrace. "I'm fine."

Rose and Zoe had grown up together, more sisters than friends. The four months they'd just spent apart seemed like four years. So much had happened. Life. Death. Loss of trust. Homelessness.

Gasping for air, Zoe extricated herself from Rose's hug. "Wait." She turned and waved out the door at Franklin. The van pulled away. Wheeling back to Rose, she asked, "What are you doing here? Wasn't I supposed to pick you up at the airport *tomorrow* night?"

"We finagled an earlier flight. Sylvia picked us up."

A teenage girl appeared in the doorway between the kitchen and the living room, cradling one of Zoe's orange tabbies. "Aunt Zoe! I'm so glad you're okay. We were worried."

Jade, the other cat, trotted past the girl to a half-empty bowl of food.

Awed, Zoe studied the teen. "Allison? What happened to you?"

Rose slipped an arm around Zoe's waist and beamed. "She grew up."

Allison Bassi had been through hell and back last winter. She'd gone from strawberry blond ponytailed innocence to black-haired Goth drug addict before crashing and starting the long road back. The fifteen-year-old woman-child standing in front of Zoe now bore little resemblance to the broken china doll Zoe remembered. A short reddish bob replaced the long hair. Instead of t-shirts bearing the logos of rock bands, she wore a western-style shirt in shades of turquoise and coral. Only the skin-tight jeans remained...except these ones were a deeper blue and had no holes or rips.

Most importantly, when the girl smiled, clarity shone in her blue eyes. "What do you think?"

"I think—you look incredible." Zoe crossed to the girl, stepping over Jade, and threw her arms around her. Merlin, the tabby Allison had been holding, wriggled free with an unhappy meow.

Zoe took Allison by the shoulders and held her at arm's length. "New Mexico agreed with you." After a glance at Rose, she added, "Both of you."

"I loved it there," Allison said. "Not at first, maybe. But the space, the quiet." She opened her arms wide. "I felt free."

Rose leaned a hip against the kitchen counter. "For the first time in her life, she wasn't plugged into her phone or her music twenty-four-seven."

"I was pretty mad when you took my phone and computer away." The teen laughed, a bright bubbly sound. "But I don't miss them now."

Zoe looked over Allison's shoulder toward the hallway. "Speaking of missing, where's Logan?"

"He stayed behind," Rose said.

Stunned, Zoe met her friend's gaze. The smile had faded.

"He has a girlfriend," Allison said.

Rose gave an exaggerated sigh. "He's eighteen now."

Allison snickered. "Which he reminds us of every chance he gets."

"I made him promise to come back for Thanksgiving or I'll go out there and drag him home, eighteen and legal or not."

"I hope you don't mind," Allison said to Zoe. "I moved your stuff across the hall to his room."

"Oh." Zoe glanced from the girl to Rose. "I was planning on having my things packed and out of here before you got home tomorrow."

Rose raised an eyebrow. "And where were you planning to move to? Pete's house?"

Zoe's cheeks warmed. "No. He's asked a time or two, but I think that's rushing things a bit." And so far, rushing things hadn't proved healthy for their budding relationship.

"Where then?"

"Earl and his wife offered me their guest room." Zoe didn't mention she'd turned them down.

"Please stay here." Allison gave Merlin a hug, burying her nose into his fur.

Zoe wondered if the teen was asking her or the cats to stick around.

"Of course she'll stay," Rose said. Case closed. "How are Mr. and Mrs. Kroll?"

Zoe's former landlords. "On the mend." She still wasn't able to talk about—or think about—the day two months ago when she'd lost almost everything she owned.

Rose knew her well enough to understand the abbreviated answer. She hiked a thumb toward the kitchen door. "So tell me about the shooting tonight. They said there was a fatality."

Fatigue weakened Zoe's knees. She dropped into one of the kitchen chairs and stumbled through the story, fighting to get the words out.

"Barry's gone?" Rose covered her mouth with one trembling hand.

Allison deposited Merlin next to the cat food and joined the two women at the kitchen table. "He was friends with Dad, wasn't he?"

"Barry was friends with everyone." Rose stood and paced to the stove before turning toward Zoe. "Why on earth would someone do such a thing?"

"I wish I knew."

"Isn't Curtis Knox supposed to get married soon?"

"Yeah." Zoe hadn't thought about that. "He and Lucy have been planning a big wedding. Everyone at the garage has been really excited about it."

"How bad is he?"

"I haven't heard."

Rose crossed the room and lovingly fingered a framed photograph on the wall—a photo of her late husband in his firefighter's uniform. "Dear God. I hope they can keep planning their wedding and not have to plan a funeral instead."

*   *   *

Sleep came reluctantly after Zoe stayed up until past one a.m. gabbing with her friend. Even so, she was wide awake by six. She managed to dress in silence and tiptoed into the hall, peeking into Rose and Allison's rooms on her way to the kitchen. Neither showed signs of stirring. Still on New Mexico time, Zoe reminded herself.

She made coffee. The aroma failed to rouse them. Although Rose had said she'd be happy to drive Zoe to Bud Kramer's Garage early this morning, she didn't have the heart to wake her.

At seven, Zoe slipped outside into a perfect early autumn morning. The humidity of summer had evaporated, leaving the air mild and comfortable. She'd often joked that southwestern Pennsylvania managed three perfect weather days per year. This might be one of them.

Too bad the death of one friend and wounding of another left a gloomy pall.

She walked two houses down and knocked on the door. A robust grandmotherly woman answered within seconds.

"Zoe?" Sylvia Bassi stepped back to allow her into the kitchen. "What are you doing here?"

"I figured you'd be awake."

"Of course I'm awake. I'm always awake."

"I need a ride to Kramer's to pick up my truck."

Rose's mother-in-law studied her for a moment. "Pete can't take you because he's still tied up with the shooting."

"I wasn't sure if you'd heard."

Sylvia sniffed. "It's all over the news. Terrible thing. Just terrible."

"Did the news mention anything about Curtis?"

"The last report on TV said he was in guarded condition." Sylvia eyed Zoe over the top of her glasses. "Are you assisting on the Dickson boy's autopsy?"

"If I can get there. My truck—"

Sylvia snatched a set of keys from a hook near the door. "Your truck is at Kramer's. Let's go."

*   *   *

The early morning sun bathed the unreclaimed strip mine's slag piles in the golden light of autumn, turning them into something almost pretty. Almost. The rolling dirt and gravel mounds bore slices and ruts, carved by local kids' dirt bikes and ATVs. Some days these desolate valleys echoed with the buzz of off-road vehicles, sounding like swarms of gigantic hornets. Today, however, cicadas trilled in the patches of tall grass, interrupted only by the squawk of radio transmissions.

Pete sipped his umpteenth cup of horrible coffee and gazed at the scene where two good men had been gunned down less than twelve hours earlier. The fire department had packed up their generators and halogen lights and pulled out. The ambulance and the overturned quad, which had baited the paramedics, had been towed away. Helicopters no longer marred the crystal blue sky above. However, the mobile command center and crime scene unit trucks remained. Teams of officers and techs searched the surrounding rocks and weeds with the painstaking precision of an archeological dig in the hopes of finding a spent round from the shooter's weapon.

"We got nothing," Wayne Baronick muttered as he approached. He'd arrived late last night, after Franklin Marshall and Zoe had removed the body.

"You're wrong." Pete resisted adding *as usual.* "Thanks to the dogs, we know where the shots were fired from."

Baronick lifted his gaze toward the trees on the western hillside. "You had that pegged before the dogs confirmed it, though."

Pete contemplated the distance. "About two hundred and fifty yards, I'd say. We can't rule out someone with sniper training, but any deer hunter could easily make that shot."

"Either way, he didn't leave us much to work with," Baronick said. "My guys have been going over the area with a metal detector and have come up with squat."

"Our shooter is smart enough to police his brass."

"But not smart enough to cover his tracks." Literally. They'd found a set of tread marks from a quad on a trail through the trees. The gunman had ridden in and out on an all-terrain vehicle. The K-9s had picked up a scent and followed it to a remote blacktopped road. Pete guessed the shooter left a truck parked there, loaded up his ATV, and simply drove away, before Kevin had even gotten the call.

"He has a thing for quads," Pete commented, more to himself than to Baronick. "He used one to gain access to the area. He used a second one to lure the ambulance crew out into the open."

Baronick took a few steps toward the spot where the paramedics had fallen. "He was willing to sacrifice the second ATV. Left it behind knowing we'd confiscate the thing. He may have policed his brass, but maybe he wasn't so careful with the quad he left behind."

Pete's gut told him they weren't gonna be that lucky.

Zoe climbed out of Sylvia's car in front of Kramer's Garage and thanked her for the lift. Sylvia fluttered a hand and sped off. Zoe's ancient Chevy pickup was parked near the fence, a sign that repairs had been completed as promised.

Zoe stepped through the garage's dented steel door. Inside, the smell of motor oil and rubber smacked her in the face.

Power wrenches whirled and screeched from a bay farther down the row.

But the sight of Medic Two in the first bay stopped her cold.

A mechanic in gray coveralls, which matched his hair, charged around the back of the ambulance toward her, a strained, polite smile on his face. "Good morning, Zoe. Your truck's ready."

"Thanks, Gabe." She pointed at the medic unit. "What's that doing here?"

Gabe Webber glanced at the ambulance as if he hadn't noticed it before. "Oh. The police asked us to tow it here so they could process it. Said they didn't have the spare manpower right now to deal with it at the township garage."

Zoe wandered around the ambulance. Mud clung to the tires and the wheel wells. A fine coating of dust coated much of the lower half of the vehicle. Her own pickup rarely saw a hose and a bucket of suds, but the EMS crews took great pride in keeping their ambulances spit shined.

Gabe tagged after her, a concerned frown on his face. "I ain't supposed to let no one near it. I was told it's evidence."

"I know. I won't touch anything." She reached the driver's side door and was about to turn and go back when she spotted the ugly, jagged hole high on the front fender. "Is that...?"

"A bullet hole? I guess it is."

For a moment, she forgot her promise to not touch, but recoiled short of fingering the puncture. Had one of the sniper's shots missed? Or had the bullet that pierced Medic Two already passed through a human body?

Her chest tightened, and she retreated.

Worried creases lined Gabe's face. "We should talk about your truck."

Zoe forced a smile. Poor Gabe probably feared he was going to have to call another ambulance for her. "Yeah, we should."

The mechanic relaxed and motioned her toward the cashier's window. "I replaced your entire exhaust system. Plus, your brakes and rotors were shot, so I put new ones on."

The weight of her empty wallet bore down on her. "That's what Bud told me when he phoned." The original work order called for repairing the muffler and checking the brakes. "It turned into a lot more than I'd planned."

The worry lines returned. "Once I got in there, I found the tailpipe was completely rotted away. And your brakes were down to metal. The boss explained all that, right?"

"Yeah." But knowing in advance didn't make it hurt any less. Zoe ran her expenses versus income through her mental calculator and came up with flashing red sub-zero balances. "You guys take credit cards, don't you?"

"Oh, sure thing."

Zoe heaved a loud sigh. "It's cheaper than a new car payment, I guess. And it should be as good as new now, right?" she offered, with more enthusiasm than she felt.

Gabe's expression didn't elicit much confidence. "I ran into another problem. When I tried to start it, it took a few tries."

"The click, click, click thing? Yeah, it's been doing that for a couple of weeks now. I just keep fussing with it until it starts."

The mechanic winced. "Except one of these days it ain't gonna. Sooner than later, most likely. You need a new starter."

Zoe struggled to pull her credit card from her wallet, as if the plastic was resisting the added burden too. "How much will *that* cost?"

"With an old truck like this, the parts shouldn't be more than a hundred dollars. Labor will only be another hundred. Maybe a little less."

Only? She choked. "Really?"

He nodded glumly, as if the money for the needed repairs was coming out of instead of going into his pocket.

"But that can wait a while, right?"

Gabe shrugged. "When it goes, she ain't gonna start for you."

"Great." Zoe contemplated asking if there was anything else, but was afraid of his answer.

The mechanic disappeared while Zoe handed her credit card through the cashier's window to Bud Kramer, the wheelchair-bound owner of the garage who no longer tackled the hands-on part of the business. "Sorry to hear about Barry Dickson," he said as she signed away money she hadn't earned yet. "He was a real decent guy."

"Yeah, he was." She didn't mention that she was on her way to his autopsy.

As she crossed the gravel parking lot, she heard someone call her name and turned to see Gabe jogging after her. He caught up, huffing. "I didn't wanna say anything in front of the boss, but I'll keep an eye out for a used starter for your Chevy. I should be able to pick one up for you lots cheaper than what we charge. And I'll install it for half of what Kramer'll gouge you." He shoved a business card into her hand. "Call me at home. I'll take care of you."

"Thanks," she said, stunned.

He gave a dismissive wave over his shoulder as he shuffled back to the garage.

She pocketed the card and studied the rusty tailgate of her beloved old Chevy. Today's repairs already had her in the hole. The additional ones, cut price or not, weren't even in the ballpark of her current budget.

But going into debt might be the high point of her day, considering her next stop.

THREE

"You're getting better at these." Only Franklin Marshall's eyes were visible above the mask.

Not enough of his face for Zoe to determine the degree of sarcasm in his words. "Am I?"

The stench of an autopsy played havoc with her every time. The sight of a body opened up on the stainless steel table didn't faze her. Nor did the pop of ribs being cut with clippers that looked like something a landscaper should be using to trim trees.

Not even the grayish face of a man she'd known for much of her life was enough to send her running. No, it was the smell that drove her out of the morgue on more than one occasion since she'd taken on the deputy coroner role.

The stupid surgical masks, worn to protect the living from whatever contagions the deceased might carry, did little to block the odors.

Franklin chuckled. "You're still in here, aren't you?"

For the moment.

Forensic Pathologist Lyle "Doc" Abercrombie straightened from leaning over the body, holding a mound the size of a fist in his gloved hands. Barry's heart.

Doc carried it to a nearby table, setting the organ down as gently as if it were still beating. "Zoe. Photos please."

Swallowing the rising nausea, she stepped forward, camera in hand. Doc pointed out the damage he wanted her to document.

Behind her, Franklin moved closer to the body, bending over to peer into the chest cavity. "This sniper is a helluva shot."

Doc left Zoe to her photography. "Not that he needed to be. He used a high-powered rifle. The bullet shattered a rib and shredded the aorta, his lungs, and everything else in its path. The victim never stood a chance."

She snapped the needed pictures and lowered the camera. She'd already photographed Barry while he was still wearing his paramedic's uniform, the same as hers only much larger, as well as after he'd been stripped. The entrance wound—small, round, and pink—exhibited very little blood, but some fibers from his shirt clung to it. On the other hand, the bullet had ripped a huge, jagged hole upon exiting.

Zoe flashed back to the night before, when she and Franklin had processed Barry's body at the scene. He'd clearly bled out in less than a minute. Died in a pond of his own blood.

She wondered who had been shot first. Barry or Curtis? What had it been like for the second victim? Seeing his partner gunned down, only then to be shot as well.

Barry had been a big, loveable lug, but he'd also made an enemy or two in his day. Simply on the basis of his size, he often acted as the protector of the weak.

A recent incident, which Zoe had heard from others at the garage, floated to the surface of her mind. A couple of weeks ago, a young, drunk badass had called Barry out. Apparently, he'd popped the thug with one fist after taking as many of the punk's insults as he could handle. According to the guys, the loudmouth ran away in tears, but had been heard around town making threats about a rematch.

Curtis was physically the polar opposite of his partner. Lean and non-threatening, he avoided altercations at all costs, telling everyone that he was a lover, not a fighter. Everyone at Mon County EMS eagerly awaited Curtis's upcoming wedding to Lucy Livingston, who some of the guys described as ten-car-pileup gorgeous. Lucy had dumped a jerk of a boyfriend for Curtis, who'd proposed after a whirlwind three-month courtship.

Zoe tried to remember Lucy's ex-boyfriend's name to no avail. Could jealousy have driven the jilted lover to try to kill his rival?

"Zoe."

She snapped out of her reverie and looked up to find Franklin staring at her over his mask. "I'm sorry. What?"

The coroner motioned toward Abercrombie. "Doc asked if you wanted to run the gut."

As if all the other aromas weren't disgusting enough, opening and washing the intestines ranked at the top of the Awful Smells List. She'd never lasted through it, even with someone else doing the deed. "Uh. No. I'll pass."

Doc snickered, smile lines deepened around Franklin's eyes, and Zoe realized both men were teasing her.

At least she thought they were teasing. "You're evil, you know."

"You make it too easy." Franklin took the camera from her hands.

"No more photographs?" she asked.

"No. I don't want you to drop my new Nikon when you pass out."

Oh, crap. They *weren't* kidding.

Pete stood in the police station's conference room, studying the crime scene photos spread across the long table. An overturned ATV. The ambulance with a bullet hole in the fender. Close-ups of the tread marks from the second ATV. Various shots of the body.

Every aspect of the case gnawed at him. The ambush. The victims. The lack of evidence. The lack of a suspect. That one really ate at him.

His cell phone rang for what felt like the twentieth time. Concerned citizens kept phoning, demanding answers he didn't have. Or offering their thoughts on who might be behind the killings. He'd taken a list of names and would follow up even though he knew most of the accusations were bogus. This time, though, the name and number on his caller ID weren't local.

Chuck Delano. His former partner from their days with the Pittsburgh Bureau of Police currently resided in Hawaii. A couple of months back, Chuck had hounded him relentlessly to accept a job at some swanky resort on Maui. At one point, Pete had been on the verge of taking it too.

Pete answered the phone. "No, I am not moving to Hawaii."

"Well, why the hell not? Oh, wait. I forgot. You're in *love*." The way Chuck said the word made it sound like a high school crush.

"I'm busy. What do you want?"

"No need to get snippy. But I do have another job offer for you. Not quite as good as the last one, at least starting out, but I think you'd make head of security within three months easy."

"I told you. I'm not moving."

"Bring the girl with you. One word for you, Petey. Bikinis."

For a moment, Pete's mind conjured up an image of Zoe in a skimpy bathing suit. He quickly filed the fantasy away for later, when he had the time to enjoy it. "I have to go."

"I don't know how you can still live around there." Chuck's tone became more wistful.

The hint of melancholy in his old partner's voice kept Pete from hanging up. "I like it here. I've told you that."

"I know. But don't you ever think about...you know?"

Of course he knew. Eleven years ago, he and Chuck had responded to a report of shots fired. A drug deal gone south. One kid lay dead in the street. A second one took a shot at Chuck, hitting him in the leg. Pete had returned fire, ending the life of what turned out to be a fifteen-year-old boy. "Donnie Moreno." He'd never forget the night or the name.

"To this day I wake up in a cold sweat remembering," Chuck said. "If I still lived back there, I'd probably have eaten my gun by now. And I wasn't the one who pulled the trigger."

"It's ancient history. We were doing our jobs. If you still can't let it go, maybe you need to talk to someone."

Pete's suggestion was met with a gruff laugh. "I do. I talk to the pretty barmaids downstairs at the lounge. I'm telling you, you need to come check the place out. Take a vacation. Bring your girl with you."

Bells jangled on the front door. "I have to go, Chuck."

"Think about it at least?"

"Yeah, yeah. I'll think about it." Pete ended the call.

He couldn't make out the words in the muffled exchange between the newcomer and Nancy, his secretary, but he heard enough to know the speaker's identity. A moment later, Baronick swaggered into the room carrying two cups from the new coffee joint in Phillipsburg.

The detective handed one to Pete. "I figured you could use this."

He mumbled his thanks.

"Do you realize you have a crew of reporters camped outside?"

"Yeah. I told them I'd give a statement as soon as we know something." Pete inhaled the aromatic steam from the cup. "So do we have anything new?"

"Not yet." Baronick took a sip. "Your officer's still overseeing things at the site. We've got teams with metal detectors trying to locate the spent bullets. What about the ambulance?"

"I sent Nate Williamson over to Kramer's to process it. We should hear something from him shortly. And Metzger's in the back on the phone trying to track down the owner of the bait ATV." Pete tapped the photo of the tread marks. "Tires aren't a match, so we're definitely dealing with two different vehicles."

Baronick set down his coffee and shook his head. "Quite the elaborate ruse, don't you think?"

"Yeah." Maybe too elaborate, which was one of the many things that bugged Pete about the case.

The bells at the front of the station jingled again. At the same time, Seth Metzger rapped on the open door to the conference room. Pete waved him in.

"I tracked down the owner of the overturned ATV." The officer handed a sheet of paper with his notes to Pete. "He's from over near Marsdale. Reported it stolen two days ago. I called Marsdale PD and they confirmed."

Baronick read Metzger's scribblings over Pete's shoulder. "Maybe my guys will be able to pull some fingerprints or fibers off it."

"Not likely. This guy's been pretty good about covering his ass."

Baronick grinned at Pete. "Don't be so negative. He's bound to slip up at some point."

Another knock at the door drew Pete's attention. Zoe, pale and sporting a matched set of dark circles under her gorgeous baby blues, leaned against the doorframe as if her legs might fail her. He moved toward her. "Are you okay?" But the reason for her pallor hit him before she had a chance to respond. "The autopsy."

She pushed away from the door and allowed him to guide her to a chair. "I don't care what anyone tells you, Vicks VapoRub does not cover those smells."

"You're just now figuring that out?" Pete offered a sympathetic smile. "What did Franklin learn?"

She shot a sickly glare at him. "Besides how fast I can run when I need to barf?"

Pete winced. "Yeah. Besides that."

"Nothing unexpected. The bullet entered the upper left quadrant of the chest, took out the aorta, broke several ribs, and shredded the lung and the liver along the way before exiting just below the posterior right ribcage. Barry died within seconds from massive blood loss."

"Any bullet fragments?" Baronick asked.

She shook her head.

Pete propped one hip on the edge of the table and leaned toward her, resisting the urge to touch her arm. "Any word on Knox?"

"I called Earl before I left Brunswick. He said Curtis was out of surgery." She glanced at Baronick. "No fragments there either." Turning back to Pete, she said, "Earl's gonna meet me here and we're driving into the city to see him."

"He's conscious?"

"Not yet."

Pete grunted. "I want to talk to him as soon as he's up to it. Maybe he can give us something to identify the shooter."

Zoe leaned back in the chair. "I wanted to talk to you about that. I was thinking about who might've wanted to kill Barry. Or Curtis. And I have a couple of ideas."

Zoe glanced at the display of primitive medical devices inside one of the glass cases lining the hallway to the South Tower of Allegheny General. They looked more like primitive torture devices to her.

"Olivia and I would love to have you stay with us," Earl said, nudging her on.

"No, you wouldn't."

"Yes. We would. Your cats could entertain our dog. I know I said your horse could sleep in Lilly's bedroom, but Olivia did put the kibosh on that idea."

Zoe bit back a laugh. "My horse still has a barn."

"Then it's settled."

"No, it's not. Rose is letting me stay in Logan's room until he comes home. Allison loves the cats, so for now, everything's good."

"For now. But the offer stands."

They reached the end of the tunnel-like hallway and crossed the large waiting area to the information desk. The woman seated behind it punched Curtis's name into her computer and gave them his room number.

As they waited for an elevator, Earl returned to a topic they'd been discussing on the drive into Pittsburgh. "You mentioned Lucy's ex-boyfriend." The elevator doors opened. Earl, Zoe, and three others stepped in. "Do you have any idea who he was?"

Zoe glanced around at the strangers sharing their ride. She didn't want to discuss her theories about who might carry a grudge against Curtis in their presence, so she answered simply, "No."

Seconds later, she and Earl stepped off the elevator.

She searched for and found the sign pointing them in the direction of Curtis's room.

"I only met Lucy one time," Zoe told Earl as they headed down the hall, "when I sat with her at the picnic this summer. I remember her talking about breaking up with her controlling ex-boyfriend. If she mentioned his name, I don't recall."

"I still think it's crazy." Earl shook his head incredulously. "Do *you* think she's worth killing for?"

"Well, of course *I* don't. But if the guy is as obsessive as she made him out to be, who knows?" Zoe checked the numbers next to each door as they got closer to the one they wanted. "I told Pete. He'll find out who the guy is and if he might be the shooter."

"I still think it's a stretch. Now Snake Sullivan? *Him* I can definitely see ambushing Barry and Curtis."

"*Snake* Sullivan? That's his name?"

"The guy Barry flattened with one punch? Yeah. It's not his given name, of course, but that's what he calls himself."

"Is he a biker or something?"

"He wishes. Mostly he just hangs out at Rodeo's Bar and talks trash. The guys think he's a big joke."

Zoe wished she'd known all this when she'd spoken with Pete. But he'd find out once he asked around.

"You know, there's one big problem with both of these theories," Earl said.

"Oh? What?"

"How would anyone—Snake or Lucy's ex—know which crew was gonna take that call?"

Zoe realized she didn't have an answer. "Good point." She spotted the number they'd been looking for across from the nurse's station. "Here we are."

They passed a patient bathroom and sink to find a large man watching his TV in the first bed. He glanced at them with a total lack of interest before going back to his television show. Beyond him, a drawn curtain blocked their view of the second bed.

Approaching it, Zoe called softly, "Hello?"

"Yes?" a strained feminine voice responded.

Zoe eased around the curtain with Earl behind her.

Curtis had never been a big guy, but lying in his hospital bed with IVs, cardiac leads, and oxygen tubes attached to him, he appeared to have shrunken. His eyes were closed. Between the bed and the window, an older woman with long gray hair pulled into a sloppy ponytail sat in a vinyl and wood chair.

"Hey, Wanda." Zoe went to Curtis's mother and bent down to give her a quick hug.

"Zoe. Earl. It's so good to see both of you." She reached a wrinkled hand to Earl, which he took gingerly.

"How is he?" Earl nodded toward the patient.

Wanda Knox sighed. "As well as can be expected, I guess. They had to remove his spleen and do a lot of work to repair the damage to his intestines. They say he's stable, but he lost quite a bit of blood."

"Has he said anything to you about what happened?" Zoe asked.

Wanda dug in her jeans pocket. "No. He's not awake all that much, and when he is, he's not very coherent." She came up with a tissue and waved it at the IV pump. "They've got him loaded with morphine."

Loud voices drifted in from outside the room. From the sound of it, someone was having a heated debate with one of the nurses.

Wanda's rheumy eyes widened as she dabbed them with her tissue. "Oh, good Lord. It's *her*."

Zoe was about to ask who "her" was when a petite, raven-haired hurricane blew into the room.

Lucy Livingston seemed torn between fury and anguish. Her makeup was flawless in spite of a flood of tears streaming down her face. "Oh my God," she wailed upon seeing Curtis. She took a step toward him, stopped, and swung to point a finger at Wanda. "*You!* Those bitches at the nurses' station won't give me any information because you told them I'm not family."

Wanda opened her mouth to speak, but Lucy let out another grief-stricken howl and flung herself on top of Curtis.

Wanda leapt to her feet, yelling. A nurse—perhaps one of the ones who'd refused to give Lucy any information—stormed in, slinging open the closed curtain, and shouting for security. The nurse grabbed Lucy, trying to pry her off poor Curtis. Earl jumped in to assist. Zoe latched on to one of the girl's arms and heaved to no avail.

"Let go of me," Lucy shrieked, clinging to her fiancé.

Curtis, however, never stirred.

"For God's sake, Lucy," Zoe said. "He's had major surgery." Not to mention having been shot. "You're going to rip open his stitches."

Lucy howled like a wounded animal.

From the corner of her eye, Zoe caught a glimpse of an older man standing inside the doorway, well away from the ruckus. Rotund and wearing a gray beard, a camo t-shirt, and a ball cap decorated with fishing lures, he leaned against the wall, chewing on a toothpick, watching the mêlée in silence.

Zoe, Earl, and the nurse dragged a kicking and crying Lucy from the bed. "Let me go," she insisted, wriggling to escape their grasp.

Curtis's mother stepped around the bed. "It's okay. Let her go."

Wanda's soft voice seemed to startle Lucy into submission. She stopped flailing.

Zoe exchanged cautious glances with the other two and released the girl. Lucy brushed off her shirt and jeans and thrust her shoulders back in an apparent attempt to regain some shred of dignity.

The nurse raised a questioning eyebrow at Wanda, who gave her a faint smile and a nod. "I'm sure she'll behave herself now."

Lucy glared at Curtis's mother, but didn't argue.

The nurse left the room slowly, as if waiting for round two to begin.

The girl shifted her gaze to Curtis and choked out a sob, pressing both hands to her mouth. She made a move toward the bed, but Zoe and Earl blocked her path. "I'm not gonna hurt him. He's my fiancé, for cryin' out loud."

Zoe took her by both shoulders. "I know it's not your intention to hurt him, but you need to get a grip."

Lucy shot her a fiery glare. "Get your hands off me. I'm fine."

"Hector," Wanda said to the man in camo, "please control your daughter."

Zoe released the girl as Hector Livingston pushed away from the wall and ambled toward them. He took the toothpick from between his teeth. "She'll mind her manners from now on. Won't you, Lucille." It wasn't a question so much as a command.

Her glare dissolved into a childish pout. "Yes, Daddy." She sniffled and some of the defiance returned. "I just needed to see Curtis." She turned again to Wanda. "We're getting married whether you approve or not. You can't keep me away from him."

Wanda's strained silence, combined with the look she gave the girl, told Zoe there was more to this relationship than the standard pre-wedding in-law friction.

Wanda squared her shoulders and fixed Hector with a stern gaze. "I'm going to talk to the nurses to find out if any test results have come back. I trust you'll keep your daughter in line."

A wordless exchange passed between the two parents' eyes. Wanda turned to Zoe and Earl. "Thanks so much for stopping by. When he wakes up, I'll tell Curtis you were here."

As the older woman walked out of the room, Zoe noticed her hands clenched in tight fists.

FOUR

Pete eyed the shabby singlewide house trailer and noticed the curtains in one of the windows shift. Good thing he hadn't been going for the element of surprise. Of course, if he had, he wouldn't have cruised into the middle of the trailer park in broad daylight in his township vehicle.

It hadn't taken long to learn the identity of the bully Zoe told him about. Nor had it surprised Pete. If Vance Township issued frequent flyer miles for visits from law enforcement, Eli "Snake" Sullivan would be a top recipient, going back to his days of riding a dirt bike on township roads when neither the bike nor the kid had a license. He'd graduated to graffiti, minor vandalism, underage drinking, and simple assault. Now that he was legally an adult, his crimes also matured. The only reason he wasn't a resident in the county jail was because his uncle was an attorney who managed to get cases dismissed, charges reduced, and fines lowered.

Pete climbed the rickety steps to a small stoop and rapped on the aluminum storm door. Through the thin walls, he heard heavy footsteps retreating toward the rear of the trailer. The faded wood panel door opened, revealing an equally faded woman who looked considerably older than her forty-some years.

"Can I help you, Chief?"

"Mrs. Sullivan. I need to speak with Eli."

The woman's eyes shifted in the direction the footsteps had gone, but she blinked and brought her gaze back to Pete. "He's not here."

Pete fixed her with a hard but sympathetic stare. "Ma'am, we both know that's not true. If Eli wants to pull off the sneaky routine, he needs to *tiptoe* into the back room."

Mrs. Sullivan sagged. She stepped clear of the door and yelled toward the rear of the house, "Eli, get your ass out here."

Pete entered a neat but tattered living room. The furnishings were probably original to the mobile home, which he guessed to be at least thirty years old. Eli remained in hiding. Mrs. Sullivan held up one finger at Pete and excused herself. She padded down the darkened hallway, shouting curses at her good-for-nothing son the entire time.

Finally, Pete heard a male voice whine, "Aw, Ma. You weren't supposed to let him know I'm here." Pete bit back a smile as he imagined Mother Sullivan dragging her offspring out from under his bed by his ear. Another muffled exchange between parent and child was followed by the same heavy footsteps, this time growing closer.

A chagrined twenty-something biker wannabe thudded into the living room. A tattooed serpent decorated one arm, which was more flab than muscle. Both ears bore piercings, as did an eyebrow.

"Hello, Eli," Pete said.

"My name's Snake," the kid said, around what Pete guessed to be a lip full of snuff.

"All right. Snake. I have a few questions I'd like to ask you."

Eli jutted his jaw. "Well, I don't wanna answer 'em."

Pete made a production of an exasperated sigh. "Now, Eli. Excuse me. *Snake.* We can do this here, or I can take you down to the station and ask you the same exact questions."

"You can't take me nowhere without arresting me. And you got nothin' on me."

The kid must have been paying attention to his uncle. "Really? I wonder what I might find if I took a look around your room. How much marijuana have you got stashed today? Or maybe you've moved up to something more potent."

Pay dirt. Eli's eyes widened in a momentary flash of panic. But he tamped it down with false bravado. "You can't search my room without a warrant. You got a warrant?"

"I don't need a warrant. All I need is your mother's permission. I think she'd give it to me. Don't you?"

The panic returned. "It's *my* room."

"In *her* house."

For a moment, Pete thought Eli was about to burst into angry tears. Instead, the young thug appeared to cave in on himself. "What d'ya wanna know?"

Pete pulled out his notebook and pen. "Where were you last night?"

Eli's eyes widened and shifted. Damn, he was a lousy liar and he hadn't even answered yet. "Last night? I was at Rodeo's Bar."

"What time did you get there?"

His eyes flitted left, then down and back again, searching for an answer that would cover his ass. "Um, I don't know. Six? Seven?"

"Which was it, Eli? Six or seven?"

"Six." He nodded approval at his decision. "Definitely six."

"I suppose everyone in the place can vouch for you."

"Oh, yeah. They all know me there."

"Names."

Eli tugged at one pierced earlobe. "Huh?"

Pete gritted his teeth. "Give me some names of the people who were there and can verify your story."

"Oh. Um." Eli thought way too hard for a moment, then rattled off the names of a half dozen not-so-upstanding citizens who frequented the dive.

Pete jotted them down. "You have a quad, don't you?"

"Yeah. No."

"Enough with the multiple choice answers, Eli. Yes or no?"

"I did. But I sold it."

"When?"

"Um, about a week—no. About a month ago."

"Who'd you sell it to?"

"Some old dude I met at the bar. He was talking about wanting one for dragging deer outta the woods this hunting season, and I needed money."

Pete considered asking what he needed the money for, but figured he'd only send Eli scrambling for another lie. "Does this 'old dude' have a name?"

Eli rolled his eyes. "Duh. We all got names."

Pete resisted the urge to choke the idiot. "What was it?"

"I don't know. He paid me cash. Don't need no name for cash."

"You do if you want to transfer ownership."

Eli gave him a blank stare. Pete decided to let it drop. Other than the questionable timing of the transaction, he suspected the story about selling the quad to a deer hunter was the first honest statement Eli had made to him. "You hunt, don't you?"

"Oh, sure. Doesn't everyone?"

"What kind of rifle do you use?"

The color drained from his face. "Why are you asking me all this?"

Pete shrugged. "Making conversation."

"Like hell. Cops don't just make conversation. Not with me."

"Do you know Barry Dickson?"

The question nudged Eli out of the land of blatant stupidity. "Oh, no." He shook his head. "I know where you're going with all this. I heard the news this morning."

"You watch the news?" Pete couldn't picture Eli "Snake" Sullivan watching anything except reality shows and cartoons on TV.

"Well, no. But Ma does, and she told me about that dude getting whacked up in the cuts."

"So I guess that's a yes."

"Huh?"

"You know Barry Dickson."

"Yeah. I—no. Wait." Eli spun and yelled toward the back of the trailer, "*Ma.* Call Uncle Andy. I think I need a lawyer."

Zoe caught up with Wanda at the nurse's station. "What on earth was that all about?"

Wanda gripped the countertop as if the thing might levitate and fly away. "I wish Curtis had never met that girl." Her voice was so low, Zoe wondered if she was speaking to herself rather than to Zoe.

Earl appeared at the doorway to Curtis's room, but stopped and glanced back inside. He must have decided to stay where he could keep an eye on the Livingstons and Curtis as well as Wanda and Zoe. Earl crossed his arms and struck a wide-legged sentry's pose.

Zoe touched Wanda's elbow. "Is Lucy always that...?"

Wanda snorted. "Nuts?"

"I was trying for a more politically correct term, but yeah. Nuts."

Wanda sighed. "Depends on who you ask. I've thought she was emotionally unstable from the first time I met her. But you couldn't tell Curtis anything. He was smitten. Love is blind, you know?"

"So I've heard."

The same nurse who had helped wrestle Lucy off Curtis approached Wanda. "Is everything okay in there?"

Wanda gave her head a sad shake. "I wish I knew." She thumped the counter lightly as if trying to snap herself out of her funk. "Have you gotten any new test results back?"

The nurse smiled kindly. "Not yet. I'll let you know the moment I hear anything."

Wanda thanked her and turned her back to the nurses' station. "I thought it was all over," she said to Zoe, "and now this happens."

Puzzled, she asked, "What do you mean?"

"Two nights ago, Curtis finally had enough of Lucy's constant drama and broke up with her. I don't think she's aware that I know about it though. Now with him hurt, she has another chance to get her hooks into him."

"Curtis broke off the engagement?" Zoe shot a look at Earl, who shrugged. He didn't know about it either.

"Yes. I was so relieved he'd finally seen through her act. Being pretty on the outside doesn't make a person good on the inside."

Zoe gazed past Earl into the room across the hall. With the curtain drawn back, she had a clear view of Lucy at the foot of Curtis's bed. Hector stood beside his daughter, a fatherly arm around her shoulders as she pressed a hand to her mouth. Nothing out of place for someone worrying over a critically wounded loved one. Had Zoe not witnessed the hysteria a few minutes earlier—and now with the news about the recent breakup—she wouldn't have given the scene a second thought.

Earl caught Zoe's eye. "We should go," he mouthed.

She held up one finger. There was a question she'd intended to ask since they'd arrived. Thanks to the outburst, she'd almost forgotten. "Wanda, do you happen to know who Lucy had been dating when she met Curtis?"

"What? No. I mean, I didn't realize she was seeing anyone else. Curtis never mentioned it." Wanda grunted. "If you find out who the guy is, let me know. Maybe I could talk him into patching things up with her."

Zoe laughed in spite of herself. "I'll do that. Call me when Curtis wakes up." She gave the woman a hug.

"Of course." Looking dour, Wanda gazed toward her son's bedside. "I need to get back in there. Maybe I can convince Hector to take his daughter home." She didn't sound hopeful.

Earl gave Wanda a quick embrace before falling into step with Zoe. "That was...bizarre," he said once they were far enough down the hall that Wanda wouldn't overhear.

"Did you know anything about it?" Zoe asked.

"About Curtis dumping Lucy? Or about Lucy being certifiable?"

"Either. Both."

Earl considered the question. "Curtis mentioned she was clingy."

"Clingy? How?"

They reached the elevators, and Earl punched the down button. "She had a jealous streak. Got kinda bent out of shape when he talked to other girls. Wanted to know where he was, who he was with all the time."

"Sounds more controlling than clingy."

Earl shrugged. "That was a month or so ago. At the time, Curtis was flattered. You know. Women were never knocking down his door. To have one who looked like Lucy treating him like he was a rock star? Couldn't blame the guy for eating it up."

The doors swished open and they joined a pair of young doctors on the elevator. Zoe pondered the situation in silence, even after they reached the main floor of the South Tower and headed back down the long hallway to the James Street parking garage. The wedding was only weeks away. She'd sent her RSVP days ago. Everyone at the ambulance garage had been chattering about the big event.

No one, as far as she could tell, had any inkling of trouble between the bride and groom.

Earl broke the silence as they reached the machine to pay for parking. "I wonder..."

"Huh?"

He dug the ticket and a five-dollar bill from his wallet. "You know what they say."

"About what?"

"A woman scorned." Earl hesitated before inserting the ticket into the machine. "From what I saw back there, I would not want Lucy Livingston's fury aimed at me."

FIVE

Pete blew off the reporters and their barrage of questions, storming into his station and past the front office, pissed that he was no closer to identifying the shooter than he had been this morning.

"Chief," Nancy called after him.

He spun on his heel.

His secretary stood at the front office door, holding a handful of pink notes. "Most of these are from residents with rattled nerves who need some words of comfort."

"And you couldn't have handled them?" he said, harsher than he intended.

She planted a fist on one hip and fixed him with a glare she could only have learned from Sylvia, his former secretary. "I did handle the bulk of them. These insisted on the kind and personal touch only you can give."

Her sarcasm forced a smile from him. She'd come a long way in recent months. She might just make it in this job after all.

The phone behind her rang, and she turned to answer it, calling over her shoulder, "The top two seem the most urgent."

Pete grabbed a cup of coffee from the pot in his office before settling into one of the chairs in the conference room to sort through the messages.

The first one was from Kevin, stating he'd found something and would be back at the station in an hour. According to Nancy's handwriting, he'd called fifty minutes ago.

The second message read: "*Chuck Delano called and said if you've reconsidered, he needs to know now.*"

Was this guy ever going to give up? Pete crumpled the note and tossed it in the trash.

The bells on the front door jangled and footsteps thumped down the hall. Expecting Kevin, Pete looked up. Instead, Nate Williamson dragged in and flopped into another of the chairs.

One of Pete's part-time officers, Nate looked battle weary. "I finished going over the ambulance." He pulled a small evidence bag from his pocket and dropped it on the table with a soft thunk.

Pete reached for it. "You found something?"

"Not really. One mangled fragment."

"That's it?" Pete tugged a glove from his hip pocket and wiggled his fingers into it before depositing the evidence into his palm. Mangled was an understatement.

"Afraid so. And I almost missed it." Nate rubbed his shaved head. "I gave Bud the okay to make repairs on the ambulance so they can get it back in service."

The bells signaled another arrival. A minute later, Kevin and Baronick tromped into the conference room.

"I thought you went back to Brunswick," Pete said to the detective.

"Why would I do that when all the excitement's out this way?" Baronick flashed his too-bright smile. "Besides, I heard Kevin here had made a big find."

Pete shot a look at his officer. Since when had Kevin started including the county police on their cases without going through Pete first?

Kevin's eyes widened and he shook his head. "The crime scene guys called it in."

Pete eased up on the kid. He already knew county would lay claim to all evidence collected. They had the lab facilities. Vance Township didn't. "What'd you find?"

Kevin held out another evidence bag. "A bullet. Found it with the metal detector."

Still wearing his glove, Pete spilled the bag's contents into his hand. The lump of lead was larger than the one Nate had dug out of the ambulance. While deformed, this one held some promise.

Kevin hooked his thumbs through his duty belt. "Considering the location of the shooter and the victims, this has to be the bullet that struck Curtis Knox."

Pete retrieved his reading glasses from his pocket and perched them on his nose before pinching the slug between his finger and thumb, holding it up for closer scrutiny.

Baronick leaned over Pete's shoulder. "Thirty caliber."

Pete grunted. "Doesn't narrow it down a whole hell of a lot." From the corner of his eye, he noticed Kevin deflate. Glancing at the officer, he nodded. "But it might help rule out some potential suspects. Good work, Kevin."

The young officer puffed up again and smiled.

Pete eyed Baronick. "Have *you* found anything?"

"More dead ends. I ran a trace on the phone used to report the so-called ATV accident. Turned out to be a burner phone. I have my guys trying to track down where it was bought, but nothing yet." He straightened. "You were off to check on Eli Sullivan. Anything there?"

"Claims he was at Rodeo's the time of the shooting." Pete returned the slug to the envelope and handed it to Baronick. "I've sent Seth over there to ask if anyone can confirm his alibi. He also claimed he had a quad but sold it for cash to, as he put it, 'some old dude at the bar.' Hopefully Seth can dig up our *old dude* while he's at it."

Baronick jotted his name on the chain of evidence tag on Kevin's bag, then scooped up the one Nate had brought in and did the same with it. "You do realize there's still one huge hole in any case you might make against Sullivan."

Pete grunted. "You mean how he would have known who would be in the ambulance responding to the call?"

"That's the one."

"Yeah. Combined with the fact that I don't see him as smart enough to pull this off, I doubt he's our man."

Baronick shoved the evidence bags in his pocket. "Which leaves us with an unknown gunman out there taking random potshots at emergency medical personnel."

Like Zoe. Who was on duty tonight. For a fleeting moment, Pete considered asking her to call off. But he knew she wouldn't.

Pete noticed Nate bracing his elbow against the table and holding his head in his hand, eyes closed. Pete barked the officer's name in his come-to-attention voice.

Nate jolted upright, eyes wide.

"Go home," Pete said, softer. "Get some sleep. This investigation is turning into a marathon instead of a sprint, and I don't want my officers conking out when I need them the most."

Nate climbed to his feet. "Yes, sir. But if something breaks and you need me..."

"I have your number. Go."

As Nate headed out, Pete turned to Kevin. "You too."

"I'm fine."

Pete aimed a thumb at the door.

"What about you?" Kevin protested. "Chief, you've been up all night after working all day yesterday and now today."

Pete held up his coffee cup. "I'm good. I'm also the boss. Go home."

Kevin stood his ground.

"Go. Home. I can't get out of here until I have some well-rested men to take over. The sooner you and Nate catch some Zs, the sooner I can do likewise."

Kevin mulled it over and reluctantly agreed.

Baronick slid into the chair Nate had vacated. "You don't really expect to get any sleep tonight, do you?" The detective's grin didn't match the concerned crease between his eyes. "Zoe's crew's on duty, right?"

Pete's cell phone rang before he could respond. He checked the screen and answered. "Seth. Did you find anything?"

Judging by the sounds coming across the phone, Officer Seth Metzger must have been standing next to a jukebox. "No one here knows anything about Snake's deal to sell a quad to anyone. Old dude or otherwise."

"What about his alibi for last night?"

There was a pause. "Well, the guy who was tending bar then isn't supposed to come back in for another hour. But there's a girl here who says she was around from six until last call."

From Seth's tone, Pete gathered the girl was quite a looker, and he visualized her next to the jukebox—and Seth—as he spoke. "And?"

"She says Snake was here all right. Was here when she arrived. But the thing is...he left around seven fifteen or so and came back a little before eight thirty."

Pete sat up. "Really?"

"I thought I'd stick around and talk to the bartender when he comes in. Unless you need me back there."

"No, that's fine. Ask around in case anyone else saw Sullivan or talked to him too. I trust you got the girl's contact information."

"Oh, yeah." Seth's smile carried through the line.

"He learned something?" Baronick asked as Pete ended the call.

"He did. Eli 'Snake' Sullivan may not have an alibi after all." Pete relayed what Seth had told him.

"Interesting. But there's still the question of—"

"Of how he would know who was in that ambulance." Pete drummed his fingers on the table. "I wonder if Eli Sullivan knows anyone at EOC."

"The Emergency Operations Center?" Baronick's eyes brightened, and he climbed to his feet. "I'm on my way there now."

Zoe stepped out of Earl's minivan in front of the police station. Pete's Explorer shared the parking lot with a pair of news trucks emblazoned with logos from two Pittsburgh area stations.

"See you in a few hours," Earl said before pulling away.

No one emerged from the trucks to approach her. Apparently they didn't believe anyone of importance would show up in a minivan.

She pushed through the station's front door and stopped at the front office. Nancy was on the phone and waved her toward the hallway.

Zoe found Pete alone in the conference room, drawing what looked like a timeline on the whiteboard. She paused in the doorway to admire the view. There was definitely something enticing about a man in uniform. Especially this man.

Pete glanced over his shoulder and smiled. "Hey."

She hoped he didn't notice her blush. "Hey yourself." She wandered over to the table and studied the array of photos, most of them from last night. "Are you making any progress?"

"Not much." Pete capped the dry-erase pen and set it on the lip of the board. "We're looking into Eli Sullivan. Calls himself Snake. He's the guy you told me about who got into an altercation with Dickson."

"I know. Earl told me the guys at the bar consider him to be a big joke." Zoe read the notes Pete had scrawled on the whiteboard. Sullivan's name had *no alibi* written under the time the shootings occurred last night. "Are you going to arrest him?"

"No." Pete motioned for her to have a seat. "Not unless you can explain how he might have known Dickson would be aboard the ambulance responding last night."

Zoe collapsed into the offered chair. "I wish I could." Pete's question was one she'd intentionally put out of her mind, because the alternative meant the shooter was gunning for random ambulance personnel.

Pete claimed a chair next to Zoe and turned it to face her. "Can you think of anyone with a grudge against Monongahela County EMS?"

"The entire ambulance service?"

"Possibly. The Phillipsburg garage, at least."

Zoe pondered recent calls. "We lose patients from time to time, but I can't think of any that raised red flags."

"Angry family members?"

"No."

"Anyone get fired? Or want a job and not get it?"

"No." Zoe's stomach did a slow roll. "You think one of *us* is behind this?"

"I don't know." Pete shrugged. "That's why I'm asking."

She thought back over recent weeks. Months. "No. We haven't turned anyone away. We haven't fired anyone. Nobody's been in trouble that I'm aware of." Her gaze drifted back to the whiteboard. "Maybe Snake was willing to take his frustration out on anyone who showed up last night. Maybe he knew Barry was on duty and took his chances. Maybe he just got lucky."

Pete looked unconvinced. "I'm not ruling him out."

Zoe's own words echoed inside her brain. "Lucky. Not so lucky for Barry and Curtis."

Pete reached over, closing his fingers over hers. "We'll get whoever did this."

She smiled at the warmth of his touch. "I know you will."

"By the way, we released your ambulance. As soon as they get it patched up, you'll be able to get it back in service."

Uneasy, she slipped her hand from his gentle grasp and leaned back in the chair. "It's going to be a weird shift."

He watched her for a long moment. "I imagine so."

"Sixteen hours straight on duty and everyone in mourning." She picked up a pen lying on the table. "And on edge."

Pete didn't say anything.

She met his gaze. He had a way of looking into her soul and her heart. Or so she believed. Sometimes the idea of him being able to read her mind terrified her. Now, it comforted her. She managed a smile. "Of course we all have that warped sense of humor to fall back on when things get tough."

"Job requirement."

"Yeah." She set the pen down and spun it on the table. "I know there's still the same problem as with Snake, but did you get a chance to look into the other possibility I mentioned?"

"You mean Knox's girlfriend's jealous ex? Not yet."

"You may want to add the girlfriend to the list."

Pete rested an elbow on the table, his chin on his fist. "Oh?"

Zoe launched into the events of the afternoon, concluding with Earl's observation about a woman scorned.

Other than the deepening of a crease in Pete's forehead, his face grew very still. She'd seen this non-expression before, during their weekly poker games. Giving nothing away. Yet she knew his neurons were firing at high gear. His voice low, he asked, "How well do you know Lucy Livingston?"

"Not very. Before today I'd only had one conversation with her. And I'm not sure you can classify today's spectacle as a conversation either."

"How about her father?"

"I know him to see him. Nothing more. He seemed to have a calming effect on her though."

Pete nodded slowly, sat up, and pulled out his notebook. He held out a palm for the pen Zoe had been twirling. She handed it over, and he jotted a note.

"Do *you* know him?" she asked.

"As well as I know anyone in Vance Township who hasn't been arrested or filed a complaint."

Zoe tried to read Pete to no avail. Either he genuinely did not know Hector Livingston, or he knew more than he was willing to share.

Pete caught her eyeing him. His face softened. "Who drove when you went into Pittsburgh?"

"Earl. Why?"

"Don't trust your truck?"

"My truck is fine. Earl's minivan fits in the parking garage easier is all."

"How much did Bud soak you for repairs this time?"

Feigning indignation, she jutted her jaw. "None of your business."

Pete chuckled. "That much, huh? You need to start thinking about trading it in. Get something smaller. With better gas mileage."

Trade in her Chevy? "I need my truck. I can't haul a horse trailer with something *smaller* that gets *better gas mileage*." She added air quotes.

"You don't own a horse trailer."

She sputtered. "I can borrow one as long as I keep my truck."

"When was the last time you hauled your horse anywhere?"

"I took him on a trail ride over in Ohio this summer."

"You didn't haul him. One of your boarders at the farm did. When was the last time you hauled *anything* with your truck?"

She hated it when he was right. The truth of the matter was she couldn't remember the last time she'd had a trailer—horse or otherwise—hitched to the back of her Chevy.

"That's what I thought." Pete made no effort to disguise his grin. "Trade it in for a smaller car. Or even a little SUV. You'd make up the expense with the money you'd save on gas, not to mention the money you wouldn't be paying to Bud Kramer."

She fumed in silence.

"You can't count on free rent from Rose forever, you know."

If Pete kept pointing out the painfully obvious, she might be getting free rent from the county jail for assaulting a law enforcement officer.

He traced a circle on the tabletop with his finger. "Of course, you could always move in with me. I still have a spare room."

She glared hard at him, hoping he might mistake the flush in her cheeks for anger. The slight upward tilt of one corner of his mouth told her he wasn't fooled. She reached over and punched him playfully. "We said we were gonna take it slow. Living under the same roof, separate rooms or not, isn't slow." Climbing to her feet, she added, "And I'll keep my truck, thank you very much. I may need to sleep in it once Logan comes home and reclaims his room."

Pete stood as well, towering over her. He caught her hand, preventing her from backing away. Struggling to catch her breath, she let him intertwine his fingers with hers. Let him draw her closer. Felt the heat radiating from him. She lifted her gaze from the front of his shirt to his mouth. Remembered what it was like to be kissed by those lips.

She slipped her free arm around his waist, ignoring the gadgets on his duty belt digging into her, and raised onto her tiptoes.

"Chief, I—oh!" Nancy stuttered from the doorway. "Excuse me."

Pulling free of Pete's hand, Zoe stumbled backwards, almost falling over the chair she'd been sitting in.

"I'm so sorry." Nancy flapped a sheet of paper at them. "I need your signature—I—can get it later." She vanished down the hall still sputtering apologies.

"Damn it," Pete muttered.

Zoe danced an awkward jig to keep from ending up on the floor. In the process she swung the chair between them. "I have to go anyhow. I need to run out to the farm before my shift. And then get a shower. And, well, I'll talk to you later."

She made it to the hall before he called to her, "Wait."

Zoe stopped. Turned. "Pete—" A subtle change in his expression silenced her. No longer teasing. Or lustful. He looked...

Worried. "Be careful."

She pictured Medic Two in the middle of the cuts last night, Barry Dickson's dead body next to it, and shivered. "I will." She started to turn away, but paused, meeting Pete's gaze again. "You too."

SIX

The old Chevy jounced up the rutted farm lane. Only the seatbelt kept Zoe from being flung around inside the cab. On her left, the burned wreckage of the mid-nineteenth-century farmhouse had been bulldozed and buried, leaving only a patch of barren dirt as its footprint.

Zoe topped the hill and rolled down the other side toward the barn. She braked to a stop next to a familiar white pickup, slid down from the driver's seat, and entered the large barn. Two dozen box stalls lined both sides of the structure, opening into a center riding arena. At the moment, only one horse stood tied outside its stall, its owner tightening the cinch.

"Going for a ride?" Zoe said.

Patsy Greene looked up. "Yeah. Care to join me?" Patsy was Zoe's cousin, friend, and right-hand woman where managing the barn was concerned.

"I wish. I'm on duty tonight."

"That's too bad. Windstar's getting fat. His owner never exercises him anymore." Patsy's expression turned somber. "I saw the news this morning. Horrible. For a minute, I was afraid it might have been you. How well did you know the guys who got shot?"

"Very."

Patsy gave one last heave on the cinch strap and flopped the stirrup down from where it had been hooked over the saddle horn. "I'm sorry. I can't imagine what it's like, doing what you do. And then to have someone shooting at you." She shook her head.

Zoe considered making light of it. *Just doing our job. All in the line of duty.* But there wasn't anything routine about coworkers being gunned down.

Patsy planted her fists on her hips. "If I were you, I'd call off sick tonight. Saddle up Windstar and let's play hooky."

Zoe gazed out the doors to the hills and woods beyond the pasture. She loved nothing more than a leisurely trail ride on a clear early autumn day. The flies wouldn't be biting. It wasn't too hot or too cold. And yet, tempting though the invitation might be, running away from her job wasn't an option. "Tomorrow. The weather's supposed to hold. You gonna be around?"

"Of course."

"I get off at eight in the morning."

"All right." Patsy slipped the halter from the Arabian's head and gathered the reins. "I'll meet you here at nine. Pack a lunch." She grabbed the saddle horn and swung onto the horse's back.

The idea of a day aboard Windstar soothed Zoe's frayed nerves. She knew better than anyone how unexpectedly life could take a turn— or be snuffed out. "You're on." A thought occurred to her. "Mind if I bring Allison along?"

"She's back? Of course I don't mind. She's a great kid. And don't worry about the barn chores. I'll make sure everyone's fed when I get back this evening."

"Thanks." At least this time of year there wasn't a lot to do. The horses stayed out in the pasture around the clock, coming in only to be grained. "Have a good ride. And be careful."

"You too. Git up, Jazzel." Patsy spun the feisty Arabian toward the open doors at the rear of the barn and booted the mare into a lope, kicking up dust in their wake.

Zoe choked, turning away until the cloud settled.

Once the air cleared, she crossed the arena, intending to walk the perimeter, peering into stalls to check for loose boards or exposed nails. Anything that might result in a nosy horse getting injured. As she strolled stall to stall, Pete's words of warning echoed in her head. The same words she'd tossed back at him. The same words she'd said to Patsy.

Be careful. Two little words that felt like lead weighing on her heart. Any other day, she wouldn't have given them a second thought. Be careful. Simply another phrase to be lumped with *see you later.* Or *have a good day...*

Except today, with Barry Dickson dead and Curtis Knox unconscious in a hospital bed, those words left her uneasy.

Be careful. Of what? More importantly, of whom?

Pete's SUV crunched up the gravel driveway to a small craftsman-style bungalow, home to Hector and Lucy Livingston. Massive maples formed a canopy over the yard letting only dapples of sunshine through. A row of pines blocked the view from the road. A detached garage with its doors yawning open listed precariously to the right. Two vehicles, an older Dodge pickup, dents marring a flat blue paint job that hadn't seen a coat of wax in years, and a silver Hyundai Accent with what looked like Mardi Gras beads hanging from the rearview mirror, sat in front. Pete wondered if the Livingstons feared the dilapidated structure might collapse on their vehicles or if they kept other things stored in there.

An ATV perhaps.

Pete parked at the top of the narrow driveway before it widened in front of the garage. If anyone wanted to leave in either the car or the truck, they would have to go through the yard to get around his Explorer.

He climbed out. There was no movement from the house. No subtle stirring of curtains or blinds. Other than a few bird chirps from the maples, all was still. Keeping alert, Pete edged around the blue pickup toward the open garage. He paused at the entrance. Thanks to the heavy shade, he didn't have to wait long for his eyes to adjust to the dark interior.

The Hyundai might have squeezed into the teetering structure, but not the pickup. The place looked like part storage shed, part workshop. Sheets of plywood darkened by age occupied part of one bay along with a rickety picnic table stacked with an assortment of poorly kept hand tools. A canoe had been shoved against the back wall. A workbench sported reloading supplies on one end, an array of fishing tackle boxes on the other. Assorted duck and turkey decoys lay scattered about. A massive generator on wheels sat off to one side. But no ATV.

"Looking for something?"

Pete turned cautiously to find Livingston standing next to the pickup. Dressed in camo, the man blended into his wooded surroundings. The fact Pete hadn't heard him approach was unnerving. "Hector. I need to speak to your daughter."

Livingston leaned against the truck's bed, appearing relaxed, although Pete suspected he could spring into action with the speed of a cat if he wanted. "What about?" Livingston asked.

Pete mirrored the man's laidback posture, resting his arms on the other side of the Ram's bed. "I have some questions about the shooting last night. I understand she broke up with a guy before she started dating Curtis Knox, and the guy didn't take it very well." Pete wasn't about to reveal his interest in Lucy as a suspect.

Livingston grunted what Pete took as a confirmation. "Lucille's in the house." He tipped his head in that direction. "Go on in." Without another word, he pushed away from the truck and ambled into the leaning garage.

Pete offered his thanks. He passed behind the pickup and almost whacked his shin on the hitch of a low flatbed trailer sticking out from beside the garage. With a quick sidestep to avoid an inevitable bruise, he headed down the fieldstone path to the back porch. The door swung open before he had a chance to knock.

A petite raven-haired bombshell greeted him with a scowl as dark as her hair. "What do you want?"

Her so-called fiancé had been shot less than twenty-four hours previous. Pete would have thought her initial reaction to seeing a cop on her doorstep might be to ask if a suspect had been caught. Unless she already knew the answer. "Lucy Livingston? I'm Chief Pete Adams, Vance Township Police."

"Yeah?"

"Mind if I ask you a few questions?" When she didn't respond, he added, "About your ex-boyfriend."

"Curtis isn't my ex," she said. "We're engaged to be married."

Pete feigned ignorance of anything to the contrary. "I realize that. I'm referring to the man you were seeing prior to Curtis."

Her face softened. "Oh." She moved clear of the door. "Come in."

The kitchen he stepped into was far from modern, but neat and clean. An off-white refrigerator bore a few hand-scrawled memos attached by an odd assortment of promotional magnets. Steam rose from a pot on an avocado green range. A box of store-brand pasta and a jar of pasta sauce sat on a spotless Formica countertop. "Sorry if I'm interrupting your supper. I won't take up much of your time."

Lucy flipped a chrome dial on the stove. "What do you wanna know?"

Pete eased his notebook from his pocket. "A name would be a good place to start."

Her dark eyes shifted. "A name?"

"Your ex-boyfriend's name."

"Why?"

Okay. They were going to play this game. "I've been told he was upset when you broke up with him to see Curtis. Is that true?"

She caught a lip between her teeth. "Yeah. He was upset."

"Upset enough to want to get payback?"

The girl's face transitioned through a series of expressions. "Payback? You mean like trying to hurt me?"

Was she really that dense? Pete suspected not. "Possibly. Or Curtis."

Her eyes widened. "You think *he* was the one who tried to kill Curtis?"

Pete wasn't buying her act. "And succeeded in killing Barry Dickson."

"Yes, of course. Poor Barry."

"What do you think? Would your ex be capable of such a thing?"

Gazing downward, she shook her head. "He might have been. But I'm afraid you're looking in the wrong direction."

"What makes you say that?"

Lucy lifted her face, her dark eyes unreadable. "Because he's got about the best alibi possible. His name was Rick Brown, and he's been dead for six months."

Something about the name Rick Brown nagged Pete as he made his way back to his SUV. According to Lucy, her ex-boyfriend had indeed been upset when she'd dumped him, and after a night of drowning his sorrows, he'd run his motorcycle into a tree.

Pete didn't remember such an accident, but that wasn't why the name set off his inner alarm.

Hector Livingston stepped out from between the blue pickup and the silver Hyundai before Pete reached his Explorer. "Did you get what you needed from my daughter?"

More or less. "What can you tell me about Rick Brown?"

Hector looked at Pete, puzzled. "Brown? Why are you asking about him?"

"Your daughter used to date him?"

"Yeah."

"And he died six months ago in a motorcycle crash?"

Hector nodded slowly. "About that, yeah. But it didn't happen around here. Why are you investigating it?"

"I'm not. Not really. Where did it happen?"

"Out in Ohio, I think. Kid wasn't from around here."

"Oh? The name sounded familiar to me."

"Brown?" Hector came close to grinning. "Can't imagine why, being such a unique last name and all. Kinda like Adams."

Pete chuckled. "You may be right."

"If you aren't investigating the kid, why are you asking about him after all this time?"

Since Hector seemed willing to chat, Pete decided to go with it. "Curtis's shooting last night. Someone suggested Lucy's ex-boyfriend was angry about the breakup and might be a potential suspect." Pete shrugged. "But he's dead, so I guess that clears him."

Hector's face grew dark, and he fixed Pete with a cold stare. "That girl of mine is quite a looker, don't you think?"

Pete studied the man. Where was he going with this? "She's a pretty girl. You should be proud."

Hector snorted. "I'll tell you a little trick I've learned. You know how you can tell when she's lying?"

Pete's mind stilled. "No. How?"

"Her lips move."

Another time, Pete might have laughed. But he had a feeling Hector wasn't trying to be funny.

"Yeah, Lucille used to date Rick Brown. And, yeah, Brown smashed his bike into an oak tree." Hector shook his head. "But he's not the one your source was talking about. That girl of mine goes through men the way most folks go through toilet paper. And they get about the same treatment."

Pete wasn't sure how to respond to that comment, so he asked, "Lucy dated someone between Rick Brown and Curtis Knox?"

"Yeah." Hector made a sour face. "Some jackass. Calls himself Snake."

SEVEN

"It's a piece of junk," Earl said.

Zoe patted him on the shoulder. "Bud Kramer said Medic Two won't be ready until sometime Monday. If the Brunswick garage hadn't sent this one out, we'd be down a unit all weekend."

The late afternoon sun warmed Zoe's back as they stood in front of the ambulance garage's open second bay, inspecting Medic Eight. As far as she was concerned, it looked fine. A few years older than their usual ride, but as long as everything worked—and she'd been assured it did—she figured they could survive one shift with it.

Earl, however, wasn't so easily appeased. "Bud doesn't want to pay anyone overtime to get the job done."

"He's only open until noon on Saturday. It would be a rush job." Zoe nudged her partner with an elbow. "Aren't you the one who always asks, 'Do you want it done fast, or do you want it done right?'"

He grumbled something she couldn't quite hear.

Zoe didn't bother asking him to repeat it. She knew full well Earl's mood had nothing to do with the ambulance. It wasn't really Medic Two he wanted back.

He extended an arm toward the fill-in ambulance. "Command could have sent us one of their regular units. This one is basically out of commission. They only use it as a last resort."

"We put in a request for a backup, and this is what they sent," Zoe said. "No one gave us a selection to choose from."

He spit out a string of profanities.

"You need to chill," Zoe said, trying to keep her voice soothing.

"Don't tell me to chill." Earl, usually the epitome of calm and reason, kicked a chunk of broken concrete, sending it skittering across the sidewalk.

She crossed her arms and waited for him to regain his composure.

After a few moments, he shook his head. "A guy shouldn't go to work trying to help people and have to worry about those same people taking potshots at him."

"Pete and his boys will catch the guy."

Earl met her gaze. "They damned well better." Shoving his hands in his pockets, he retreated into the office.

Alone in front of the open bay, Zoe eyed the fill-in ambulance. Even when Medic Two returned to service, nothing would be the same again.

Crunching tires made her turn to see a blue Subaru Outback pulling up to the curb. Earl's wife stepped out from behind the steering wheel.

Zoe strode over to her. "Hey, Olivia. What are you doing here?"

She held up a cell phone. "Earl walked off without this. I'm taking Lilly to cheerleading practice, so I thought I'd bring it to him."

Zoe leaned over to wave at the young girl strapped into the backseat before holding out a hand. "I can give it to him. He's a little crabby right now."

Olivia held onto the phone and rolled her eyes. "Tell me about it. He's been on edge since last night. Didn't sleep hardly at all. I had hoped he might be in a better mood after the two of you got back from seeing Curtis, but no such luck." She turned the phone over in her hand. "Still, I think I'd rather give it to him myself. You know?"

"Yeah." Zoe didn't need the blanks filled in. *Just in case.* She aimed a thumb at the office door. "He's inside. I'll stay with Lilly."

Olivia smiled. "Thanks."

Zoe took a seat behind the Outback's steering wheel and turned to smile at the small cheerleader. "How're you doing, Lill?"

"Okay." The girl's eyes sparkled. "Daddy says you might come stay with us."

"Afraid not, kiddo."

Lilly jutted out her lower lip. "But I hoped you'd bring your cats. I want a kitten."

Zoe laughed. Once again, Jade and Merlin were the welcomed guests. She was simply the human that came with the package. "I heard you want a pony too."

"Well, yeah." Lilly dragged out the word to make it sound more like duh. "But Daddy won't let me." She perked up. "Maybe I can come to your farm and ride one of yours?"

Her farm? The Kroll farm never had been hers, but it used to feel like it. Not that she was going to explain her homeless status to a seven-year-old. "I'll talk to your dad."

"Great." Lilly beamed as though it were a done deal.

They chatted about Lilly's two older brothers and about the family dog—Lilly made no bones about preferring the dog to the brothers—until Olivia returned.

"Thanks for keeping Lilly company," she said, reclaiming her seat from Zoe.

"No problem."

Olivia turned the key, reached to close the door, and paused. She looked up at Zoe, her eyes moist and worried. "Take care of him. Okay?"

The tremor in Olivia's voice was as uncharacteristic as Earl's foul mood. Zoe searched for words to comfort her partner's frightened wife. Finding nothing adequate, she replied, "Of course."

Zoe watched the Subaru pull away and disappear around the bend. Within less than twenty-four hours, an unknown monster with a gun had taken one life and left another person unconscious in a hospital. But he'd also taken so much more.

She scanned the town around her and wondered who he was and what he had planned next.

Pete punched Wayne Baronick's number into his cell phone as he parked in front of Sullivan's mobile home for the second time that day. When the detective picked up, Pete asked, "What'd you find out from EOC?"

"Nothing yet," Baronick replied. "From the dispatchers I've talked to, no one has any connections with, or knowledge of, Snake Sullivan."

"Keep digging." Pete eyed the mobile home. A shadow passed in front of a lamp burning inside, but with the curtains closed, he couldn't tell if it was Snake or his mother. "And while you're at it, find out if anyone there is friends with Lucy Livingston."

"Knox's girlfriend?"

"Ex-girlfriend." Pete gave Baronick a quick rundown of what Zoe and Hector had told him.

"I'll ask around and get back to you."

Pete ended the call and shoved the phone back in his pocket before climbing out of the Explorer. Deep gray clouds had taken over the sky, and the air smelled of rain.

He was being watched. Not only by whoever was inside the Sullivan home, but probably by every other resident of the trailer park. He knocked on the door and noticed a lack of heavy footsteps from inside.

The door swung open to Mrs. Sullivan's battle-weary face. "Eli's not here. For real this time. He left an hour ago."

"All right." Pete took off his ball cap. "Could I talk to *you* for a few minutes?"

She gave the request a moment of thought before nodding and stepping clear.

The place hadn't changed since Pete's earlier visit. "I understand Eli used to date Lucy Livingston."

Mrs. Sullivan's eye twitched. "Yeah."

"What can you tell me about the relationship?"

The woman gave a tired sigh. "I'm not sure what you want to know. They dated for a few months. But he hasn't seen her in quite a while."

"Who ended it?"

"The girl did. Eli talked about asking her to marry him." Mrs. Sullivan laughed without a hint of humor. "Like he could afford a wife. He probably would've wanted to move her here and let me pay their bills."

"Was he upset when Lucy broke up with him?"

"You could say that." Mrs. Sullivan wandered over to a battered recliner and sank into it as if her legs couldn't hold her any longer. "He was a brute for a while. Busted a bunch of my stuff. Most of the time he was out getting drunk." She shot a glance at Pete. "Or high. Frankly, I didn't care as long as he wasn't here. I know that's horrible for a mother to say. But I can't control him. He's got a mean streak. Got it from his father."

Pete felt sorry for the woman. Hauling her son off to prison might be the best thing for her. "Does your son have any friends who work at the 911 center in Brunswick?"

The question seemed to startle her. "I don't think so. I doubt it. To be honest, I don't know Eli's friends, but I seriously doubt any of them can hold down a real job."

Pete had to agree. "Do you have any idea when Eli will be home?"

She laughed, again without humor. "Probably not until morning, after he's drunk himself into a stupor and needs to sleep it off."

"When he does come back, could you ask him to come down to the station first thing tomorrow? I'd like to ask him a few questions."

"I doubt he'll talk to you."

"Tell him life will be easier for him if he does."

"He'll just have me call my brother-in-law."

The attorney. "Fine. Have him come along too." Pete didn't really expect to get any direct answers from the kid, with or without Uncle Andy present. But one or the other might just let something slip. Like where Snake was between seven fifteen and eight thirty last night.

"I'll tell him, but I ain't making any promises."

Pete tugged on his ball cap and thanked the woman.

As he made his way down the rickety steps, his cell phone rang. Caller ID showed the station's number.

"Chief," Nancy said when he answered, "I was about to leave for the day when Wanda Knox called. Curtis is awake."

Pete stopped, one hand on the door of his SUV. "That's great." He might finally catch a break in this case.

"Do you want me to ask Kevin or Nate to drive into Pittsburgh to talk to him?"

"No." Pete checked the time. It was already after five. "I'll go. Is Kevin there?"

"Yeah. He rolled in a half hour ago."

Pete slid behind the wheel and slammed the door. "Patch him through."

The television in the crew lounge blared some sporting event that no one was watching. Zoe thumbed through a tattered magazine from a pile somebody had brought in from home. Two years out of date, the smiling celebrity couple on the cover had long since divorced. Not that it mattered. The words could have been written in Greek for all she comprehended.

Earl and the other guys on the crew stared at the TV, their faces blank. Zoe wondered if they would even be able to tell her the score if she asked. She doubted it.

Tossing the magazine aside, Zoe hoisted herself out of the too-soft, too-worn armchair and headed for the office.

Crew Chief Tony DeLuca sat at the desk doing paperwork. A police scanner on the shelf above him squawked with activity from an assortment of emergency response departments around the county.

Zoe crossed to the closed door leading to the ambulance bays. On a warm summer evening, both the outside bay doors and the office door would have stood open to catch a breeze. But the sky had grown dark and ominous.

Through the window, Zoe noticed the wind kicking up, fluttering the awning on the flower shop across the street and sending dust devils scurrying along the sidewalks.

"The weather suits the mood around here, doesn't it?" Tony said.

Zoe spun to see the crew chief watching her. "I guess it does."

He tapped the report in front of him with his pen. "I read the same line four times and still can't tell you what it says."

"A lot of that going on."

The Monongahela County EMS radio on the desk crackled to life. "Phillipsburg, this is Control. Medical response requested to two-five-five Franklin Run Road. Seventy-five-year-old male complaining of chest pains."

Tony snatched the mic. "Ten-four, Control." He jotted the address down on a slip of paper and aimed a thumb at the doorway to the crew lounge with his free hand. "Zoe, tell Mike and Tracy they're up."

A moment later, Medic One roared out of the garage. Zoe and Tony watched from the window.

"I really hate this," he said. "After last night, I wonder what I'm sending them into."

Zoe hugged herself against a sudden chill. "I was thinking the same thing."

Behind them, the phone rang. At the same time, the scanner on the shelf above the desk emitted a series of tones on the county fire channel. Tony blew out a noisy breath. "Sheesh. Is it going to be that kind of night?"

The crew chief reached up to silence the scanner and answer the phone. Zoe watched a woman step out of the flower shop carrying a bundle wrapped in green tissue and duck her head against the breeze as she hurried to her car. Just another day. For some people.

"Thank God," Tony exclaimed into the receiver. "That's great news. Thanks for letting us know."

Zoe turned away from the window as Tony hung up. "What's great news?"

The crew chief lowered his head, his eyes closed for a moment. When he lifted his head again, he was smiling through tears. "Come on. I'll tell all of you at once."

Zoe followed him into the lounge. Earl looked up from the TV.

"Curtis's mom just called," Tony said. "He's awake. His vitals are stable and everything looks like he's gonna be fine."

Earl let out a whoop. Zoe slumped against the doorway in relief.

"We should all go see him tomorrow," Earl said.

Tony chuckled. "We could take him a six-pack and a pizza."

Earl heartily agreed.

"I hate to burst your bubble," Zoe said, "but I doubt they'll allow him to have beer when he's been on morphine."

"Curtis can have the pizza," Tony said. "*We'll* take care of the beer."

The shrill ring of the phone pierced their raucous laughter.

Zoe waved off Tony. "I'll get it." She left them to planning their hospital keg party and retreated to the office.

"Monongahela EMS. May I help you?" she said into the phone.

Sirens blasted through the earpiece, drowning out the gruff voice on the other end.

The back of Zoe's neck prickled. "I'm sorry, can you repeat that?"

"I said, this is Deputy Fire Chief Onderick. We need a medic unit out here, *now*."

Zoe grabbed a pen and paper. "Give me your address and the nature of the medical emergency."

"The old Carl Loomis farm," Onderick shouted above the din. "Shots fired."

Zoe's fingers froze on the pen.

Through the receiver, the deputy chief's voice bordered on hysterical as he added, "We have two men down."

EIGHT

"How are you doing?"

Curtis Knox had always been as thin as a marathon runner, but in the hospital bed plugged into IVs and oxygen, he looked frail, almost skeletal. "I've been better."

Pete had sent Wanda down to the cafeteria with orders not to return until she'd had a good meal. He hoped the paramedic might be more willing to share the horrors of his experience without his mother present. "Are you up to answering some questions?"

Curtis shifted in the bed with a pained grimace. "I'll try."

Pete pulled a chair closer to the bedside, sat down, and took out his notepad. "What can you tell me about last night's call?"

Curtis's eyes clouded with the memory. "It happened so fast."

"Just do your best." Pete started for him, "You responded to a report of an ATV accident?"

"Back in the cuts. Yeah. We—me and Barry—" Curtis's voice cracked.

"Take your time," Pete said gently.

The paramedic rubbed his nose then readjusted the nasal cannula. "We found an overturned quad on the access road. I should have suspected something was off. The thing was right there on the road. On the level. No reason for it to be tipped over like that."

Pete waved away his concerns. "You had no reason to expect trouble. Did you see anyone?"

"No. Nobody was near the thing. At least we didn't see anybody. I radioed in that we were on scene. Barry and I got out..." Curtis's voice again grew ragged. "We got out and were gonna walk over to the quad." He fingered the IV tubing. "Then, I don't know. Things went sideways. There was a crack. Like you hear during hunting season."

"A rifle," Pete prompted.

"Yeah. *Boom.* And—Barry went down. For a second, I didn't know what was going on. I ran around the front of the ambulance. Or started to." Curtis paused, twisting a handful of sheet into a knot.

Pete remained silent, giving him time. On his notepad, he jotted, *Dickson hit first.*

"Next thing I know, I'm on the ground. I don't really remember hearing the second shot. And I don't remember realizing what had happened for a second or two. Then...*man,* everything hurt. Burned like fire." He touched the bandage on the upper right of his chest.

"Did you see anything? Anyone?"

"No." Curtis lowered his hand to rest, clenched on the sheet covering him. "I just laid there. Afraid whoever it was would shoot again. So I played dead." He met Pete's gaze, his eyes wide with pain and sorrow. "I played dead. Because I was scared. I let Barry die because I was too scared to move."

Pete reached over to place a comforting hand on Curtis's uninjured shoulder. "According to the coroner, he bled out fast. The bullet tore him up so bad inside, nothing you could've done would have made a difference."

"I could have kept him from dying alone, lying in the dirt."

"Or you could have died with him."

Curtis turned his head away. "Right now, I don't care."

Pete withdrew his hand. Survivor's guilt was a powerful thing. "Okay, but you didn't die. You're still here. Help me catch the son of a bitch who did this."

"I would if I could." Curtis met Pete's gaze again. "But I didn't see shit."

"Did you *hear* anything?"

"Things got fuzzy pretty quick. I must have passed out from blood loss." Curtis rubbed his head as if trying to massage away the fog. "But...now that you mention it, yeah. Far off. I remember thinking someone was revving up a chainsaw to cut wood."

"A chainsaw?"

"I don't know. Could've been a weed whacker. Or a dirt bike."

"How about another quad?"

"A quad? Yeah." Curtis nodded. "Yeah. Could be."

"Anything else?"

He thought for a long moment. "No. Sorry."

Pete jotted in his notebook. "Can you think of anyone who might've wanted to kill you or Barry or anyone else on the ambulance service?"

The question appeared to puzzle him. "No."

"Has anyone made any threats?"

Curtis shook his head.

"Any disgruntled patients or patients' families?"

"No."

"Can you think of any patients you or anyone else with the county EMS lost that maybe you shouldn't have lost? Or that the family members felt you shouldn't have lost?"

Curtis's brow furrowed as he pondered the question. "I can't think of anyone."

Pete paused for a moment before asking the next one. "What can you tell me about Snake Sullivan?"

The paramedic stiffened. "Snake?"

Before Curtis could say more, Pete's cell phone rang. He jerked it from his pocket. Caller ID showed the call was coming from his station. Probably one of the men reporting in with lab results. He pressed *ignore*. "Yeah. Snake," he said, pocketing the phone.

"He's an idiot. And he's mean. Likes to push people around just for fun."

"I hear he and Barry got into it."

"It wasn't a big deal. Snake was running off at the mouth. Saying stuff about...well, just being a jackass. He started pushing Barry around and Barry flattened him with one punch. It was over. Done."

"Was it?"

"You think Snake did this?"

"I don't know. I'm trying to find out."

Pete's phone rang again. Five more minutes. That's all he needed with Curtis. He yanked out the phone. He hovered his thumb over the ignore button, but paused. It was the station again.

"I should take this," he told Curtis before answering the call.

"Pete? Where the hell are you?" Sylvia's voice sounded tight.

"I'm talking to Curtis Knox. What are you doing at the station?"

"All hell has broken loose here, that's what I'm doing at your station. You need to get back here now. Bruce Yancy's been shot."

"You should have stayed back," Earl said to Zoe as they followed Medic Three along the tarred and chipped country road, approaching the Loomis farm.

Every nerve fiber in her body agreed. The last time they'd responded to the now-abandoned Loomis farm, they'd discovered a burned corpse. "I'll be fine." But Carl Loomis's charred remains weren't what haunted her. The memory of another burning structure—one she'd been inside—was too fresh, too vivid.

Everyone at the ambulance garage knew about her demons. Tony had offered to let her stay behind and man the radio. He said he could call in someone off-duty to take the call with Earl. But she wouldn't hear of it. She had to face the monsters lurking in the flames sooner or later.

They topped one last hill and rounded the blind curve leading down the other side. Deep gray smoke, almost the same hue as the rain clouds, billowed over the trees blocking the view.

Less than a minute later, the pair of ambulances turned into the gravel farm lane. Ahead, the barn was ablaze, flames devouring the old wood. A trio of firetrucks, including one tanker—no hydrants out here—were parked near the structure. Men in bunker gear poured water on the inferno.

Their radio hissed as Tony in the lead ambulance radioed that both EMS units were on scene. Control responded with a ten-four and the time. Eighteen twenty-six. Almost six thirty. Zoe noted it on the call report.

Deputy Fire Chief Onderick lumbered toward them, waving his arms. Both Zoe and Earl powered down their windows. A gust of rain-laden wind sliced through the ambulance's cab. Sirens and blasts of air horns, some distant, some closer, along with the stench of burning wood and hay, filled the air. Onderick shouted something at the guys in the first rig. Zoe couldn't make it out over the din.

Medic Three pulled forward. Earl followed, and Onderick waved them on rather than repeat whatever orders he'd given.

Zoe caught a glimpse in the rearview mirror of a pair of police cruisers, neither of them Pete's.

Medic Three parked in the grass alongside the farm lane, leaving room for more fire apparatuses. Earl parked Medic Eight next to the other ambulance as the first fat raindrops splattered on the windshield. Zoe jumped out, instinctively reaching for the rain slicker she kept behind the seat. Except this wasn't her regular ride. With no time to search for errant weather gear, she tugged on her EMS ball cap and grabbed the jump kit from inside the side patient compartment door.

"We'll take care of the kid," Tony bellowed over the diesel rumble of idling fire trucks and the vicious popping crackle of the fire. "You two treat Yancy."

Zoe and Earl trailed behind at a jog. Zoe was able to keep her eyes averted from the burning barn, but the sounds and smells triggered flashbacks. Trapped in the basement of a doomed farmhouse, waiting for the groaning timbers to collapse onto her. She choked.

Earl slowed and glanced at her. "You gonna be able to do this?"

"Yeah." She shook it off and nudged him forward. "Go."

They circled to the front of the rig closest to the fire. Two men were on the ground. Fire Chief Bruce Yancy cradled a young man in his arms. Blood soaked through the junior firefighter's turnout coat and covered Yancy's fingers where he bore down on the gunshot wound with his left hand. The chief's right arm hung limp at his side, more blood saturating a tattered sleeve that was half torn away.

Tears filled the chief's eyes as he looked up at the paramedics. "Save him," he pleaded.

"We got him, Yancy," Tony said. He eased the kid out of the fire chief's arms.

Yancy winced, his breath a sharp hiss.

Zoe tugged her cap down lower as a gust of wind and rain threatened to rip it from her head. She studied the entrance wound, relatively small compared to the hole in the back of his arm. "Are you hurt anywhere else?"

"Nope." Yancy swallowed hard. "Bullet shattered my arm," he said through clenched teeth.

Earl dug into the jump kit and pulled out a triangular bandage, which was quickly soaked from the rain. He fashioned a makeshift sling to immobilize the arm. "If you can walk on your own, let's get out of this rain and into the ambulance."

"I can walk." Yancy looked over at the other team working on his young charge. "Is Jason gonna be all right?"

"They're the best. You know that," Zoe said. Not a real answer, but the best she could offer at the moment.

Zoe helped Earl ease the bandage around the broken arm. A loud crack drew her gaze to the burning barn in time to see the roof give way, disintegrating into the hungry flames. She shivered and looked away, taking a glance at the landscape. Overgrown pastures surrounded the barn, house, and a few other decrepit outbuildings rolling in waves upward to the tree line at the top of the hill.

Was the shooter still out there? Had he sufficiently gotten his jollies, picking off helpless rescue personnel? Or had the rain driven him into hiding?

She caught Earl watching her and guessed he was asking himself the same questions.

They helped the fire chief to his feet. As they trudged back to Medic Eight, Tony caught up to them. "Can one of you give me a hand with the gurney?" From the look on his face, no one needed to ask how the junior firefighter was doing.

"I got Yancy," Zoe told Earl. "You go."

Earl and Tony veered away at a slushy jog. Yancy leaned on Zoe with his good arm and they pressed on through the deluge.

She yanked open the ambulance's back doors and helped him climb in. After pulling the doors closed, the sound of the flames and the diesel engines were muffled, leaving only the drumming of raindrops on the roof.

"Jason's mother's gonna kill me for letting her boy get hurt," Yancy stuttered through chattering teeth as he took a seat on the jump bench.

Zoe pulled her trauma shears from her pants pocket, glad she'd sprung for the heavy duty variety. "It wasn't your fault." She wanted to add the boy would be fine, but she had a bad feeling it would be a lie.

Wishing she had Earl's extra set of hands to help keep Yancy's arm stabilized, she removed the temporary sling and started cutting the heavy sleeve of the bunker coat.

The fire chief groaned. "You got any good drugs in this meat wagon?"

"I sure do. As soon as I can get this coat off you, I'll start an IV and slip you something for the pain."

The going was slow and tough, and Zoe had to use both hands to cut through the layers of fabric.

Yancy watched her work. "You want me to do that?"

"I got it, thanks."

"You do realize that's a five-hundred-dollar coat you're destroying." He forced a grin that was more of an agonized grimace.

"I think whoever shot you took care of that already."

He grunted. "This stuff is made to stop projectiles—falling debris, nails and shit. Doesn't do squat against bullets."

With the sleeve slit from cuff to shoulder, Zoe helped Yancy ease out of the decimated coat. She tugged a blanket from under the straps on the gurney and settled it over the fire chief's shoulders.

"You're soaked to the core," he said, resisting the blanket as much as he could with only one functioning arm. "You need this more than I do."

"Forget it, Yancy." Zoe grabbed a bottle of saline and some clean towels. "Behave yourself. You're the patient. I'm the boss here."

He grumbled something she couldn't make out.

She doused the wound to wash away some of the blood and debris. The entrance wound didn't look bad at all. But the back of the arm was a ragged mess. Blood soaked through the bandages as fast as she applied them. She hoped the air splint she applied to immobilize the break would also act as a pressure bandage and help stem the bleeding.

She expected a battle from the grizzled old fire warrior when she told him to lie down on the gurney, but he gave her no argument. A check of his blood pressure confirmed what the lack of color in his cheeks already told her. She leaned toward the back doors, trying to spot Earl around the Star of Life emblems plastered to the back windows.

"What's going on out there?" Yancy asked.

"I can't see a thing." Until her partner returned, she was on her own. She flipped open several storage compartment doors and gathered IV and oxygen tubing, a non-rebreather mask, and a bag of fluids. Within minutes, she had her patient on O2 and started him on IV fluids. As she unlatched and opened the portable EKG, a shadow fell over the rain-streaked back window. For a second, she thought Earl had returned, but instead, someone pounded on the door.

"Zoe? It's Wayne Baronick."

She heaved the door open and almost didn't recognize him. The detective wore a plastic weatherproof hooded slicker, covering his usual all-business dress suit.

"Mind if I come in and ask the chief some questions?"

Zoe slid down the jump bench to make room. "Watch your—"

Too late. He slammed his head as he climbed in. "Damn it," he said, wincing.

"Don't knock yourself out. I'm busy with the one patient I already have."

Wayne flipped his hood back and rubbed his scalp. "The depth of your compassion is astounding."

She clipped a blood oxygen sensor on Yancy's finger. "Have you seen Earl out there?"

"They're still working on the young fireman."

Yancy pulled the non-rebreather mask from his face, perching it on his chin. "How's Jason?"

"Jason? Oh. The kid." Wayne glanced at her askance, his eyes telling her it wasn't good. "They wanted to bring in Life Flight, but the helicopter's grounded because of the weather."

"That's not an answer," Yancy said.

Zoe replaced the mask over his mouth and nose. "This doesn't do any good unless you wear it right."

He glared at her. "You gonna get me something for this pain or do I have to get it myself?"

"I'm calling the hospital next. You know the protocol. On a scale of one to ten—"

"Twenty-five," Yancy snapped.

She looked at Wayne. "He's all yours, Detective."

"Thanks a bunch."

Zoe moved to the seat at the front of the patient compartment, allowing Wayne to slide into her vacated spot on the bench. She picked up the phone and punched in the Brunswick Hospital's emergency department's frequency, keeping one ear on the conversation between the two men.

"Did you see anyone when you first pulled up?" Wayne asked Yancy.

"Didn't see anyone at all, other than my guys. The son of a bitch never showed his face."

"Can you give me an idea of where the shots came from?"

The doctor came on the line, drawing Zoe's attention back to the task at hand. She relayed her patient's vitals and condition and was granted permission to administer a dose of morphine sulfate, repeating every five minutes as needed.

"What's your ETA, Medic Eight?" the doctor asked.

"ETA thirty minutes."

Provided Earl showed up to drive.

She hung up and pulled out the key to the locked drug compartment. "I hate to interrupt, but I need to get Yancy started on some pain meds."

"About gawddamned time," Yancy muttered.

The detective pocketed his cell phone. "I'll talk to you some more at the hospital," he told the fire chief.

"I doubt I can tell you anything else. Like I said, I didn't see much."

Zoe caught Wayne's arm as he moved toward the rig's back door. "I also need to get to the hospital. Could you go find my partner?"

Before the detective could respond, someone else pounded. Wayne opened the door to another firefighter. Instead of turnout gear, he wore a dark coat with wide fluorescent bands, and he appeared on the verge of tears.

"Earl told me to drive this ambulance to the hospital," the firefighter said to Zoe. "They needed an extra man to..." He shot a glance at his chief. "To work on Jason." He again met Zoe's eyes and gave an almost imperceptible shake of his head.

If she hadn't already been sitting, her knees would have given way. They needed Earl because they were using heroic measures to keep the young man alive.

NINE

For the second time in as many days, Pete found himself racing back to Vance Township to deal with a shooting. His headlamps and red and blue emergency lights carved through the veil of rain. The winds ripped a crop of early-turning leaves from the tree branches, scattering them across the dark, glossy pavement.

Roadblocks had been set up, same as the previous night. However, unlike last night, the weather would prevent the state police helicopter from searching, and the rain would offer a challenge to the K-9s. Pete wondered if this elusive shooter had intentionally used the inclement forecast to his advantage.

One other difference between tonight and last...Zoe wasn't in the passenger seat beside Pete. He knew who the victims were from the phone conversations he'd had with his men. He knew Zoe was unharmed. But damn it, some maniac was going after first responders. Paramedics. Firefighters. They may not have been part of the brotherhood of law enforcement, but they were definitely close cousins.

And Zoe was closer yet.

The narrow country road approaching the Loomis farm was clogged with police and fire vehicles. By the time Pete made it into the driveway, the old barn had succumbed to the flames. Fire crews continued to pour water onto the still-burning debris.

He eased off the lane, making room for an exiting tanker headed for the nearest hydrant. Or farm pond.

Figuring he wasn't about to find a parking spot any closer to the action, he turned off the ignition, pulled on a slicker, and stepped out of the Explorer.

Pete located Baronick standing outside the Mobile Command Center being briefed by a pair of county officers and a state trooper.

They acknowledged Pete before excusing themselves. Baronick motioned for Pete to follow and led the way to the big truck's door.

Once inside, the detective swept his hood back. Water splattered everywhere, earning him a dirty look from the computer techs. "Sorry, guys," Baronick said.

"What have we got?" Pete asked.

"Not very much. Just like last night, he pulled a hit and run. Two men down." Baronick held up one finger. "But unlike last night, he left a pair of uninjured witnesses. There were four firefighters manning the first truck on scene. The first two off the truck were gunned down. The other two stayed inside and radioed EOC for police backup."

"Did either of them see anything?"

"They were able to give us an idea of where the shots came from. Not exact because it happened fast. *Bam bam* and outta here."

"That's it? They didn't see our guy?"

"Nope. They said the shots came from the tree line about two-hundred yards away. I have men over there searching along with the K-9 unit, but with this rain..."

Pete shook his head. "Last night, he used a stolen ATV as bait and the setting sun to his back to conceal himself. Tonight, he sets a barn fire on a night when evidence is going to be obliterated before we can find it. Is he that lucky or that smart?"

Baronick raised an eyebrow. "I had an instructor in the academy who taught me there are no such things as coincidences. And in my mind, luck constitutes a coincidence."

"Must have been a good instructor."

"He was all right." Baronick gave a hint of a grin. "Some guy named Adams."

"Smartass." Pete dug out his notebook, trying not to drip on it. "Looks like we're back to square one where suspects are concerned. Even if Snake had a motive to go after firemen, he has the IQ of a wood duck. No way he'd think to plan a hit around the weather forecast."

"Rules out the girl too." Baronick's phone rang. He turned away to answer it, plugging his other ear with a finger.

Who the hell was doing this? Pete dug out his own phone, hesitated, then punched in Zoe's number.

*   *   *

The Emergency Department of Brunswick Hospital was jumping. As if two shooting victims from Vance Township weren't enough, one of the nurses told Zoe there had been a multi-vehicle accident on the eastern side of the county with five patients either already arrived or in transit.

After transferring Yancy to a cubicle where a nurse and an aide had taken charge of his care, Zoe found a quiet spot in the hall, parked her empty gurney, and stripped the soiled linens from it. As she tossed them into a nearby bin, her cell phone burst into its rendition of "I Fought the Law and the Law Won." Her pulse quickened.

"Hey, Pete," she answered.

"How's Yancy?"

She glanced toward the cubicle where she'd left the fire chief. "Bullet went through his right arm. Shattered his humerus and he lost a lot of blood. Not life-threatening, but I don't know about nerve damage."

There was a brief silence on the other end of the line. Pete was probably wondering the same thing she was. How would big rough and tough Bruce Yancy handle losing the use of his arm? After a moment, Pete asked, "What about the other fireman?"

"I haven't heard." Earl and the others from Medic Three had pulled in a few minutes after she had, but considering she still hadn't seen any of them, she knew it was bad. Real bad. Most of the time when they arrived at the ER with a patient, the hospital's staff took over, and the paramedics changed sheets on their gurney, restocked their supplies, and got back in service. Only when it was dire did the doctors enlist their help. "Please tell me you've caught the guy."

A sigh came through the line. "I wish I could. Are *you* all right?"

The truth or a lie? The truth being *hell no.* But that would lead to choking tears, and this was not the time or place. "I'm hanging in there. Pete...what's going on? Who's shooting at us?"

"That's the sixty-four-thousand-dollar question, isn't it? We have every law enforcement officer in three counties looking for him."

But would they find him before or after anyone else died? She knew better than to ask the question, though. Movement at the end of the hallway drew her attention. The three paramedics stepped out of the cubicle where they'd been working on the young firefighter. "Hang on a second," she told Pete. "Here comes Earl." She lowered the phone and waited.

Her partner spotted her and shuffled toward her, shoulders sagging, hands stuffed in his pockets. She knew without asking.

Earl met her gaze, his eyes damp. He shook his head.

Zoe took a raspy breath. Blew it out. And again lifted the phone to her ear.

"Pete? Jason didn't make it."

"You look like shit." Sylvia had never been one to pull punches.

But at least she thrust a cup of coffee into Pete's hands as he dragged into the station after a second long night at a shooting scene. He inhaled the aroma and sipped. "You, on the other hand, are beautiful."

She blew a raspberry and then grew serious. "You find anything?"

He shuffled down the hallway to his office, Sylvia trailing behind. "They pinpointed where the shots came from. Mostly we were trying to cover the area with tarps to protect what we could from the rain. Now that it's stopped and the sun's coming up, they're starting to do a more thorough search." He sagged into his chair. "Thanks for manning the station all night."

A sad smile crossed her face. "It almost felt like old times." The smile faded. "I can't believe Jason Dyer's gone. He was such a sweet kid. Ted was the one who got him interested in firefighting, you know."

"No, I didn't know." Sylvia's son, Ted Bassi, had been a pillar of the Vance Township VFD prior to his tragic death last winter. "So you knew Jason?"

She took a seat opposite Pete. "He spent a lot of time at Ted and Rose's house. He and Logan were great pals. Have you talked to Jason's folks yet?"

"Last night." Death notifications. One of the worst parts of his job—telling a parent his child won't be coming home again. "They didn't take it well."

Sylvia stared into space, her eyes glazed. Pete had given her the same news less than a year ago.

He knew full well she was reliving that moment right now. "You should stop in and talk to them."

"I intend to. As soon as Nancy gets here." Sylvia checked her watch. "Which should be any time now."

He sipped his coffee and shook his head. "It's Saturday. She's off today. So am I, for that matter."

"Do you need me to stay?"

"Always." He gave her a weary smile. "But no. We'll manage. The Dyer kid's mother needs you more than I do right now."

"You have my number if—"

Pete waved her off. "We'll be fine. Any word on Yancy?"

"Not since last night. They were prepping him for surgery. Have *you* heard anything?"

"Nothing."

"I don't suppose he'll make it to the poker game tonight." Sylvia managed a somber smile. "Pity. I always earn my week's lunch allowance from him on Saturday nights."

Pete rubbed his tired eyes. "I think the weekly poker game might be cancelled just this once. Half the gang will be on duty. Or, if we nail this guy, catching up on sleep." He hoped they wouldn't be dealing with a third night of shootings.

Sylvia fixed him with a stern gaze. "Have you talked to Zoe?"

The question carried a truckload of innuendo, but Pete wasn't about to delve into the subject of their relationship.

Not now.

"Last night. She's the one who told me the kid didn't pull through." Pete didn't mention how many times he'd looked at his phone during the long night, nearly placing a call just to check on her. Make sure she was okay. Just to hear her voice...

He may not have spoken his thoughts, but somehow he suspected Sylvia read them. "Uh-huh. When are you two knuckleheads gonna quit this dance of yours and get together?"

"We *are* together."

Sylvia raised a very doubtful eyebrow.

"We're seeing each other." Sort of. "Hey, I'm here, aren't I? I didn't take that job in Hawaii."

"Yeah, well. *Being here* isn't all there is to a relationship."

Pete traced the rim of his mug with one finger. "It's a good start. Even though I turned down that gig last month, Chuck keeps calling with other private security job openings. I can't seem to get it through to him that I like my life here."

The bells on the front door jangled, and Sylvia climbed to her feet with a groan. "I'll see who that is. Then I'm heading home. Provided I can fight off the growing media encampment in the parking lot."

"Tell them I'll give them a statement at noon."

"A statement? Telling them what exactly?"

"I don't know yet."

Sylvia snorted. "Right. Keep me posted."

"About the case or about my job situation?"

She shot a dirty look at him. "You aren't going anywhere unless you take Zoe with you."

"There's a thought."

Sylvia shambled into the hall. Over her shoulder, she called, "It's that detective from county."

"I'll meet him in the conference room in two minutes." Two minutes should be enough to sneak a quick call to Zoe. To make sure she hadn't responded to any last minute runs. Damn it, he had to catch this guy. Otherwise he was going to be sorely tempted to assign her an armed escort every time she climbed into an ambulance.

Baronick's voice boomed from outside Pete's office door. "Tell him I don't have two minutes to wait."

"Stuff it, bub," Sylvia said.

She'd never warmed up to Baronick. Pete doubted she ever would.

The detective appeared in the doorway. From the dark circles shadowing his eyes, he hadn't slept in the last forty-eight hours either. "I wanted to touch base with you before I head back to Brunswick."

Pete motioned to the chair Sylvia had occupied, but Baronick shook his head. "If I sit, I'll fall asleep."

"Should make for an interesting drive. You plan on standing the whole way?"

"No, but I'll open the windows and crank up the air conditioning." Baronick scrolled though the notes in his phone. "The state fire marshal arrived at the Loomis place a little bit ago, but we all know we're dealing with arson."

"I'll talk to him later."

"They're still searching for spent casings, but the place is mud soup over there. The crime scene techs did manage to salvage one set of tracks near the spot we figure the suspect fired his shots. They appear to be a match to the same quad he used the night before."

"Our guy knows the area." Pete drained his mug and thunked it down on the desk. "He knows how to get into remote areas, where to hide, how to slip out unseen."

Baronick grunted. "And he pays attention to the weather channel. Guess you can give up on Snake and the Livingston chick."

"Looks that way. Except Eli 'Snake' Sullivan is still AWOL. Once again, he has no alibi."

"He also has no motive. Whoever's doing this isn't going after individuals. He's gunning for emergency personnel as a whole." A strange look crossed the detective's eyes. "When's Zoe on duty again?"

Pete held Baronick's gaze, knowing the detective carried a not-so-secret torch for her. "Her shift ends..." Pete checked his watch. Five minutes to eight. "Right about now. And she'll be off duty until Tuesday at four."

The faint smile that crossed Baronick's face might have been a smirk if he weren't so exhausted. "That gives us a little over three days to catch this asshole."

"Let's not wait that long. I don't want to give this guy a chance to go gunning for any more of our fire or ambulance personnel."

Baronick nodded and turned to leave. "I'm going to the Dyer kid's autopsy, if I can stay awake. I bet Zoe'll be there."

Pete tamped down a quick rush of jealousy. Zoe had no interest in the detective. They both knew that. Baronick was egging him for sport. "Possibly."

Baronick took two steps out the door and then backed up. "You mentioned our shooter aiming for fire and ambulance personnel. Be careful out there, Pete. He might just include law enforcement in his vendetta."

TEN

"I've never been so glad to see eight a.m. come around," Earl said, digging his car keys from his pocket.

Zoe stood at the door between the EMS office and the ambulance bay. "Me too." However, she wasn't looking forward to the day ahead. Earl would go home to his wife and kids and spend his Saturday off enjoying family time.

Zoe, on the other hand, planned to make a quick stop at the Vance Township Police Department, followed by another quick stop at Rose's to get washed up. Then she'd go by the barn to make sure nothing required her attention. And finally on to the morgue in Brunswick for the young firefighter's autopsy at nine. She'd be late, but so be it. Afterward, she intended to look in on Yancy.

Tony charged into the office from the back of the station carrying a clipboard. "Hey. You two still okay with pulling an extra shift on Monday so B crew can take off and be at the funeral home for Barry?"

"Yeah," Earl said somberly. "Absolutely."

Zoe nodded. "Count on it."

"Good." Tony jotted on the notepad clipped to the board. "We'll take turns going to visitation both Monday and Tuesday as emergency calls allow. The funeral's Wednesday morning. We'll all go as a group, in uniform."

"Let's just hope the cops will have caught the guy by then," Earl said, voicing what Zoe had been thinking.

"Amen to that." Tony set the clipboard on the edge of the desk. "Enjoy your weekend."

The clouds, which had dumped so much rain on them last night, appeared to be breaking up. Patches of blue peeked through in spots. With a little luck, it might turn out to be a gorgeous autumn day. Zoe and Earl crossed Main Street to the parking lot cattycorner from the garage.

"See you Monday," Earl said without any enthusiasm.

"Give Olivia and the kids a hug for me."

A smile lit his face as he chirped open his minivan's front door. "You bet."

Zoe climbed into the Chevy's cab, tossed her purse on the passenger side of the bench seat, and turned the key.

Click.

"Come on, baby," she cooed.

Click. Click. Click.

"Come on. Start."

Click. Click. Click. Click.

It may have required some tinkering to get the truck started lately, but not usually this much. Zoe watched Earl drive away as Gabe the mechanic's words echoed in her ears. *Except one of these days it isn't gonna. Sooner than later, most likely. You're gonna need a new starter.*

She sat and stared at the dashboard. Tried again. Still nothing but a click. Crap.

She slammed the steering wheel. "I don't have time for this," she told the truck.

It responded with passive-aggressive silence.

Several more attempts yielded the same results. With a defeated sigh, Zoe pulled her cell phone from her pocket and punched in the number for Bud Kramer's Garage. Did the fact that she kept his number saved in her contact list hint that Pete's advice to buy a new vehicle might have some validity?

Standing outside her truck, she thought she heard Bud chuckle gleefully as he told her a flatbed would be there in fifteen minutes.

So much for her plans for the morning. She pulled up Franklin Marshall's number on her phone, but before she could punch the send button, "I Fought the Law" started playing. "Good morning, Pete."

"Hi." He sounded drained. "So you made it through the rest of your shift okay?"

Zoe leaned against the Chevy's fender, breathing in the rain-washed breeze. "Yeah. It was a quiet night. Except for..."

"Yeah. Have you heard any news on Yancy?"

"No." And she now had no way to get to the hospital to visit him. "I'll call later. Maybe he'll be in a room and able to talk."

There was a pause. "I thought you'd stop in to see him after the autopsy."

She cringed. If she told him she wouldn't be attending it, she'd have to explain why, which would be followed by a round of I-told-you-so's. But she wasn't about to lie to Pete either. "I'm not going to the autopsy."

Another pause. "Have you fulfilled your commitment already?"

"No. This would have been number six."

"And you're skipping it because...?"

A litany of excuses played through her mind. She couldn't deal with an autopsy on a kid. She had to give a riding lesson. She'd already decided against a career in the Coroner's Office. With a defeated sigh, she said, "Because my truck won't start."

The third silence from Pete's end of the call was followed by his deep, rumbling laugh. A sound she rarely heard. But liked.

"Don't you dare say 'I told you so.'"

"I wouldn't think of it." The laughter evolved into almost a giggle, and Zoe pictured Pete wiping tears from his eyes. "Where are you?" he asked.

"Waiting for one of Bud's guys to come get me with the flatbed."

"Then what are you going to do?"

Good question. "I guess I'll call Rose to come get me."

"Forget it. I'm on my way."

He hung up before Zoe had a chance to argue. She stared at the phone's screen pronouncing the call ended. And smiled.

Gabe Weber was behind the wheel of the big flatbed when it pulled into the parking lot a few minutes later.

"That was quick," Zoe said as he climbed down. "Not that I'm complaining."

Gabe gave her a broad grin.

"I aim to please." He planted his fists on his hips and eyed the Chevy as if it were an insolent child. "*You* again."

Defensive of her truck, she protested, "In all fairness, this is the first time it's needed to be towed."

"True. I apologize. Up until now, she's always managed to limp in under her own power." Gabe gave Zoe a teasing grin. "What seems to be the problem today?"

She slouched. "I guess that starter you warned me about finally quit altogether."

The mechanic tsk-tsked. "I told you so."

She had a feeling she was going to get sick of hearing that.

Without any further heckling, Gabe headed to the cab of his flatbed. Zoe stood back and watched him maneuver the big truck into position in front of the Chevy, blocking one lane of Main Street. Small town that Phillipsburg was, the disruption in traffic amounted to an occasional car needing to wait for oncoming vehicles before going around. Minutes later, Gabe secured the pickup aboard the flatbed and motioned for Zoe to climb in. "Unless you wanna walk," he said.

Bud's place was less than a quarter mile away, but she opted to ride. With the luck she was having, she'd probably get hit by a car while crossing the road.

Gabe parked in front of the garage's second bay and left the diesel engine idling. Zoe slid down from the passenger side and followed the mechanic inside.

Medic Two still sat where she'd last seen it. She patted its hood on her way past, offering comfort to an old friend.

Bud Kramer wheeled his chair over to the cashier's window. "Long time no see."

Zoe forced a sour smile. "I couldn't wait to give you more of my money."

He chortled with the same glee she'd heard over the phone.

Gabe leaned on the counter next to Zoe. "It's the starter, boss. Spotted it when she was in before."

Bud scribbled on a form. "Do you happen to know if we've got the part in stock, Gabe?"

"I checked. We don't."

Bud nodded. "I'll call the auto parts store."

Zoe envisioned more dollar signs. And an emptier bank account.

He glanced up from the work order. "How's Yancy?"

She really needed to call and get an answer to that question. "I haven't heard anything this morning."

Bud shook his head. "It's damned scary. Stuff like that just don't happen around here."

"Yeah," Gabe agreed. "Some nut out there shooting at anyone driving something with a flashing light on top. You never know who's gonna be next. Maybe even a tow truck driver."

Zoe opened her mouth to point out tow truck drivers weren't usually first on the scene, but decided against it. She had no clue what was in the shooter's mind. Gabe might be right. "We all have to be careful out there."

Gabe nodded. "That's for sure."

The door from outside scraped open, and Pete strolled in. Bud glanced up. "Hey, Chief."

Gabe straightened and thumped the counter with his fist. "Guess I better get back to work."

"That would be a nice change," Bud said. "Park her Chevy over by the fence."

"You got it, boss." Gabe ambled away.

Bud looked at Zoe. "We've got a full house with that ambulance holding top priority. Probably won't have your truck done until late Tuesday, early Wednesday, depending on what we find when we get in there." He separated the carbonless copies of the work order and slid the pink one across the counter to her. "I'll call you."

She stared at the paper.

Late Tuesday or early Wednesday? She pictured riding Windstar to and from work.

Pete leaned one forearm on the counter next to her. "Bud, you're the biggest thief in Monongahela County."

The garage owner gave Pete a gap-toothed smile. "And you can't even arrest me. Drives you crazy, don't it?" Bud executed a perfect one-eighty in his wheelchair and rolled away.

Both Pete and Zoe stepped back from the window and faced each other. For the first time, she noticed the dark circles under his eyes, the pallor of his skin. "You look like you haven't slept in a month."

He rubbed the space between his brows. "More like two. What time's the autopsy? Nine?"

"Yeah." She checked her phone. 8:35. "I forgot. I need to call Franklin and let him know I won't be there."

Pete rested a gentle hand on the small of her back, walking her toward the door. "You can call him from the car. Tell him we'll be late, but we're on our way."

She glanced down at her uniform as they stepped outside. So much for stopping at Rose's house and changing. "Okay. But I need to call Patsy too and see if she can make sure everything's okay at the barn. I was planning to stop on my way—" Another forgotten plan for the day surfaced. "Oh, crap."

"What?" Pete opened the Explorer's passenger door for her.

"Patsy and I were supposed to go riding this morning."

"I'm sure she'll understand."

He was right. She would. She always did. That was the problem. Zoe tried to remember the last time she and Patsy had gone trail riding together and couldn't. For a moment, Zoe considered telling Pete to drop her off at the farm. Forget the autopsy. Forget that Yancy and Curtis were hospitalized. Forget the upcoming funeral for Barry.

Forget everything. Leave her cell phone behind, pack a lunch, and ride off into the woods.

"Zoe?" Pete roused her from her daydream.

She blinked. He was still holding the door for her. With a wistful sigh, she climbed in and dialed Patsy to cancel their horseback date.

By the time they reached Brunswick, the sky had cleared to a beautiful blue. The trees and grass still glistened from last night's rain, a few splashes of gold and orange leaves even more vivid against the green. Pete shot a glance at Zoe, whose face was turned away from him, and wondered if she wished she hadn't cancelled her riding plans.

The dashboard clock read 9:34 as he pulled into the underground lot at the hospital and parked outside the entrance marked Authorized Personnel Only. No other signage labeled it as the morgue. Zoe didn't wait for him. She stepped out of the SUV and approached the glass doors, hesitating long enough for Pete to catch up.

He put a hand on her shoulder and squeezed. "You'll be fine," he whispered into her ear.

For a moment, she leaned against him. A simple gesture of accepting his support. But it sent a fire through him. He longed to take her in his arms and never let go. To shield her from all her fears and doubts. To protect her from the maniac out there gunning down her coworkers and friends. But she steeled herself and pushed away.

Side by side, they stepped forward. The doors swished open, and they entered the hallway to the morgue.

The outer office was empty. A window between it and the autopsy suite revealed Wayne Baronick and Franklin Marshall observing the forensic pathologist and a tech work on the body.

Zoe grabbed two sets of disposable scrubs from a cart in the corner and handed him one. They suited up in silence before stepping into the other room.

Marshall and Baronick turned toward them. "You're late," the coroner said.

"I had car trouble," Zoe said.

Baronick glanced from her to Pete and back. He grinned. "Nothing like having the Chief of Police as your personal chauffeur."

Pete aimed a scorching look at the detective.

Zoe ignored the comment and asked Marshall, "What do you want me to do?"

Without looking up from his work, Doc Abercrombie called over his shoulder, "You're just in time to run the gut."

Pete noticed the color fade from Zoe's cheeks. He had a feeling he'd missed an inside joke and would have to ask her about it later.

His suspicions were confirmed when Marshall snickered. "I'm going to give you a pass this time." The coroner grew serious. "You've had a rough couple of days."

Pete motioned toward the body on the table. "Have you found anything?"

"So far I can tell you there's only one gunshot wound. Unlike the first victim, the shot wasn't through and through. The bullet entered here." Marshall thumbed the area at the base of his own left ribcage. "It shattered the tenth rib. We're still examining the abdominal tissues and organs, but x-rays show fragments all through the right lower quadrant. I'm willing to bet we find the bullet caused massive organ trauma before hitting the ilium and fragmenting."

"Fragments," Baronick echoed. "Anything that looks like it might be big enough to be identifiable?"

Marshall shrugged. "Doubtful. I'll let you know as soon as we have anything more."

Pete thanked him, and the coroner headed back to the table.

"As much as I appreciate the company, there's no sense in all of us hanging out here." Baronick nudged Zoe. "Especially if you aren't gonna jump in there and give us a show."

She shot him a dirty look.

As much as Pete detested agreeing with the smug detective, this time he had to. "You stick around and collect any evidence they find and get it to the lab. I'll head upstairs and see if Yancy's up to answering questions." He touched Zoe's arm. "You with me or do you want to stay here?"

She snorted. "What do you think?" She spun on her heel, stripping out of the scrubs as she headed for the door.

"I'm hurt," Baronick called after her.

Pete chuckled. "I may not have much of a way with women, but I can tell you this much. There are better options than a date at an autopsy."

ELEVEN

Zoe was relieved to have escaped the smells of autopsy, but seeing big, tough Bruce Yancy wearing a hospital gown and attached to monitors, IVs, and oxygen didn't strike her as a huge improvement. The head of his bed was raised, but he slumped more than sat. An unopened plastic cup of juice and a full container of green Jell-O with a spoon stuck in it occupied the bedside tray in front of him. A haggard young woman wearing a stained and wrinkled t-shirt perched on the edge of a chair next to the bed.

"Hey, Yance," Pete said, striding toward the patient. "How are you feeling?"

Yancy seemed to have difficulty finding and focusing on his visitors. When he did, he made a sour face. "How the hell do you think I feel?" His voice sounded mushy. He attempted to hoist his right arm, which was in a brace and strapped to his body. "That son of a bitch blew out my humerus."

The young woman touched Yancy's shoulder. "Take it easy, Dad."

Pete extended a hand toward her, which she took. "You must be Nicole. Pete Adams."

Zoe introduced herself too. She'd heard Yancy talk about his only child, although the impression he'd created didn't quite match the pale, disheveled woman in front of her. Spending a night in a hospital chair wasn't conducive to restful sleep.

Yancy's eyes wavered and settled on Zoe. With his left hand, he pointed a shaky finger at her. "That there's my angel," he slurred.

She glanced at a quizzical Pete and then took note of an IV line leading to a morphine pump. She smiled to herself. Yancy was stoned.

He continued to point at her. "She saved me last night," he told his daughter. To Zoe he said, "I owe you my life."

She met the daughter's questioning gaze and shook her head. "I was in the ambulance that brought him in is all."

Pete stepped forward. "You up to answering some questions?"

"Yeah." Yancy looked at his daughter. "Nicole, why don't you go down and get yourself something to eat?"

"I'm fine, Dad."

"Go. You've been sittin' there all night." He nodded at Pete and Zoe. "They'll make sure I don't escape."

"That's not what I'm worried about." But she stood and stretched before moving around the foot of the bed. She stopped next to Zoe. "Can I give you my cell number? We're waiting for the doctor to come in, and you know darned well he'll show up the minute I leave the floor."

"Sure." Zoe pulled out her phone and punched in the number Nicole gave her.

With a worried glance at her father, Nicole left.

Yancy watched her go. His eyes steadied. "She won't let me turn on the news or call anyone. How's Jason?" From his expression, he already knew.

Pete shook his head. "He didn't make it."

Yancy took a deep ragged breath. Blew it out. And blinked away tears. "Goddamn it. That boy never did nothin' to nobody. Best worker I had. Never complained. Always wantin' to help."

Pete grabbed a second chair, dragged it closer to the bed, and sat. "So help me catch the bastard."

"I'd love to. But I don't know what I can tell you."

"Did you see anyone?"

"No. One second we were rolling up to the fire, climbing down from the truck, then *boom boom*." Yancy took a couple of labored breaths.

Zoe reached for the pink pitcher on his tray. "Can I pour you some water?"

"No."

She poured a glass anyway and set it on the side of the tray closest to his one functioning arm.

"Next thing I knew I was on my knees, my arm burnin' like a son of a bitch. Blood all over me." Yancy took another moist breath. "And

Jason was on the ground. Not moving. I knew it was bad. I tried to get to him, but the SOB shot at me again. Backed me off."

"Three shots?" Pete jotted in his notebook. "You heard three shots?"

Yancy appeared to contemplate the question. "I guess. No. Four. Two real close together. Then two more. The one that pinned me down and another one. I think the other boys started to get out of the truck and he was shootin' at them."

Baronick had mentioned the other firefighters too. Pete thumbed through his notes. "What were the names of the other guys on the truck with you?"

"Stu Wilkins and Dex Alvarez. I guess they stayed in the truck. Sure wish Jason had."

Zoe gingerly took a seat at the foot of Yancy's bed. "Maybe one of them saw something."

Pete met her gaze, but before he had a chance to say anything else, a tall dark-haired man in a white lab coat breezed into the room, a binder in his hands.

He introduced himself as Yancy's doctor. Zoe sent a quick text to Nicole as Pete shook hands with the physician.

Pete tucked his notebook into his pocket and turned back to Yancy. "I'll stop back later if I have any more questions." The two men shook left-handed. "Call me if there's anything I can do."

"The only thing I want you to do is catch that son of a bitch."

Zoe and Pete passed Nicole in the hallway.

Yancy's daughter threw up her hands in exasperation as she breezed by them. "I knew I wouldn't have a chance to eat. Never fails."

At the elevator, Pete jabbed the down button. Something was going on inside his head.

Zoe faced him, folding her arms. "You think one of the other guys on the fire truck might have seen something?"

His faraway gaze settled on her. His mouth was stretched into a thin line. "I hope so."

"I get the feeling you heard more in that conversation with Yancy than I did."

Pete's jaw tightened. "Maybe. Maybe not."

"What's that supposed to mean?"

He shook his head slowly. "I'm still sorting it out. But I'll let you know when I do."

Pete dropped Zoe off at Rose's front door with a promise he'd go home and get some sleep.

As soon as he checked in at the station.

On the short drive up the hill, he called Baronick. "Anything new with the autopsy?"

Instead of answering, the detective asked, "Where are you now?"

"Dillard, heading back to my office. I'm supposed to give the press a statement in..." He checked the clock on the dashboard. "Ten minutes ago. Why?"

"I'm five minutes out. Meet you there."

The line went dead in Pete's ear.

The station's parking lot was filled to capacity with vehicles bearing logos from various local stations and newspapers, forcing him to park on the township offices side of the building. He cut the engine and placed calls to the rest of his officers, summoning them to come in for a briefing.

By the time he reached the station's front door, reporters had piled out of their trucks and cars and hovered, blocking his path.

Pete held up one hand. "I know I'm late with my statement. I need to meet with my men to get updated and then I'll be out to speak with you in one hour."

The crowd responded with an impatient rumble, but backed away, except for one dark-haired kid in a rumpled white shirt and even more wrinkled khakis. "Do you think we have a serial killer in the area? Do you have any suspects yet?" The kid continued to bark questions as Pete pressed through the front door.

Minutes later, Baronick ambled into the conference room. Pete had already started a pot of coffee and updated the whiteboard with what he'd learned from Yancy.

The detective slapped a folder down on the table. "You look like you should be next in line for an autopsy. Go get some sleep."

Pete grunted. Putting his reading glasses on, he opened the file. "How about the short version."

"Nothing earth shattering. You heard the bulk of it when you were there. Doc removed a half dozen fragments from the kid's abdomen. I dropped them off at the lab, but I can tell you there's not enough to help us identify the gun. Did you get to talk to Yancy?"

The bells on the front door jangled. "Yeah. Let's wait until everyone is here."

Five minutes later, Baronick, Nate Williamson, Kevin, Seth, and two part-time officers whom Pete had called in gathered around the table with somber faces, open notebooks, and cups of coffee.

Baronick went over the autopsy findings again with the men.

Pete studied the whiteboard. "Kevin, did you find anything more about Snake Sullivan?"

"I've been trying to track him down since you called me about him yesterday." The young officer skimmed through his notes. "No one's seen or heard from him. And no one knows where he was between seven fifteen and eight thirty Thursday night."

Baronick drummed a pen against the table. "You can't possibly still think he's involved in this."

It was a question he'd been asking himself over and over. "Do I think he's smart enough to pull it off? No. Do I think he's hiding something? Oh yeah. And until we can positively say he wasn't involved, I'm not clearing him of anything."

"I did find out one thing," Kevin added. "That ATV he claimed to have sold? The DCNR has no transfer of title recorded for it."

Pete scrawled on the whiteboard: *Snake's ATV* and three question marks. Something else to ask the kid whenever they found him.

"So what about Bruce Yancy?" Baronick asked. "You talked to him this morning, right? How is he?"

Pete turned his back on the board. "They have him loaded with pain meds right now, but he's not doing bad, all things considered."

"He's alive," Seth said. "That's pretty huge at the moment."

"True." Pete went on to tell about Yancy's report on the shooting, including the four shots fired. "Who questioned the other men on that first truck?"

Seth raised a hand. "I did. Dexter Alvarez and Stuart Wilkins. They said there were four shots too. Wilkins was pretty shaken up. I think he probably hit the floor when the shots rang out. Claims he didn't see a thing. Alvarez, though, spotted the muzzle flash and was able to help us pinpoint the shooter's location."

Baronick tapped his phone with the pen. "Which enabled us to find the tire marks from his quad. Because of the rain and mud, we couldn't get a clean cast of the tread, but the measurements match the one he used when he shot the paramedics."

"What about spent shells?" Pete asked.

"None. He's still policing his brass." Baronick set the pen down on the table. "So we have four shots." He held up one finger. "The first one hits Yancy in the arm. Through and through." Baronick held up two fingers. "The second one hits Jason Dyer and fragments inside his body." The detective raised two more fingers. "Shots three and four were misses." He closed his hand into a fist. "So our guys with the metal detectors could potentially find a couple of bullets out there in the mud. And with a little luck, they'll be intact enough to ID a weapon."

"We just have to find a weapon to match them to first," Pete said.

"Yeah. There is that."

Pete faced away from the men and rubbed a hand across his eyes. The exhaustion of the case and over forty-eight hours with virtually no sleep was catching up to him. As much as he wanted to push ahead, he needed rest. He turned back toward the table and pointed at Seth and Kevin. "You two. Go home and get a few hours' sleep."

Seth straightened. "But—"

Pete shushed him with a wave of his hand. "We need to work this in shifts until we nail this guy."

"What about you?" Kevin asked.

"I'm going home too." To Nate and the part-timers, Pete said, "Find Eli 'Snake' Sullivan. Or find out where the hell he was last night and between seven fifteen and eight thirty on Thursday night. And keep an eye out for that quad he says he sold."

Baronick folded his arms. "I had the impression you didn't believe he did this."

Pete spun on the detective. "I don't believe anything one way or the other. Sullivan's lied about his whereabouts during the first shooting. We're looking for a quad, and he has or had one. If nothing else, I want to clear him so I can eliminate one possibility."

The two men glared at each other for a moment before Baronick nodded. "I'll get on my men to find those stray bullets buried in the mud at the Loomis place."

Pete stepped back. "Good. And one more thing. I want a police escort on every emergency call in Vance Township tonight."

Nate gave a low whistle. "On a Saturday night? I hope everyone stays off the streets and out of the bars. We're gonna be busy."

"What about the rest of Monongahela County?" Baronick asked.

Pete held up his hands. "That's your problem. I have to take care of my own jurisdiction." And if he had any say in the matter, no more first responders were going to die on his watch.

Rose paced her kitchen, a tissue clenched in one fist. "I can't believe this is happening. First Curtis and Barry. Now Yancy and—" Her voice cracked. "Jason Dyer." She gestured toward the kitchen chair Zoe currently occupied. "Jason used to sit right there with Logan while they did their homework."

"I didn't realize they were so close," Zoe said.

Rose paused at the sink and stared into it as if it held answers to the unfairness in life. "Jason and Logan went to school together, were lab partners, played football and basketball together. After Jason's dad died, Ted stepped in and kind of filled the void a little. Ted would take both boys to the fire station with him. Logan had no interest in joining the department, but Jason was in love with the idea of fighting fires and saving lives. He was a good kid."

Zoe gazed through the screen door.

The warm sunshine and low humidity outside mocked the sorrow and anxiety blanketing the inside of the Bassi house. "Are you gonna call Logan and tell him?"

"I guess I have to." Rose opened the dishwasher and rolled out the bottom shelf. "I really don't know how I'm gonna break the news to him. Or Allison. She kinda had a crush on Jason for a while. I hope this doesn't set her back."

The memory of a suicidal and drug-addicted girl flashed through Zoe's mind. She brushed it aside. "Allison's stronger now. And we're both here for her."

Rose cast a strained glance over her shoulder at Zoe. "We've all lost so much this year."

"Where is she anyway?"

Rose started picking through the dirty plates and containers in the dishwasher, rearranging them. "She's spending some girl time with my mom."

"How's your mother doing?" Zoe asked. The older woman had been having a string of minor health issues over recent months.

"Better. The doctors finally seem to have her meds adjusted right." Rose inspected a warped plastic storage box she'd removed from the bottom rack. "Who loaded the dishwasher?"

"Me." Zoe squirmed. She hadn't had one at the farm. Nor had she used Rose's while staying there alone. However, now that Rose was back and had been sticking dirty plates and glassware in the thing, Zoe figured she'd make herself useful and help out. "Why?"

Rose turned and held up the now oddly shaped box. "Plastic goes in the top rack so the heating element doesn't melt it."

"Oh. Sorry."

She slid the upper drawer out and removed a dirty pot. "And big stuff goes on the bottom. Otherwise, it doesn't get clean."

Oops. "Yes, Mom."

Rose shot her a dark scowl. But the look quickly softened. "You look worn out."

Zoe rubbed her eyes. "I am." She thought of Pete and suspected he had to be even more exhausted than she was.

Rose continued to reconfigure the dishwasher contents. "Go take a nap."

"I supposed I'd better. If this gunman makes it three nights in a row..." Zoe shivered at the thought.

Rose, a glass in her hand, spun to face Zoe. "Don't say that. Don't even hint at it. I can't stand the thought of losing anyone else. I'm hoping he's done. Or—Heaven forgive me for wishing this horror on another town—but I hope he moves on to someplace else."

Zoe didn't answer. Didn't want to destroy Rose's fantasy. But she knew that's what it was.

No one in Monongahela County could rest easy until this monster was caught.

TWELVE

If Pete could have avoided the press camped at the station's front door, he would have. But he'd stalled them as long as possible. The group swarmed them the moment they stepped outside. Pete used a lot of standard keywords like "ongoing investigation" and "persons of interest" without giving away too many details. The reporters had done their homework and already knew about Yancy's and Knox's conditions as well as the coroner's findings on the deceased. Pete and Baronick, as well as the State Police, had agreed to keep the ATV aspect quiet for now. They didn't want their shooter to dump the only good link they had tying the cases together.

After Pete gave his statement, the members of the media hurled questions at him. He pointed at a young woman he recognized from a local paper.

"Is there a connection between the victims?"

"They're all emergency personnel," Pete replied. From the look on her face, he knew that wasn't what she had in mind, but before she could ask a follow-up question, he pointed to another reporter.

"Do you think the shooter is randomly targeting ambulance and fire responders in general, or is he going after specific people?"

"We're still investigating." Pete gave the same answer to the next three variations on the same question.

One young man elbowed his way to the front of the crowd and shoved a microphone toward Pete. "Do you think the 911 Killer will strike again tonight?"

There it was. Someone in the press had given the guy a name. "Not if I can help it," Pete said, his words greeted by a barrage of serial-killer-on-the-loose questions. Knowing he was on the verge of saying something he'd regret—and would no doubt see on every newscast on every network for the foreseeable future—he slapped his ball cap on his head and muscled his way through the crowd toward his car.

Behind him Baronick gave a more politically correct closing to the briefing before trailing after Pete.

"That went well." Sarcasm oozed from Baronick's words.

Pete grunted. "The 911 Killer. Just what we need."

"You knew it was bound to happen. Now what?"

Pete glanced back at the reporters, some climbing back into their vehicles, some texting, a few setting up to film their on-air personalities filling in the blanks. "Now we catch the son of a bitch before he lives up to his reputation."

Pete phoned Deputy Fire Chief Todd Onderick and asked to meet him at the ambulance garage.

The EMS crew on duty was uncharacteristically subdued. Black bands adorned their sleeves. When Onderick arrived, he wore the same symbol of mourning on his arm, plus a black band across his badge.

Pete gathered everyone in the ambulance crew lounge.

"What's goin' on, Chief?" Onderick asked. "Do we all have targets on our backs?"

"Until we catch this guy, we have to assume the worst. That's why I wanted to speak to all of you." Pete gazed around the room at the various expressions. Worry. Sadness. Anger. But if anyone was afraid, they were covering it well. "It's my hope that we'll have an available police officer to respond to each and every emergency call that comes in tonight. Even so, there are some precautions I want all of you to observe. If the call takes you to a remote location or vacant structure, make sure you request police backup if we aren't already there. And stay in your vehicle until we've secured the scene."

One of the paramedics, a young woman with long red curls, raised her hand. Pete nodded to her.

"What if the delay results in a critical patient not being treated?" she asked.

"So far there haven't been any patients involved in one of these ambushes. Keep in mind the shooter set up a staged accident scene with the overturned ATV. But there was no patient."

"In other words, as long as we can see a victim, we can go in?" another paramedic asked.

Myriad scenarios danced through Pete's brain. If the shooter got wise to their precautions, would he be so brazen as to fake illness or injury to lure a crew into his trap? "Be alert to anything that seems not quite right. If there's any doubt, wait for the police. Keep your eyes open. And for crying out loud, if you don't see a patient, stay in your vehicles."

"I just don't want to put a patient in jeopardy because of this idiot," the redhead said.

Pete covered a smile. He could imagine Zoe saying the same thing. "And I don't want to put any more EMS or fire personnel in jeopardy because of him either. Be smart. You won't be able to help anyone if you're—if you become the next patient." He caught himself before saying *if you're dead.*

He turned to face Onderick. "Same with the fire department. If responding to a fire in a questionable area and no one is in clear and present danger, wait for backup."

"This is crazy," the deputy fire chief said. "Because of one psycho, we're putting lives and property at risk." He shook his head. "I understand if it's a situation like these last two. A barn on an abandoned farm. A desolate location like the cuts. But I'm not taking unnecessary precautions just because we're paranoid."

Pete stepped toward Onderick and fixed him with a hard glare. "We don't know how this guy is going to change things up. One night it's an overturned quad. The next it's a barn fire. We can't expect him to be predictable or obvious. You may not want to take what you feel are unnecessary precautions with your own life, but what about your men?"

The deputy fire chief lowered his gaze.

Pete did a slow turn, pausing to meet every one of the seven sets of eyes watching him. "We can't afford to lose any more brave men and women. As I said before, I hope to have at least one officer respond with each call so the scene can be cleared as quickly as possible. But odds are good there will be cases in which you arrive first. Use your heads. We know this guy is still out there. He's hit two nights in a row. I see no reason to expect him to skip one at this point."

The brutal truth sent the room into silence.

After a moment, the paramedic Pete recognized as the crew chief for the shift stood and approached him with his hand extended. "You've got our full support. Just do me one favor."

Pete clasped the offered hand. "What's that?"

"Catch this nutcase. Tonight."

Zoe's attempt at an afternoon nap resulted in a mishmash of nightmares, most of which she was grateful she couldn't remember. Feeling more drained rather than less, she decided to head to the farm to do some barn work. Except her truck sat at Bud Kramer's Garage. Not only was she homeless, she was now stranded as well, dependent on Rose for room, board, *and* wheels.

"Take me with you," Allison said when Zoe asked to borrow Rose's car.

Zoe hesitated, shooting a questioning look in Rose's direction.

"If it's okay with Zoe, it's okay with me," Rose said, digging through her purse and coming up with a set of keys.

The teen fist-pumped. "I'll be right back. I need to get my boots."

Rose gave an exasperated sigh. "I should warn you. What she really wants is to drive."

Drive? Little Allison? "She's not old enough," Zoe said. "Is she?"

Rose shrugged. "She'll be sixteen in November. She'll ask to drive on the road. The answer is no. I made the mistake of letting her get behind the wheel out in New Mexico on some of the back roads. But traffic is way different here."

Allison clomped back into the kitchen, hopping on one foot while tugging a boot onto the other. "Okay, I'm ready. Can I drive?"

Rose raised an eyebrow at Zoe—a wordless I-told-you-so.

"Your mother says no."

"How about once we get there? On the farm lane?"

Zoe detected a minute nod from Rose. "Sure. Why not."

During the short trip from Dillard to the Kroll farm, Allison talked nonstop about starting back to school on Monday as a junior. In some ways the girl was a typical teen, but Zoe knew what she'd gone through almost a year ago. Therapy and the escape to New Mexico had taken her a long way from those dark days. Hopefully Allison had developed the strength and coping mechanisms to handle high school life where everyone knew—or thought they knew—what had happened to her.

No sooner had Zoe turned into the farm lane, than Allison started fidgeting in the passenger seat. "Can I drive now?"

Zoe braked on the bend where the lane swung toward the back of the house, or what had been the house. Currently, three white pickups sat hillside above the lot. Someone on a Bobcat was digging what appeared to be a footer and several other workmen nailed boards together into forms along the portion already dug out.

Shifting into park, Zoe opened the door. "Trade me seats."

Allison leaped out and passed Zoe in front of the car. Sliding into the passenger seat, she clicked her seatbelt.

Allison rolled her eyes. "We're only going a few hundred feet."

Zoe wagged a finger at her. "Doesn't matter. Buckle up, kiddo."

With an exaggerated sigh, Allison did as ordered. She shifted into drive and gave the old Taurus a little too much gas, kicking up gravel. "Oops."

The short jaunt up the hill and over, rolling down the other side to the barn, took less than a minute, but Allison seemed pleased by her effort. No dents were added to Rose's car or any of the half dozen or so boarders' vehicles parked in front, so Zoe was equally happy.

Laughter rang out from inside. A group of riders—all female—stripped saddles from their sweaty horses. Patsy spotted the new arrivals and waved. "You're too late. We just got back."

"It was an awesome ride," one preteen girl in a pink baseball cap gushed.

"A perfect autumn day for being in the saddle," added the girl's mother.

Zoe's annoyance wasn't entirely an act. "Rub it in a little more, why don't you?"

After a moment's pause, Allison skirted the crowd and crossed toward the far end of the barn, where the doors opened to the pasture. Zoe headed for the tack room, wondering if the girl was simply eager to check out the rest of the horses, or if she was avoiding the trail riders.

Patsy patted her Arabian's glossy neck and stepped away from the group, catching Zoe at the tack room door. "How'd the autopsy go?"

"We were late getting there, so Franklin gave me a reprieve."

"You should have come riding."

"I know."

"How about tomorrow?"

Tomorrow. What would tomorrow bring? Another autopsy? She shook her head.

Patsy planted her fist against her hip. "Why not?"

"Oh. I wasn't saying no. I was..." What? Shaking off a recurring nightmare? "I'd like to, but it depends on..." She couldn't say the words. *It depends on if someone else gets shot tonight.*

"I'll come pick you up."

"Can I call you in the morning and let you know for sure?"

Patsy made a sour face. "Tell you what. I'll pick you up at ten. Call if you can't make it."

She spun on her heel and walked away before Zoe could object.

She watched the riders brush out their sweaty mounts, taking turns leading their horses to the faucet at the far end of the indoor arena. In the middle of summer, there would have been water battles with no one caring about getting soaked. The cool fall air had the kids working a little harder to keep themselves dry.

"Windstar's gotten fat." The voice behind her made her flinch. Allison stood there gazing at the ground, her mouth tense.

"He needs exercise," Zoe said. "I didn't see you come back."

"I walked around the outside rather than cut through the mud where they're bathing the horses."

A legitimate excuse. But there was something in the girl's expression that convinced Zoe it wasn't the real reason. And then it hit her. "Oh my God, Allison. Have you not been out here since—?"

The teen shook her head, then tipped it toward the spot on the ground where her gaze was fixed. "I almost died there."

Zoe didn't know whether to pull the girl into her arms or smack herself in the head. How stupid could she be? Of course Allison hadn't been back to the barn since that awful night last January. "Why didn't you say something?"

Allison lifted her gaze to meet Zoe's. "I was afraid you wouldn't let me come with you."

"Of course I would." A little forewarning might have been nice.

A wan smile crossed the girl's face. "I didn't want to stress you out any more than you already are."

When did Allison get so grown up?

The teen wandered over to the spot where she'd nearly bled to death. Zoe noticed her absentmindedly rubbing the scars on her wrists. Allison stood motionless, staring at the dirt, as if standing over a grave.

Zoe waited. Should she say something? Should she go stand next to the girl? Put an arm around her? But that would draw the attention of the kids still grooming their horses. Patsy already cast a puzzled gaze in her direction. Zoe mouthed, "It's okay" at her.

Minutes later, Allison and Zoe sat side by side on the dusty tack room floor, leaning against the wall. Over the years, this had been the location of many of their intimate chats, although usually the topics had been more along the lines of scraped knees, bruised egos, and stupid boys.

Allison fingered a stray piece of hay. "I needed to come here and face this." She looked over at Zoe. "But I didn't want it to be a big deal. I was afraid you'd get all weirded out over it if I told you. I'm sorry."

Zoe waved the apology away. "Did your mom know why you wanted to come out here?"

"No." She smiled. "Maybe. Mom's not as clueless as she used to be."

Now it was Zoe's turn to smile. Maybe Allison had matured beyond believing her mom was an idiot. "So how are you doing?"

The teen didn't answer right away as she pondered the question. "Mostly good. A little shaky sometimes. Everything was so different out west, it was easy to pretend last winter never happened." She studied the piece of hay. "Coming home didn't really feel like coming *home*. Some stuff is the same. But Logan's not here. Dad's...not here."

Zoe draped an arm around her shoulders. "Your mom, your grandmothers, and I are all here for you though. You know that, don't you?"

"Oh, sure. I'm okay." Allison shot a sideways glance at Zoe. "What I mean to say is while some stuff is the same, I'm not. I'm stronger."

Zoe raised a clenched fist. "I am woman. Hear me roar."

Allison laughed. "Exactly." She tossed the piece of hay. "I think I'm ready to come back here to ride without getting all whacked."

"Good. How about tomorrow? You. Me. Patsy."

"Maybe." Allison shifted to face Zoe. "Yeah. Definitely. Life's too short to put stuff off, right? Look what happened to Jason."

A knot rose in Zoe's throat. "Your mom said Jason and Logan were good friends."

A faraway look clouded Allison's eyes. "Yeah. Jason was super nice. And cute. Really cute."

Zoe caught the girl's emphasis on *really*. "You liked him."

Allison nodded. "A lot. And I think he liked me too."

Zoe waited for more.

"I think he and I might've, you know, gotten together. Except..."

"You got mixed up with Matt," Zoe said.

"That too. I guess Jason and I both got mixed up with the wrong people. Me with Matt." Allison shook her head sadly. "And Jason with Lucy Livingston."

THIRTEEN

Allison hadn't wanted to talk any more about Jason. She especially didn't want to talk about Lucy, leaving Zoe stewing with unanswered questions. Key among them—was it mere coincidence that Lucy Livingston's name kept being linked to local men who were now either in the morgue or in the hospital?

Back at Rose's house, Allison thanked Zoe and disappeared down the hall to her room. Zoe deposited her barn boots next to the door and headed for the coffeepot, emptying the last of the brew into a mug.

Rose looked up from her seat at the table where she was sorting the stack of mail that had accumulated during her absence. "How did she handle it?"

Zoe flopped into a kitchen chair across from her friend. "You knew why Allison wanted to go with me?"

"I had a pretty good idea." Rose gathered one of the piles and stood, crossing to the trash can and dumping the flyers and junk mail. "We'd talked about things she needed to confront once we came back. That night in the barn was one of them."

"You could've warned me."

"Would it have made a difference?"

Zoe sipped the lukewarm coffee and pondered the question. "No. Maybe. I don't know."

"Some things have to happen in their own way. In their own time. If you knew in advance, you might have opened up the subject before Allison was ready." Rose shrugged. "Honestly, I didn't know if she was ready to talk about it with you."

Zoe had a feeling Allison wasn't the only one who had returned home from their western sabbatical a little wiser. Leaning forward, Zoe asked, "Do you know Lucy Livingston?"

Rose eyed the barn boots Zoe had left next to the door. "Isn't that the girl you said was engaged to Curtis Knox?"

"Yeah. Sort of. Besides that, though. Do *you* know her?"

"I don't think so. Should I?" Rose picked up the boots, opened the door to the basement steps, and plopped them on the landing.

"Allison suggested that Lucy and Jason were involved at one point."

"Jason Dyer? I thought this Lucy Livingston was older than that."

"She is. I mean, I think she's in her twenties."

Rose made a disgusted sound. "Jason is—was—Logan's age. Eighteen."

Zoe didn't mention the age difference between Allison and the monster who had nearly ruined her had been way more than the difference between twenty-something Lucy and just-barely-legal Jason Dyer. "You've said Jason hung out here. Did he ever mention her?"

"If he had something going with an *older woman...*" Rose made air quotes. "He didn't say anything in front of me."

"But he might have said something to Logan."

"Probably."

"Can you reach him? Ask him what he knows?"

Rose returned to her chair. "Why are you so interested in this girl? Do you think she might have something to do with Jason's murder?"

Zoe took a long draw from her mug and made a face at the tepid stuff. "I don't know. She says she's engaged to Curtis, only she's not. He's lying in a hospital bed with a gunshot wound after being bushwhacked. She may or may not have had something going on with Jason Dyer, and he's lying in the morgue after being bushwhacked. Coincidence?" Zoe shook her head. "Pete doesn't believe in them."

Rose studied her. "How is Pete, by the way?"

Zoe got up and dumped the rest of the coffee down the sink, placing the mug in it. She wasn't up to facing her jumbled feelings right now. "He's exhausted. I don't think he's slept in days. He promised to try and get some this afternoon."

Rose wrinkled her nose. "Not what I meant. And you know it."

A rap on the screen door saved Zoe from having to delve into the convoluted mess that was her relationship with Pete Adams.

Sylvia blew in without waiting to be invited. She looked at Zoe. "Good. I'm glad you're here."

"Me? Why?"

Rose stood and moved next to Zoe at the sink.

"You're not on duty tonight, right?" Sylvia asked.

"Right." Zoe watched from the corner of her eye as Rose removed the mug from the sink, opened the dishwasher, and placed it on the top rack. Next to the warped plastic container.

"But you aren't gonna get any sleep either. Until this beast is caught, none of us are."

"Us?"

Sylvia gave Zoe a look, which she translated as *get with the program*. "Anyone who responds to 911. Or anyone who cares about those who do."

Oh. "Yeah. You're probably right."

"Probably, my ass. You know I'm right."

"What are you driving at, Sylvia?" Rose asked, closing the dishwasher again.

"I'm not driving *at* anything. I'm driving *to* the police station. If tonight is anything like the last two, Pete's gonna need all the help he can get." Sylvia aimed a finger at Zoe. "You've had dispatch training."

"I have."

Sylvia turned her hand and crooked the finger. "Then you're coming with me. I'm not trusting the lives of our boys to those high-tech computer jockeys sitting in the EOC in Brunswick."

All five full- and part-time Vance Township officers sat at the conference table wearing expressions ranging from eager to solemn. Pete looked over his men and wondered how much flack he was going to catch at the next supervisors' meeting when the topic turned to overtime pay. Right now he didn't give a damn. Hell, he'd kick back his own pay if it helped nail this guy.

One of the part-timers raised a hand. "What if the call is something really petty?"

"Petty?" Pete fixed the man with a hard glare. "*Petty* and *emergency* are really oxymorons, don't you think?"

"You know what I mean. A cat up a tree or duck in a drainage pipe stuff. We don't have to go to those too, do we?"

Pete took three slow, deliberate strides to stand in front of the man, leaned down, and braced one hand against the table next to him. "Do you know what the shooter has planned for his next ambush?"

The officer's jaw tightened. "No, sir."

"Do you know who his next target or targets might be? How he plans to lure them into his next trap?"

"No, sir."

Pete slammed the table with the hand he'd rested there. The officer flinched. "Then, yes, you have to respond to cats up trees and ducks in drainage pipes and every other damned call that comes in."

The part-time officer slouched in his chair. "Yes, sir. I see your point."

"Good." Pete turned and stalked back to the head of the table. "Any other stupid questions?"

The room fell silent—except for the ringtone on Pete's cell phone. He snatched it out of his pocket. Caller ID indicated Chuck Delano. Pete sent the call to voicemail. In a calmer tone, he again asked, "Any more questions?" When the response was negative, he thumbed toward the door. "Get out there. And be careful."

The men rose and filed out of the room as Pete's phone rang again. This time caller ID showed Baronick's name. "What've you got?"

"One of the CSU guys located a beautiful intact bullet at the fire scene."

"Wonderful," Pete said, letting his sarcasm show. "Now we just need to find the gun to match it."

"But when we do, we'll have him. Also, the fire marshal found evidence of an accelerant in the barn. And not just a can of gas or kerosene. He says it was all over. So the Loomis barn was definitely torched."

Pete rubbed his forehead. The evidence had caught up to what they already knew, but it didn't help right now. "Anything else?"

"I've got our county officers on alert. We'll have extra patrols in your area in case they're needed."

"Appreciate it."

There was a moment's lull on the line.

Then Baronick said, "I hope we don't see each other tonight."

"Yeah."

The bells on the front door jingled as he ended the call. Now what? He stepped into the hallway to find Sylvia and Zoe heading into the front office.

Zoe stopped and met his gaze. For a moment he set aside the strain of the upcoming night to admire the sight in front of him. In tight jeans and a curve-hugging v-neck shirt, she looked damned good. Why the hell were they always finding excuses to avoid what he knew they both wanted? It had been months since the one and only time they'd made love. And it had been incredible. But he'd botched the whole morning after thing. Next time would be different.

Next time.

What if Zoe had been on that call to the cuts? What if the shooter didn't care who was in the ambulance or on the fire truck? What if the killings were completely random? What if Pete never had a chance to tell Zoe what she really meant to him?

Sylvia stepped back out of the front office, blocking his view. "What's going on—?" She spun to look at Zoe, who lowered her head. Sylvia rolled her eyes. "I wish you two would just hit the sheets and get it over with. But now is not the time. We have work to do."

Apparently Sylvia wasn't aware that they had already *gotten it over with*. Pete cleared his throat. "What are you doing here?"

"We're going to man the radios and phones," Sylvia said.

"You added yourself back onto my payroll?" He feigned annoyance. "The supervisors might have a problem with that."

"I have some pull in that area. Besides, we're volunteering our services." Sylvia slapped Zoe on the back. "Let's get busy. I'll show you which buttons to push."

Sylvia shuffled into the front office again.

Zoe paused, holding Pete's gaze for a moment longer before a sexy smile crossed her lips. Then she sauntered after Sylvia.

Pete released a breath. Damn. Tamping down the sudden rise in temperature, he moved toward the front of the station, stopping in the doorway to the office where Sylvia was giving Zoe a quick tutorial.

"I appreciate the help, but Monongahela County EOC knows the situation and will notify us of all emergency calls."

Sylvia dismissed him with a shake of her head. "That's all good and well, but Emergency Ops is twenty miles away from the action. No one knows this corner of the county better than the three of us. And you..." She aimed a finger at Pete. "You need to be out there, not in here."

She was right, of course.

"Besides," Zoe added, "we can field local calls. If something happens, folks might call to report anything out of the ordinary."

Pete held up both hands in surrender. "Hey, I'm sold. Just make sure you coordinate your efforts with the EOC."

Sylvia thumbed at Zoe. "That's going to be her job."

"Okay then." Pete snatched his ball cap from a hook on the wall. "I'll leave my station in your capable hands."

He'd made it to the front door when he heard Zoe call after him. He stopped and turned. She stood there, her baby blues wide with concern. He almost asked what she wanted. But before he had the chance, she covered the distance between them, flung her arms around his neck, and pressed a kiss to his lips. He pulled her closer and she melted against him. Damn, he wished he didn't have his Kevlar vest on. She clung to him, her mouth warm, intense. When she broke the kiss, she pressed her face to his neck.

"Come back safe," she said, her voice tight, almost desperate.

"I will. I promise."

He could easily have stayed right there for the next hour. Hell, for the rest of his life. But he had work to do.

Like catching a killer before Zoe's next shift. Pete took her by the arms, gently backing her away. Her eyes glistened, and he brushed a thumb across her cheek. "I have to go."

She nodded. "Sylvia and I will have your back."

He smiled. Took one more long look at the woman he loved more than life. And turned away, stepping into the warm early evening sun.

Zoe stood at the front door, watching through parted blinds as Pete climbed into his Explorer. She rested her forehead against the smooth glass. Why hadn't she told him she loved him? What if she never had another chance?

"He'll be fine." Sylvia's voice behind her made her heart jump.

Zoe spun. "How long have you been standing there?"

The woman's omnipotent smile told Zoe *long enough.*

Cheeks warming, she looked down at her sneakers. "I'll get us some coffee."

Sylvia followed her into the front office. "Pot's empty. I'll make fresh, but you can check the one in Pete's office."

Appreciating a moment to regroup, Zoe headed down the hall. Pete's coffeepot held less than a cup of cold sludge. Worse than the stuff at Rose's.

She carried it into the restroom, dumped the disgusting muck, and rinsed and refilled the pot with water. Back in his office she set up the brewer with a clean filter and loaded the basket from the nearly empty container of Maxwell House. All Pete needed to do was flip the power button when he returned.

As she approached the front office, the familiar static-laced voices of emergency radio broadcasts drifted through the station.

"What's going on?" she asked, pausing in the doorway.

Sylvia sat in the chair she'd once occupied on a regular basis and jotted a note. "Medical call, forty-nine-year-old male. Insulin shock."

"Sounds legit."

"Yeah. Nate's responding with the ambulance just in case."

The coffeemaker hissed and gurgled, so Zoe slid into the second chair. "How do you want to handle this?"

Sylvia tapped the paper in front of her with the pen. "For now EOC has the lead. I'm keeping track of calls—locations and responding units, as well as where each of our boys are."

Zoe knew Sylvia's definition of "our boys" was the Vance Township Police. She leaned toward the older woman to read what was on the page. Pete's name was at the top with a notation of the time and his most recent location—driving south on Route 15 toward Covered Bridge Road.

The radio crackled with another call directed at the Phillipsburg EMS garage. A sixty-eight-year-old female who had fallen earlier in the day and was complaining of abdominal pain. Her location was only a mile or two from Pete, but the Emergency Ops Center dispatcher requested Kevin to accompany the medics.

Sylvia aimed her pen at Zoe. "Get on the horn to those idiots and tell them we'll take care of dispatching our officers. And that I'm having Pete take this call."

Grateful that a sixty-eight-year-old fall victim sounded innocuous enough, Zoe dialed the non-emergency number for the 911 command and relayed Sylvia's orders.

"Vance Base, this is Unit Thirty-Five," Nate's voice boomed.

Sylvia keyed the mic. "This is Vance Base."

"It's all clear here. Show me as back in service."

"Roger that, Unit Thirty-Five." Sylvia glanced at the clock. "Nineteen thirty-four."

Zoe stood and crossed to the window, sweeping aside the vertical blinds. Outside, the sun appeared to perch on the treetops on the distant hillside. Shadows grew long. If the shooter stuck to his routine of striking as dusk fell, they were fast approaching a dangerous window.

Her cell phone buzzed in her hip pocket. The number on the screen wasn't familiar. "Hello?"

"Zoe?" The feminine voice sounded weak. Far away.

"Yes?"

"This is Wanda Knox."

A lump rose in Zoe's throat. "Is Curtis okay?"

"He's holding his own. He wants you and Earl to come see him."

Before Zoe had a chance to reply, the EOC fire tones blasted over the radio.

"Oh. I didn't realize you were working." Wanda must have heard them over the phone.

"Yeah." Zoe tried to focus on Curtis while keeping one ear on the radio. "Um, do you think it can wait until tomorrow morning?" As soon as she said the words, she cringed. Would he still be alive tomorrow?

"That'll be fine," Wanda said. "He's just eager to talk to both of you about something. He wouldn't tell me what."

The lump in Zoe's throat softened. "Tell Curtis we'll be there first thing."

The tones repeated, followed by the dispatcher's voice. "Control to Station Eighteen. Report of a vehicle fire, state game lands, exit one, Route 33. Time out, nineteen thirty-seven."

"Thanks," Wanda said. "Whatever's on his mind seems to be pretty important."

The phone clicked in her ear. Important? Had Curtis remembered seeing something and she'd just put him off?

"Dear lord," Sylvia whispered.

Zoe turned to see Sylvia gripping the edge of the desk, all color drained from her face.

The location—exit one, state game lands—sent a chill through Zoe, a chill as bitterly cold as that night last January when she'd responded to the same spot.

Sylvia looked up, meeting Zoe's gaze. She knew the spot as well and as painfully as Zoe. It was where Sylvia's son's body had been found.

But Zoe pushed the memory aside. That was eight months ago. Right now the location carried another reason to freeze her heart. It was lonely. Desolate.

Sylvia drew an audible breath and echoed what Zoe already knew. "This is it."

FOURTEEN

The sixty-eight-year-old female with abdominal pains was exactly what she claimed to be. Pete left the ambulance crew in her kitchen taking vitals and headed back to his SUV. Over the radio, Sylvia sounded more on edge than usual.

"Unit Thirty-Two, this is Vance Base."

"Unit Thirty-Two here." Kevin's voice crackled over the radio.

"Respond to a report of a vehicle fire, game lands, route 33 exit one. Station Eighteen is en route."

Damn it. No wonder Sylvia sounded tense. That exit. Those game lands. Besides the nightmarish memories, it was the perfect location for an ambush. Pete broke into a jog.

"Copy that, Vance Base," Kevin said. "On my way."

Pete grabbed the mic clipped to his shoulder. "Vance Base, Unit Thirty-Two, this is Unit Thirty. I'm on my way too. ETA ten minutes. Base, who else do we have in that area?"

"Unit Thirty-One is about six miles out," Sylvia said.

Seth's voice cut through the static. "Unit Thirty-One responding. Make my ETA five minutes."

Pete slid behind the wheel and jammed the gas pedal to the floor. "Base, get the State Police helicopter over the game lands. Call in County too."

"Already handled."

Of course it was. Sylvia was an old hand at this.

During the drive to the scene, the radio chatter increased by the minute. The fire department arrived first. They reported a burning four-door sedan about a mile southwest of the exit. There were no bystanders. Following orders, they stayed in their truck.

Pete prayed no innocent victims died in that fire.

Kevin arrived next. Minutes that felt like hours passed before the officer's next transmission. "I hear an ATV or a dirt bike. Sounds like it's west of here, heading away from the scene."

"Where's the helo?" Pete barked into the mic. He tried to press harder on the accelerator, but his boot was already to the floor.

"State Police report their helicopter is one minute out," came Sylvia's reply. "And they have troopers in route along with County."

By the time Pete roared off the highway and rolled up to the smoldering remains of an older model sedan, the fire crew had knocked down the flames. Dusk was settling in. Clouds in hues of pinks and purples billowed along the treetops to the west. Under different circumstances, he might have taken a moment to enjoy the sunset.

Kevin, his face flushed, approached Pete's SUV as he climbed out. "I'm sorry, Chief."

"About what?"

"I should've had him."

"Did you see him?"

Kevin's shoulder's sagged. "No."

Pete surveyed the scene. Firefighters doing their job. Two county officers stringing yellow police tape. "Were there any shots fired?"

"No."

Pete clipped him on the arm. "Then you have nothing to apologize for. You secured the scene and reported our suspect's location." He almost added there were no fatalities, but decided to hold off until the fire crew had a good look inside the car.

"Vance Base to all units," Sylvia said over the radio. "The State Police pilot reports he's sighted four ATVs on a game lands trail approximately two miles west of the fire location."

Pete dove back into his Explorer, pausing to point at Kevin, who appeared ready to bolt for his own car. "Stay here. Keep the scene secured."

The young officer looked like a teenager who had been grounded the night of the big dance. But he sucked it up and gave a nod. "Yes, sir."

"Vance Base, this is Unit Thirty responding." Pete slammed the shifter into drive and punched the accelerator. "Get me better directions."

Within a minute, every available unit from Vance Township, Monongahela County, Pennsylvania State Police as well as from three other neighboring jurisdictions were closing in on the game lands.

The access roads left much to be desired. Pete hit ruts and rocks harder than he should, jarring his spine. Only his seatbelt and his death grip on the steering wheel kept him from bouncing his head off the roof. He hoped someone ahead of him caught this guy before it got any darker.

Guy. What had Sylvia said? The pilot reported seeing *four* ATVs? Not one. Four.

"They're on a double-track trail heading west-southwest," Sylvia reported. "Approximately a half mile east of Hillman Road."

Nate's voice cut in. "This is Unit Thirty-Five. I think I know that spot. There's a parking area off Hillman that a lot of dirt-bikers use to access the trails. I'm coming up on it now."

Pete knew the area and was headed straight for it. He grabbed his mic. "Sylvia, get more units there *now*." The last thing he wanted was one of his men in a firefight with a stone cold killer. Or killers.

"I'm on scene," Nate said. "Four pickups in the parking lot. I can hear the ATVs coming and have eyes on the helo."

"County's ETA to your location is two minutes," Sylvia reported.

Damn it. Two minutes could be a lifetime. Pete pushed the Explorer as hard as he dared into a bend. The SUV bucked sideways on the washboard ruts, but managed to hold the road.

"I have eyes on the ATVs," Nate said. "I count four. Coming right at me."

Pete muscled the steering wheel one-handed, keying the mic with other. "Sylvia. Where's his backup?"

"En route," she responded. "Closest is still a little under two minutes away."

Pete came out of the turn to be hit full in the face with the setting sun. Blinded, squinting, he tugged the bill of his cap down. Jammed the accelerator to the floor. Through the dust-streaked windshield, he made out a straight stretch. He could make up some time.

"All four ATVs are stopping," Nate said, his voice tight, edgy.

Pete pictured his officer, weapon drawn, ordering them to stop. So far they were complying. So far.

As he pressed harder on the gas pedal, the front driver's side of the Explorer dropped. Hurled Pete against his shoulder harness. Then a jolt, pitching him the other way. He wrestled the steering wheel. But the SUV careened on two wheels. Threatened to tip. Slammed back to earth. Hard. And sideways. Pete hit the brakes, but it was too late.

The Explorer nosedived into a ditch next to the road. The immediate stop was accompanied by a sickening metallic crunch and the explosion of the deploying airbag.

Stunned, Pete sat pinned to his seat as the airbag deflated. His Kevlar vest cushioned the impact where the seatbelt grabbed him, but his hips and sides ached from the throttling his duty belt had given him.

Choking on dust, he fought to clear his mind. What the hell just happened?

From the radio, Nate's voice shouted, "One of them's rabbiting. He cut across onto the access road, heading east."

East?

"Unit Thirty-Five to Unit Thirty. *Chief.* He's coming your way."

Pete batted away what was left of the airbag, his senses clearing. He fumbled for and found the mic. "Roger that."

He released his seatbelt. Hit the button on the center console to release the Remington Model 870 shotgun from the rack between the seats. He tried the door. Hoped it wasn't too damaged to open and said a silent prayer of thanks when it did. He stepped out of the car. For the moment, he heard nothing of an approaching ATV, so he took a look around.

His Explorer was nosed off the road into a ditch. But what had he hit? He turned. With his back to the sun, he could clearly see the deep gully carved across the road by recent heavy rains. He'd been blinded coming out of the curve and hadn't noticed it. Hitting the thing at the speed he was going? He'd have broken a spring or an axle for sure. Not that it mattered now.

Damn it.

In the distance, a whining buzz of a million pissed-off bees—or one ATV hightailing it away from law enforcement—grew louder.

Pete took cover behind his vehicle and racked a round of double-zero buckshot. He hated his disadvantage of facing the sun, but in another minute or so, it would drop below the horizon, leaving him and the killer in shadows.

Of course, judging from the sound, the quad was going to beat sunset by a good minute and a half.

Pete braced against the Explorer. Fixed on the stretch of road reaching to the west. And waited. The revving engine grew louder.

The ATV roared into view, rounding the next bend, racing straight at Pete. He raised the shotgun and anchored it against his shoulder.

The rider slammed on the brakes. Tires crunched the gravel as he skidded to a stop. A cloud of dust rose and rolled toward Pete, further obscuring his view.

Pete held his position. Waited. He wanted a good look at this bastard. Silhouetted in the last vestiges of daylight, his face was unidentifiable. But Pete could tell he wore no helmet.

The dust cloud parted. The horizon swallowed the last blip of the sun. At the same moment, the rider hit the gas and spun the quad away from Pete.

But not before Pete got his wish. "Police! Stop!" he bellowed, knowing the guy couldn't hear him over the engine.

The ATV sped off in another cloud of dust.

Pete lowered his shotgun and grabbed for his mic. "Unit Thirty to all units. Suspect is heading west on the access road." He hesitated before adding, "Be advised. The suspect is Eli 'Snake' Sullivan."

"You'll never make it as a police dispatcher."

Sylvia's words echoed in Zoe's ears as she approached the game lands exit ramp. The moment they'd heard Nate report the suspect was headed toward Pete, Zoe had lost focus on everything else. And the tone of Pete's voice on the radio set off warning bells and whistles in her head.

It felt like hours before he reported the suspect—Snake Sullivan— was headed the other way. And added that Pete's vehicle was in a ditch.

Sylvia may have acted annoyed about Zoe's less-than-professional reaction to the news, but it hadn't taken much prodding for the older woman to hand over her car keys. After years behind the wheel of an ambulance or a three-quarter-ton pickup, Zoe felt like her ass was dragging on the ground in Sylvia's Escort. But unlike the truck, the car started.

A state trooper flagged her to a stop at the end of the ramp, waving for her to turn left when she was determined to turn right. She lowered the window to a cacophony of songs from night insects.

The trooper, a young woman, stepped toward the car. "Road's closed, ma'am."

Ma'am? "I'm with the coroner's office," Zoe said, trying to sound official. *Ma'am?*

The trooper eyed the small white car, and Zoe read her mind. *Not a very official-looking vehicle.*

"You can radio Chief Adams or anyone from Vance Township PD and confirm it." She fumbled in her purse for her wallet, coming up with her driver's license and holding it for the trooper to examine. "Or anyone from the Monongahela County PD too."

The trooper took the license, excused herself, and walked back to her idling cruiser.

Two minutes later, license back in her wallet, Zoe was headed into the game lands, relieved that whoever responded to the trooper either knew Zoe or accepted her at her word.

The access road was a mess, carved with deep ruts, punctuated with exposed chunks of rock. At one point, the Escort's undercarriage scraped and she hoped she didn't end up with yet another repair bill. She rounded a turn and jammed the brakes, stopping before the car dropped into an especially vicious-looking washout. Ahead of her, Pete's SUV was nose down in the drainage ditch that ran alongside the road. A cruiser from the county PD sat angled with its headlights shining on the debilitated Explorer. A pair of men in uniform—one of them Pete—stood between the two cars. And there wasn't an ambulance in sight.

A knot of tension Zoe hadn't realized she carried released from her neck.

Pete was okay.

She didn't dare attempt to drive Sylvia's car through the washout. Cutting the engine but leaving the headlights on, Zoe climbed out of the car—a process that felt like climbing out of a hole—and picked her way over the rough terrain.

If the other officer hadn't been there, she would have launched into Pete's arms. As it was, she wondered how unprofessional she would appear if she gave him a hug. After all, he'd faced down a killer less than an hour ago. Who would blame her? Yet Pete had an image to uphold.

No. Best save the clinch for later.

"What are you doing here?" he asked. "I thought you were manning the radio with Sylvia."

"I was." Zoe caught the curious raised eyebrows of the county officer and decided *I was worried about you* might also be construed as less than professional. "When we heard you'd wrecked your car, we thought you might need a paramedic."

"We" sounded good. Never mind that she had no idea if Sylvia carried so much as a Band-Aid in her glove box.

A subtle grin tugged one corner of Pete's mouth. The other officer might be buying her excuse, but Pete wasn't.

"You okay, Chief?" the officer, suddenly concerned, asked. "Should I call for an ambulance?"

"No, I'm fine. Zoe made the trip out here for nothing."

The officer appeared relieved. Zoe, on the other hand, wasn't sure whether to feel relieved or chastised.

Pete clapped the officer on the back. "Make that phone call. I need to talk to this paramedic a moment. And let me know if there are any developments."

"Will do, Chief." The officer turned away, keying a number into his cell phone.

Pete rested a hand on the small of Zoe's back and guided her out of the headlight beams. Wrapped in the illusion of privacy the shadows provided, he pulled her into his arms for a quick embrace. Had the county officer noticed, he might have mistaken it for a friendly hug.

"I made the trip for nothing, huh?" she whispered into Pete's ear.

He eased her away, but kept his head bent forward and his voice low. "Yeah. I'm glad you did though."

"Are you okay? I mean *really* okay?"

"I'm fine. Really." He grinned, or at least she sensed he grinned in the dark. His voice dropped even lower. "You can give me a complete physical exam later if you aren't convinced."

Her cheeks warmed, and she was thankful he couldn't see the blush. "Could happen." She cleared her throat. "Have you caught Snake yet?"

Pete straightened. Back to business. "No. But we will."

"You're sure it was him?"

"I saw his face. And we caught the guys he was riding with. As soon as Bud Kramer sends one of his trucks out to tow my vehicle in, the officer here will give me a lift back to the station to question them."

Zoe blew out a breath. "I'm glad you know for sure who did all this, but I'll be even happier when you lock him up."

The rumble of an approaching diesel engine ended their private conversation. "That must be Kramer's man," Pete said. He took her by the arm and escorted her the two steps back into the light.

The officer pocketed his phone. "Sullivan's mother claims she hasn't heard from him since yesterday afternoon."

"Do you believe her?" Zoe asked.

Pete gave her a look. "What do *you* think?"

From his tone, she gathered he had his doubts.

The diesel grew louder, and the glow from its headlights grew brighter. A moment later, the truck appeared around the bend behind Sylvia's Escort. Zoe cringed, hoping he spotted the small car in time and didn't flatten it. She relaxed when the flatbed swung clear of the little Ford and lurched through the washout before hissing to a stop in front of them.

The driver's door opened, and a young man in dark coveralls emblazoned on the back with Bud Kramer's logo stepped down.

Pete intertwined his fingers with Zoe's, drawing her close to him. "You might as well go," he said, just loud enough for her to hear over the idling diesel. "It's going to be a long night."

She looked up into his icy blues and grinned. "What about that physical exam?"

The corner of his mouth tipped up. "I'll meet you back at the station. If we nab Eli the Snake quick enough, I'll let you examine anything you want."

FIFTEEN

"What do you mean you *lost* him?" Pete's temples throbbed. This case might be the one to give him a stroke.

For once, Baronick wasn't flashing his devil-may-care smile. "Sullivan ditched his ATV and took off through the game lands on foot. We lost him in the thick underbrush and trees."

"So we have the ATV?"

The detective brightened. "Oh, yeah. Plus we have the entire area locked down and the search dogs on the way. As soon as it gets light, we'll nail him."

Pete closed his eyes for a moment and leaned back in his office chair. He wished he felt as confident as Baronick sounded. They'd had this punk "locked down" twice before and he'd gotten away. "I want the report on the tire treads ASAP."

"Lab's already working on it."

"Any firearms stashed on the quad?"

"None."

Pete came forward in the chair. "So he may still have his weapon on him."

"I indicated that much on the BOLO."

"All right." Pete placed his palms on the desk and stood. "Let's see what Sullivan's buddies have to say for themselves."

The trio was cooling their heels in the station's conference room with Nate nearby in case they tried to get their stories straight prior to questioning. He assured Pete and Baronick the only words spoken by any of them was a request for a smoke from one muscled and tattooed brute wearing a buzz cut and sporting a nervous twitch.

Pete had that one brought into interrogation first. With the recorder running and Baronick standing in one corner, arms crossed,

Pete read the guy his rights and established his name was Lathan Stegenga.

"But I go by Steg," he added.

Pete could understand why. "How old are you, Steg?"

"Twenty-two." He squirmed in his chair. "Hey, I really need a cigarette, man."

"Sorry. No smoking." Pete tapped the table between them with his pen. "But you answer my questions and I'll make sure my pal here takes you outside so you can light up."

Baronick narrowed his eyes at Pete.

"I don't know nothin'," Steg said.

Pete shrugged. "Then we may have to order out for some nicotine patches."

The kid bit his lip. "Okay. Ask. But I really don't know nothin'."

Pete opened a folder and removed a photo, which he spun toward Steg. "You know this guy?"

"Oh, sure. Snake. What'd he do?"

"You tell me."

Steg shook his head, a movement that looked as much like a small seizure as a negative response. "How should I know?"

"You were with him this evening."

"Yeah." He dragged the word out and ended with an uptick.

"What were you doing?"

"Riding our quads." Again, it sounded more like a question that a statement.

"What time did you first meet up with Snake?"

The kid wiped his upper lip. "He'd texted me and the boys this afternoon and told us to meet out there at that parking lot to ride at six o'clock. I got there a few minutes early, but everyone else showed up between six and maybe six fifteen."

"What about Snake? What time did he get there?"

"He was on time. Six. Maybe a couple minutes after."

"And the four of you rode together the whole time?"

"Yeah. Until Snake spotted the big cop waiting when we was coming back. Then he took off."

Pete made note of the times. "So you were with him when he set the car on fire?"

The kid's eyes widened. "What? No. What car? We didn't do nothin' like that."

"You said you were with him the whole time. From about six to almost eight."

"Yeah, but we just rode our quads. We didn't set no cars on fire. Hell, we didn't even see a car the whole time we was back there."

Pete studied the kid. Antsy. Jonesing for a smoke. And terrified. If he was lying, he was damned good at it. "Did Snake take off on his own at some point?"

"No."

"Not even to maybe go explore on his own?"

"No, man. I told you. We was all together. None of us took off alone."

Pete stared at the kid. Watched him squirm under the scrutiny. Finally, Pete shrugged and turned to Baronick. "Okay then. Take him back to the conference room with his buddies."

"Wait." Steg came forward in his chair. "What about my smoke?"

Pete knew the kid wasn't under arrest—yet—and could get up and walk any time he wanted. But Steg clearly hadn't figured that out. "You didn't tell me anything." Pete started to rise.

"Wait. There *was* something a little weird."

Pete shot a smile at Baronick and sat back down. "I'm listening."

Steg chewed his lip for a moment before going on. "We don't usually ride there. I mean like ever. Me and the other guys tried to talk Snake into goin' to one of our other spots." He shifted in his seat.

Pete read between the lines. He'd come across these "spots" on occasion. Evidence of a campfire with assorted trash indicating drug use and other assorted activities they'd prefer to keep hidden from law enforcement. Or parents.

"But Snake insisted we had to meet *there* at *that* time. It was kinda odd, ya know? Not normal."

"Did he say why you had to ride in that particular area?"

"No. Well, sorta. He didn't come right out and tell us, but he hinted around about maybe having a buy or something set up out there. But nothin' happened."

Pete traced invisible circles on the table with his pen. Nothing Steg said fit with the scenario he'd worked out. And admitting they'd anticipated buying drugs didn't seem like the smartest lie. "Detective, take Mr. Stegenga out back and let him light up."

Baronick gave Pete a look. "Seriously?"

Pete fixed him with a look of his own that didn't require clarification.

"Fine," the detective muttered.

Two hours later, all three bikers marched out of the station having provided similar accounts of the evening. They agreed Snake was with them the entire time. None of them knew anything about a burning car. And the second two confirmed Steg's statement about that part of the game lands being an unusual area for them to meet and ride.

No one knew where Snake might be, and the BOLO on him hadn't produced so much as a possible sighting.

Pete sat in the conference room updating the timeline on the whiteboard when Baronick ambled back in, covering a huge yawn with the back of his hand.

"Go home," Pete told him. "Get some sleep."

"You should do the same."

He studied the board while rubbing the ache above his right eye. "Yeah. Maybe next week."

Baronick leaned against the doorjamb. "What's your take on the terrible trio? Are we chasing the wrong guy? Or are they all providing each other with alibis?"

Pete had been asking himself the same questions. "Have you heard from the lab about Sullivan's quad?"

"Not yet." Baronick glanced at his watch. "It's after midnight. Come on, Pete. Let's get out of here and start fresh in the morning."

He hated to admit the detective was probably right. They hadn't accomplished a whole hell of a lot. Snake Sullivan was still in the wind, meaning the county's emergency personnel were still in danger. But at least he was without his mode of escape. Maybe they'd get a reprieve until he could replace it. "We need to contact all the dealerships that sell ATVs to keep an eye out for Sullivan. And check the newspaper ads for anyone selling used ones."

Baronick pulled out his phone. "And Craigslist too."

"Who's Craig?"

The detective chuckled. "Crawl out of your twentieth century cave once in a while, Pete. It's an online classified ad site."

Oh. Pete tossed the dry erase marker onto the whiteboard's shelf. "Fine. Anyone who's selling an ATV, new or used, needs to be keeping an eye out for this kid and needs to contact us if they hear from him."

"On it. Now are you going home on your own power, or do I have to drag you?"

Pete gave him the Look. *Just try it, buster.*

Baronick held up his hands in surrender. "Well, I, for one, am outta here."

Pete followed the detective to the front door, let him out, and flipped the lock. Nate, Kevin, and Seth were still out patrolling, checking on all of Snake's haunts. County and state had officers manning roadblocks. But Pete had a feeling the rest of the night was going to be quiet.

Snake most likely had taken after his namesake and slithered into a hole somewhere. With a desk piled high with reports, Pete had no plans to go home, knowing he'd only lie awake until dawn.

He glanced into the front office. Sylvia had left at some point. He thought she'd given Zoe a lift to Rose's.

But there Zoe sat—on the floor, her back in the corner, her legs stretched out, and her chin tucked toward her chest—asleep.

Pete paused in the doorway and smiled. Her short blond curls framed her face. She'd been so tense lately, but at that moment, she was the picture of tranquility. A slumbering angel.

His angel.

He eased toward her, keeping his footsteps light, and knelt at her side. "Hey," he whispered, brushing a honey-colored lock from her forehead.

She drew a deep soft breath, and her eyes fluttered open. "Hey, yourself." She covered a yawn with her fingers.

"Why are you still here?"

"My truck's in the shop."

Lame excuse. "Why didn't Sylvia give you lift?"

Zoe caught her lower lip in her teeth for a moment. "Uh. I...thought you might still need help?"

He smiled, glad she'd stayed even if he didn't buy her excuse. Hell, she didn't sound like even *she* bought it. "Well, I don't. Now what are you going to do?"

She stretched and gave him a sleepy smile. A damned sexy sleepy smile. "Don't suppose I could bother you to drive me home?"

"Sorry," he said, feigning total disinterest. "I have a ton of paperwork to do."

With an exaggerated sigh, she said, "Guess I'll have to walk home. In the middle of the night. With a killer on the loose." Zoe drew her legs in and started to push up.

Pete stood and offered a hand, which she took. She popped to her feet, but he didn't release her, drawing her closer instead. "You still owe me an exam after my wreck this evening."

"What about your paperwork?"

"It's not *that* important."

She glanced toward the security camera. "What if someone sees the tape?"

"I'm the chief. I'll burn it." He planted one fist against his hip. "Besides, do you really think anyone around here would be shocked by video of us?"

"I guess we're not the best-kept secret in town."

"Not really." Pete let his imagination play out for a moment. Pictured Sylvia viewing the resulting video footage. He could hear her now. *"It's about goddamned time!"*

Of course, the one night he and Zoe had spent together—one spectacular night—had been followed by a disastrous morning, which had taken weeks...months...to recover from.

Maybe his dream of spontaneous sex in the police station wasn't such a good idea.

Damn it.

He studied Zoe's lips, slightly parted, so close to his he could taste her warm coffee breath. "Come on. I'll walk you home."

"Walk?"

"The Explorer's in the shop too. Remember?"

She stepped back, her gaze locked on his. He could tell she was thinking, but he had no clue what about. Was she remembering that night and the next morning too? Was she silently rehearsing how to let him down once they got to the door—because the home he planned to take her to was not Rose's.

I was only kidding.

I have a headache.

We should stick with being just friends.

Zoe opened the bottom desk drawer and retrieved her purse. "I'm ready."

Pete stepped to one side, allowing her to brush past him out of the office.

And the phone rang.

He bit back a string of profanity.

Zoe choked out a desperate laugh. "Maybe it's a telemarketer." But she retraced her steps and snatched the receiver from its cradle. "Vance Township Police Department."

Pete watched as Zoe's smile faded.

"That's right." She grabbed a pen and slid into the chair, tucking the phone between her shoulder and ear. "When did you notice it missing?"

Pete moved behind her, reading the notes she scribbled over her shoulder. The name she'd written—Jack Utah—wasn't familiar to him, meaning either he wasn't local or hadn't had any run-ins with law enforcement.

She added *one a.m.* next to the name.

"What kind of car was it?"

He watched her write *1986 Chevy Cavalier.* She glanced back at him and tapped the paper.

The burnt car from the game lands had been an older model Cavalier. He held out his hand for the phone.

"Hold on, Mr. Utah. I'm going to put Chief Adams on the line." Zoe covered the mouthpiece and whispered, "He's calling to report his car's been stolen. He'd heard the news earlier, but just got home and noticed the car was gone."

Pete traded places with her and took over questioning Utah.

"So, you think that was my car?" The man's voice sounded a tad boozy.

"I can't say for sure, but it matches the description."

"Was it green? 'Cause mine was green."

Pete had no idea what color the torched car had been. Any paint had been burned off. "Can you give me a license number?"

Utah mumbled a response, which Pete noted. "If it *is* my car, when can I get it back?"

"Sir, if it is your car, I'm afraid there isn't much left."

"Oh." The line fell silent for a moment. "Shit. I knew I shouldn't have gone out drinkin' tonight."

A question popped into Pete's mind. "Mr. Utah, out of curiosity, where were you tonight?"

"I wasn't drinkin' and drivin', if that's what you're gettin' at. I had a—a desig—a designated driver." He stumbled over the word, carefully enunciating each syllable.

"Good. Happy to hear it. But I'd still like to know where you were drinking."

"We was at Rodeo's."

Jack Utah babbled on, assuring Pete he could ask anyone about his innocence regarding any potential DUI charge.

But Pete only half heard him. The part that interested him was the bar. Rodeo's.

Snake Sullivan's hangout of choice.

SIXTEEN

Zoe and Earl stood at the coffee cart next to the hospital's gift shop. She sipped hers and winced at the bitter brew.

He doctored his with creamer and sugar. "Wanda didn't give you any idea what Curtis wanted to talk about?"

"She didn't know. He just told her it was important." Zoe removed the lid and added some of the stuff passing as a dairy product to tone down the coffee's burnt taste. "Sorry I volunteered you to come along without asking."

Earl sampled his before turning away from the cart. "That's all right. Olivia was a little miffed because I backed out of helping her take the kids to church, but it's Curtis. If he needs to talk to us, we have to come, right?"

Short of dumping more creamer into the cup than coffee, Zoe decided the stuff was as good as it was gonna get. "Right. I felt bad because I had to put him off until this morning. He wanted to see us last night."

They crossed to the elevators and waited with a dozen or so others.

"So have you heard anything more from Pete?" Earl asked.

On the drive into the city, she'd told her partner about the events of the night before. She left out the part about nearly going home with Pete prior to the phone call reporting the stolen car. Instead, he'd walked her to Rose's door before going home to pick up his personal vehicle and heading out to speak with Jack Utah. "Not a word. Hopefully he got some sleep after taking the report about the Cavalier."

One set of elevator doors swished open and the waiting crowd drifted toward them.

Zoe and Earl managed to squeeze in.

When they stepped off at their floor, Earl asked, "Do you think they'll have police respond to all calls again tonight?"

"I think Pete hopes to catch this guy before it gets to that."

Earl nodded in agreement.

Curtis had the head of his bed raised when they walked in. The tray in front of him held a mostly untouched plate of scrambled eggs and bacon. Wanda stood over him, wearing a stern motherly expression.

"Are we interrupting something?" Zoe asked.

Curtis gave them a weak grin. "Yeah, thank God."

Wanda only glanced at them before fixing her displeasure back on her son. "You aren't going to regain your strength if you don't eat."

Curtis pushed the tray away. "I'll eat if they bring me something edible."

She shoved the tray back in front of him. "Eat it anyway."

Zoe widened her eyes at Earl. "Maybe we should come back later."

"No," both Wanda and Curtis said at once.

Curtis picked up his fork. "Please stay."

Zoe noticed that he still didn't use the implement on his food though. "Your mom's right, you know."

Wanda crossed her arms and winked at Zoe.

"Yeah, yeah." The patient rolled his eyes.

The bickering was a good sign. Better than Friday's drug-induced stupor.

Curtis studied the plate for a moment. His gaze shifted to his mother and then to Earl and Zoe. He set the fork down and looked up at Wanda. "Mom, why don't you go down to the cafeteria and get something for yourself. You talk about me, but you haven't been eating either."

She patted her girth. "I can afford to miss a few meals. You can't."

"Tell you what. You go eat, and when you're done, bring something back for me. Something that actually tastes like it's supposed to. You do that, and I promise I'll eat."

Wanda appeared to consider the deal. Zoe suspected Curtis was simply trying to get rid of her so they could talk.

"Fine. But you *will* eat what I bring back, no matter what."

"Yes, Mom." Curtis dragged the two words out like a ten-year-old.

Wanda scruffed his hair—like that same ten-year-old—and excused herself from the room.

Earl and Zoe claimed two chairs as Curtis shoved his tray away once again. This time no one argued.

Earl tipped his head at the empty bed next to him. "What happened to your roomie?"

"Discharged. For the moment I have the place to myself."

Zoe slid her chair closer. "Your mom said you had something important to talk to us about."

Curtis played with the button on his side rail, raising the head of the bed a little more. Then lowered the foot of it. "Yeah. Once my mind cleared a little, I started thinking. Mom tried to keep stuff from me, but between what I heard on the news and finally pried out of her, I learned about Bruce Yancy and the other fireman."

"Jason Dyer," Zoe said.

"Yeah." Curtis shot a nervous glance toward the door. "I didn't know Dyer very well. But when I heard Yancy got shot, I remembered something that happened about a month ago. Maybe a little less."

Zoe came forward, resting her elbows on her knees. "What?"

"It was a call for a traffic accident out on Oak Grove Road. We didn't think it was gonna amount to much, except—"

Approaching footsteps and a rumble of voices in the hall distracted Curtis. Zoe noticed his jaw tighten, as if he sensed what was coming a moment before its arrival.

Lucy Livingston swept into the room as if surfing a wave of drama. "Good morning, my darling," she said with an oversized smile before noticing Zoe and Earl. Lucy's demeanor darkened, which she made no effort to disguise. "I didn't realize you had company."

Earl, who'd had his back to the door, jumped to his feet, turning to face her.

Zoe faked a smile. "Hey, Lucy. Wanda had called me and—"

"Told them I was awake," Curtis interrupted, "so they decided to drop in for a visit. Nice surprise, huh?"

Zoe caught the look Earl shot her and gave a quick nod she hoped only he saw. Curtis clearly didn't want Lucy to know he'd asked to speak with them.

The young woman sneered. "Lovely."

"I told you not to come back in," Curtis said. His voice suggested he'd told her a lot more than that.

"And I told *you* it was no trouble."

"You shouldn't be driving into the city with all the traffic and construction."

"It's Sunday morning. There's no traffic. I buzzed right through the tunnels."

"There'll be traffic later. The Pirates are playing at home."

"They're playing in Cincinnati today. I'll be fine." Her voice dripped with honey. Poisoned honey. "I intend to spend the entire day with my Curtie Boo."

Curtie Boo?

A self-conscious Curtis looked from Earl to Zoe, his eyes silently pleading for...what? She wasn't sure if he wanted them to stay or leave. Or throw his ex-fiancée out the window.

Lucy tossed her purse onto the empty bed and elbowed past Earl, leaning over Curtis to plant a kiss on his lips.

He placed his hands on her shoulders and pushed her away. "Lucy, stop." This time his tone left no doubt of his intentions.

Her face flushed, but she didn't back off. "Am I making you uncomfortable, darling? You shouldn't be. They're your friends. And we're about to be married. Little displays of affection are nothing to be embarrassed about."

"Lucy..." Curtis dragged her name out.

She crossed her arms. "Yes, Curtie Boo?"

"Stop it. Just stop it. We are *not* about to married, and you know it. This fantasy of yours has to stop. Now."

Zoe stood slowly, afraid any quick movement might set Lucy off. The girl was unstable. No doubt about it.

"You are such a kidder." Lucy grabbed the chair Earl had vacated and dragged it to the head of the bed, knocking the thing against his legs in the process.

An uncharacteristic flash of anger narrowed ever-patient Earl's eyes. Zoe feared for a moment he might snatch the chair back. Or snatch the girl by the throat.

Zoe stepped around the foot of the bed and caught her partner's arm. "Maybe we should go."

"Yeah." Curtis dragged the word out. "Thanks for dropping in. It was a nice surprise."

There was that lie again.

Lucy lowered the bed's side rail and settled into Earl's chair, leaning over to finger Curtis's hair. He ducked his head away, but she ignored his hard-to-miss body language. She also ignored Zoe and Earl as they headed for the door.

"Whoever said 'beauty is only skin deep' surely had *her* in mind," Earl muttered as they waited for the elevator.

"And what's with Curtis?" Zoe huffed. "'Nice surprise.' *He's* the one who insisted we come in."

Earl frowned in the direction of the room they'd left. "He doesn't want her to know."

Zoe replayed the last few minutes in her mind. "Is it just me or does he seem scared of her?"

"Hell, *I'm* scared of her. She's psycho."

"Maybe we shouldn't leave her in there alone with him."

Earl appeared to contemplate trying to remove the girl from Curtis's bedside and made a sour face. "If you want to try, go ahead. But the nurse's station is right outside his door."

Zoe agreed. "What about that call he was telling us about before she got here? Do you have any idea what he was talking about?"

"None."

The elevator doors dinged open, and they stepped inside.

"Traffic accident a couple of weeks ago on Oak Grove Road," Zoe said as much to herself as to Earl. "It shouldn't be too hard to look up."

Pete tramped through a tangle of dried grass and still-green weeds in the game lands west of where the burnt Cavalier had been discovered. The morning's blue sky was quickly being blotted out by encroaching dark gray clouds. Any evidence out there would likely be decimated by rain, so every available cop had joined the crime scene team to scour the area. According to the crumpled map in Pete's pocket, one of those double-track trails the bikers and quad riders used was dead ahead.

As he picked his way up a hillside, his mind meandered back to last night. Damn that Jack Utah.

Instead of a night with Zoe—alone at Pete's place—he'd spent the wee hours following up on the man's story. First he'd swung by Rodeo's Bar before it closed. The bartender and several self-proclaimed regulars confirmed Utah's story. He'd been there. A buddy had driven him home. And while the patrons admitted to knowing Snake, none of them believed Sullivan and Utah were more than acquaintances. Nor did they recall having seen Snake recently.

Utah was still awake—more or less—when Pete arrived at his house, a rundown hovel with an uneven sidewalk leading to a poorly lit concrete stoop and a door with a shredded screen. Utah staggered as he showed Pete into a space he guessed was a living room. He'd heard of a TV show about hoarders, and this guy could have been a headliner on it. Utah squinted at the photo Pete held up and acknowledged he knew Snake from the bar, but they didn't socialize elsewhere. Utah didn't know Snake's last name or where he lived. Claimed he didn't run with the same crowd. The way he said it, wrinkling his nose and curling his lip, Pete suspected Jack Utah did not approve of Snake's friends.

Still, Snake might have known more about Jack Utah than the other way around. Pete scribbled a note linking Snake and the stolen Cavalier.

The wind in the game lands picked up, hissing through the browned late-summer grass. The terrain swept up an increasingly steep hillside. According to Pete's map, the trail was at the top of the rise.

By the time he reached the crest, he was breathing hard. Damn, he was out of shape. Hunting season was a little more than a month away. He'd better get out and do some hiking to build his stamina if he intended to lug his new muzzleloader around the woods.

As he caught his breath, he surveyed the scenery around him. To his back, the rolling grassland from which he'd come.

At his feet, the trail he'd been looking for swept in both directions, following the ridge. Ahead of him, the ground leveled out for a hundred yards or so before dropping off again, and all of it was wide-open grassland with the exception of a few saplings too scrawny to obstruct his view.

To his left, the trail headed west-southwest—toward the parking lot where Nate had rounded up three of the four ATV riders. That view also stretched wide open for at least a quarter of a mile before disappearing into a tree line.

To Pete's right, the trail vanished into a stand of trees and underbrush only a few hundred feet away. His head told him to turn away from the woods and start toward the parking lot. But his gut drew him in the other direction.

He strode east and slightly north, away from the parking lot, away from the location of the burning car, but toward a great place to hide. He glanced down at two dusty paths with a strip of weeds separating them. Neither of the dirt tracks bore the imprint of a tire tread. When was the last rainfall? Friday night.

No one had been on this trail since the deluge of the night before last erased all previous tread marks. Snake and his buddies had not traveled this trail last night.

Pete almost turned around. But the woods called to him.

The musty aroma of leaf mold and damp soil enveloped him as he stepped into the shadows. He paused to let his eyes acclimate. The trail carved a narrow path through the trees. Branches and grapevines arched overhead, creating a tunnel of green with dapples of gold and red.

Pete again considered reversing direction, but his gut urged him on. Ten feet down the path, a spider web enveloped his face. Sputtering and spitting, he swiped it away, hoping the resident arachnid hadn't been home. Swearing, he trod onward.

Ahead, something that didn't belong caught his attention. He stopped. Squinted. It was hard to make out. He eased closer. Instinct brought his hand to his sidearm.

A recognizable shape took form in spite of the camouflage fabric. A hunting blind—a big one—perched a few feet off the trail, mostly concealed by the saplings and brambles.

Pete took one slow sidestep to place a tree between him and the tent-like structure. He released his Glock. If Snake Sullivan—or anyone else—was inside, they had a clear shot at him. The tree behind which he'd taken cover felt like little more than a twig, but it was the best he could do.

He reached to the mic clipped to his shoulder. "This is Vance Township Unit Thirty. I've located a hunting blind in the woods off the

ATV trail east-northeast of the parking lot and about a half mile west of the site of last night's vehicle fire. Unknown occupant. Requesting backup."

Immediately, four officers responded, including Nate and Baronick, who were two minutes away.

With backup en route, and their response loud enough that anyone inside the hunting blind would have been able to hear, Pete raised his Glock. "You! Inside the blind. Throw out your weapons and then come out. I want to see both your hands."

The harsh buzz of insects and a few birdsongs were the only reply. A breeze smelling of rain kicked up, fluttering the material.

Pete held his position. Kept his gun fixed on the blind. And waited. If Snake was in there watching him, the kid had made no move to surrender. He'd already taken two lives and left two more good men in the hospital. Pete wasn't about to give him a clear shot.

A distant rumble grew louder. A vehicle approaching from the direction Pete had just come.

"We're about to get company," he yelled. "And things could get sticky for you. Show me your hands and come out *now*."

Still nothing.

The vehicle grew closer. Or perhaps it was two vehicles. Yeah. Definitely two. The cavalry had arrived.

His radio hissed to life. "Chief?"

Pete recognized Baronick's voice and replied, "Follow the trail into the woods."

"Officer Williamson and I are on our way."

The engines quieted. Two car doors slammed. The trail wasn't wide enough for a motor vehicle.

Still no movement from the hunting blind.

A minute later, jogging footsteps, muffled by the soft earth, grew close.

"I'm here," Pete shouted. He waved to catch their eyes and pointed toward the blind, then motioned for them to spread out. "It may be empty, but let's not take any chances."

"Roger that," Nate called.

The Vance Township officer and the county detective moved into position, flanking the hunting blind.

"Last chance," Pete yelled again. "Throw out your weapons and step out, showing me your hands."

When he received no response, he signaled to the others. Then the three men moved in with guns trained on their target.

SEVENTEEN

Pete closed in first, his Glock at the ready. Nate and Baronick approached from the flanks. Brown camouflage fabric with mesh windows concealed the interior until Pete was inches away.

"It's empty," he said.

Nate holstered his sidearm. "Some hunter probably left it behind once the season was over."

"I doubt it." Pete stashed his Glock too. "It's in too good of shape. If it'd been sitting here since winter, or even spring turkey, it would show more wear and tear from the elements."

Baronick pulled open the flap serving as a door. "I'd say you're right about that, Pete. Look."

He and Nate circled to the opening. Inside, the grass and weeds had been flattened. A set of tires had left a mashed path in their wake— a path that led toward the trail. Careful not to step on the tracks, the men followed them. Once they hit dirt, the indentations became distinct tread marks.

Baronick yanked out his phone. "I'll get the techs in here to photograph and cast these to see if they match Sullivan's ATV."

While the detective made his call, Pete bent over, studying the tracks closer. "There are two sets," he said to Nate, pointing. "Both from the same tires. He drove in from the east, stashed the quad in the blind, and then drove out, heading back east again."

Nate scowled down the wooded path. "East?" He turned the other way. "But I caught up to them *west* of here."

Baronick pocketed his phone. "CSU's on their way. Did you say he went east?"

"Yeah." Pete showed the detective the incoming and outgoing tracks.

Baronick slapped at the side of his face. "Damned mosquitoes."

"Wood flies," Pete corrected.

"Whatever." Baronick scratched the bite. "He came and went here. But Nate caught him…" The detective pointed to the west. "There. He must have circled around to throw us off."

Pete didn't like it. None of it. "Maybe." He shook his head. "But I don't think so. This guy stashed his quad here, not expecting us to find the blind, so why head east to go west? Besides, I don't think Snake Sullivan is capable of this much thought and planning."

All three men turned toward the shady trail heading east.

"Baronick, you wait here for the crime scene techs," Pete said. "Nate, you're with me. Let's follow these tracks and see where they go."

Zoe had Earl drop her off at the ambulance garage in spite of his argument about leaving her stranded. She'd argued that at least there she could beg a ride from someone. If he took her "home" to Rose's, she'd be stuck.

She needed her truck back.

C crew had the long weekend shift, and every medic in the building wore their exhaustion, fear, and grief on their faces. After Zoe updated them on Curtis's medical status—leaving out the part about his crazy girlfriend—most of the crew drifted out of the office, some headed for the bunkroom to catch up on sleep, others to the lounge to watch TV.

Randy Nichols, whose sister Tracy was the youngest member of Zoe's crew, stayed behind. He handed her a cup of coffee and motioned for her to have a seat on the bench in front of the window.

"Actually, I want to dig through the files," she said.

He propped a hip on the corner of the desk. "I thought you looked like you were after something more than just giving us the latest on Curtis's condition."

"You thought right." Zoe crossed to the pair of metal filing cabinets where they stored the run reports. "Do you know anything about a traffic accident on Oak Grove Road about a month ago?"

Randy slid from the desk into its chair. "Oak Grove Road? No. Was it on this shift?"

"No." She set her cup on top of the cabinet and opened the drawer containing the most recent reports. "Curtis and Barry took the call, so it was B crew."

"Was it a bad one?"

"Curtis said they hadn't thought it would amount to much."

"But?" Randy raised an eyebrow at her.

"I don't know." Zoe thought of Lucy's interruption. "Someone came in before he could tell us the rest. But he hinted it might have something to do with what's been happening."

Randy tapped some keys on the computer keyboard. "Do you have a patient's name?"

"Sorry. I've told you all I know."

"Huh. You don't have much to work with. Then again, Oak Grove Road? Not exactly a lot of traffic out there."

"That's what I was thinking." She shuffled through the papers, searching for dates from last month.

Randy rolled the chair back and stood. "I'll go in the back and ask the other guys if they remember hearing anything."

"Thanks."

The latest dates in the drawer Zoe opened went back three weeks. Curtis had said a month or less, so she started pulling each call sheet to check the call's location. She'd made it through a half dozen records when the front door crashed open.

Lucy stormed in, fists clenched at her sides.

Zoe let the report she was scanning drop back into its folder and closed the drawer with a metallic clunk. "Hey, Lucy." She glanced toward the door to the back and wished Randy hadn't left. "I thought you were spending the day with Curtis."

The girl marched across the office toward Zoe. "He made me leave."

Taking an involuntary step back, Zoe bumped into the filing cabinet, rattling it and the coffee cup on top. "I'm sure he must be tired and wanted to rest."

Lucy stopped inches in front of Zoe, glowering up at her. "He's not tired. I'm just not the one he wants to be with anymore."

The admission startled Zoe. "Oh. I'm sorry."

"No, you're not."

Well, she was right about that.

"*You* wanted him to break up with me," Lucy hissed.

Zoe opened her mouth, but Lucy shoved her before Zoe had a chance to say anything.

She staggered into the filing cabinet again, harder this time. The cup tipped, slopping hot coffee on her shoulder before crashing to the floor and exploding into shards.

Zoe ignored the bite of the burn and shoved Lucy back. "Back off," she told the girl while tamping down her own rising anger. Lucy was shorter and thinner, and in a catfight, Zoe knew she'd be able to take down the crazy little bitch, but somehow she didn't think beating the crap out of Curtis's ex would do much to help him.

Besides, heavy footsteps from the back told Zoe help was on the way.

Zoe's retaliation seemed to stun Lucy, but it didn't cool her down. She raised fists as if ready to come out of her corner swinging.

Randy and the other five C crew members appeared in the doorway. Randy rushed forward, snatching Lucy from behind and pinning her arms. "What on earth is going on here?"

Zoe rubbed her stinging shoulder. "I wish I knew." She took a step toward the restrained hellcat, glass crunching underfoot. "What is your problem, Lucy?"

The girl squirmed against Randy's grip, but he had a foot of height and close to a hundred pounds on her. Angry tears brimmed in her eyes. "Curtis broke up with me because of *you*."

Randy shot Zoe a questioning look over Lucy's head.

"*Me?*" Zoe choked. "I don't *think* so."

"You've got the hots for him. And he's in love with you too."

"I—*what?*"

"So he dumped me for you—you *whore*."

Zoe flinched. The last time someone had called her that was in high school. Both she and the other girl had been expelled for the resulting fight. The other medics must have sensed the potential for fisticuffs. They all piled into the office, taking positions to block or tackle as needed.

The potential scene flashed through Zoe's mind. Pete being summoned to a brawl at the Mon County EMS garage. Finding Zoe and

Lucy tussling on the floor. He would side with Zoe, of course, and toss Crazy Lucy in jail. On the other hand, he was a little busy trying to solve a couple of murders and didn't need the added aggravation.

Zoe inhaled a calming breath. Blew it out slowly. "All right...look. Curtis isn't interested in me, and I'm definitely not interested in him."

"Liar," the girl snapped. "I'm not blind. I can see how he looks at you. And how you hate when I'm around."

She had that much right. Only her reasons were way off base.

Randy must have given Lucy's arms a squeeze because she let out a whiny yelp. "Let go of me, you Neanderthal."

He started walking her toward the still-open front door. "I'll let you go once you're off EMS property."

She stagger-stepped until she realized she was out-muscled. "Fine. I'm leaving." She squirmed. "Now let me go."

He released her, but stood firm, letting her know the only direction available at the moment was out.

With a growl, Lucy slouched her way to the door, but paused and turned back toward Zoe, shaking a finger at her. "This isn't over. Curtis is mine, and I *will* win him back. You just watch your step." Her jaw set, she blew out of the office.

"What the hell was that all about?" Randy asked.

"She's nuts." Zoe tugged her damp shirt away from her skin, pumping a little cool air against the burn.

"I got that much. Are you okay?"

"I think so." She glanced at the mess on the floor. "Looks like we're down one mug."

"Don't worry about it." He directed two of the guys to clean up the mess. "You," he said to Zoe, "go have a seat in the back. I'm gonna get something and then I'll be right there to take a look at that burn."

"But—"

He extended one arm with a finger pointing at the doorway to the lounge. "Go."

No longer in a fighting mood, Zoe acquiesced.

After collapsing onto the lumpy couch, she stretched the neck of her t-shirt over her shoulder, craning her neck to get a look at the damage from the hot coffee. Her skin was pink rather than angry red with no sign of blistering. A little aloe should do the trick.

A few minutes passed before Randy joined her, carrying another cup in one hand, a file folder and a box of gauze squares in the other, and a bottle of saline clamped under one arm. He offered her the cup first. "I thought you might want a refill on the coffee. Try not to wear it this time."

She made a face at him. "Ha, ha." But she accepted the mug.

He took a seat next to her, eyeing her shoulder. "Doesn't look so bad."

"No." Zoe sipped the hot brew. "And I don't need all that." She nodded toward the saline and the bandaging he'd set on the couch between them.

"I guess not." He held up the folder and removed a sheet of paper. "But you may want to see this."

She set the mug on the end table and reached for the report. "What is it?"

"You were talking about the run out on Oak Grove Road. It didn't strike a chord with me until your little scuffle with Loco Lucy."

Zoe was glad she'd already swallowed the coffee. Otherwise she'd have choked on it. "*Loco* Lucy?"

Randy shrugged. "It's what some of the guys call her."

"How did I not know this?"

"You don't hang out with us at the bar." He tapped the paper. "Anyhow, I remembered hearing about a call and thought it might be the one you were asking about, so I pulled the report."

Zoe scanned the nearly indecipherable scrawl on the page. Dated three weeks ago, it indicated Barry and Curtis had been on the crew responding to a vehicular collision on Oak Grove Road. Vance Township VFD had also responded, although the report didn't name which firefighters had been at the call. Nothing unusual there. Two cars had been involved in the accident. Only minor injuries noted, with no one requiring transportation to the hospital, and the ambulance returned to the garage.

Disappointed, she said, "This doesn't tell me much."

"No, it doesn't. It was a very forgettable call. On paper."

"What do you mean?"

Randy removed another sheet of paper from the folder. "One of my guys stopped in that day after they'd gotten back. I remember he mentioned Curtis was acting jittery. When asked about it, Curtis dodged the questions, and Barry just waved them off, saying it was nothing. But he got the impression that it was definitely *not* nothing."

She reached for the second paper. "What's this?"

Randy handed it to her. "The reason Loco Lucy's appearance reminded me about the call."

The second sheet of paper was one of the release forms they required patients who refused transportation to sign. Considering what Randy had said, she expected to see Lucy's signature at the bottom.

Zoe was close.

The signature on the form belonged to Hector Livingston, Lucy's father.

EIGHTEEN

The gray clouds grew darker as the wind hissed through the leaves overhead. Pete could smell the approaching rain on the breeze. Rain that would obliterate the tire tracks he and Nate were following. He picked up the pace.

"Any idea where this trail leads?" Nate asked.

Pete dug the crumpled map from his pocket and handed it to his officer. "Unfortunately this one branches off a couple of times. Hard to tell which trail our guy took."

Nate kept stride for stride with Pete while studying the map. "He was on an all-terrain vehicle. Didn't necessarily need to stay on the trail."

Yeah, there was that too.

They broke into a rolling open expanse of grassland dotted with scrub trees. The wind, unbroken by the wooded cover, had shifted. Coming from the north, it carried a chill and threatened to snatch Pete's ball cap from his head. He tugged it down tighter.

No way were they going to beat the rain. He pulled out his phone. Knowing there was no one at his station manning the radio on a Sunday morning, he punched in the non-emergency number for the county EOC. When they answered, he stopped walking and gestured for Nate to do the same. He needed to catch his breath, and stopping to look at the map was a good excuse. "Send officers in the area out to Gayle Road and T920 where the double-track trails intersect. Tell them to look for quad tracks consistent with our shooter. He may have used one of those trails to escape."

"Ten-four, Chief Adams."

Stuffing the phone back in his pocket, he started off again.

"We can rest a bit longer if you need to," Nate said.

Pete noticed his officer wasn't breathing hard at all. "I'm fine. Let's move."

He calculated they'd hiked about a half mile before they came to the first split. The tracks veered right at the Y, following the trail at a slight downgrade into another patch of trees. A minute later the pitter-patter of rain in the tree canopy pushed Pete into a jog. At least the cover of leaves and branches bought them a little time.

The next half mile felt like ten. Damn, he needed to get into shape. Another trail from the right joined theirs and brought with it multiple sets of new tracks.

"Our shooter wasn't the only one out here," Nate said.

Pete noticed his officer still wasn't winded.

They trudged on, the pace slowing from a jog to a long-striding walk. Even with the additional tracks, Pete hoped they'd be able to pick out the one set they were interested in.

Overhead, the light pitter-patter grew into a steady whisper. Drops worked their way through the leaves, pelting his hat and shoulders.

A hundred or so yards ahead, the trees gave way again to rolling grasslands blanketed with a gray haze. The tread-mark mishmash in the dirt dissolved into a glistening sheen of mud, melting discernable prints into generic grooves along the trail.

"Damn it," Pete said.

Nate stood at his side looking at the blank ribbon of slop stretching from their feet into the foggy distance. "I'm not sure if this guy is good or just lucky."

"Both." And while Snake Sullivan might have luck on his side, Pete still didn't believe the kid had the smarts to be classified as good. Nor did Pete believe the tracks they'd been following doubled back at some point. Which meant not only was the gunman still out there, but Pete didn't have a clue who or where.

Or if there really was only one shooter.

"What do you know about Hector Livingston?"

Having begged a ride home from Randy, Zoe stood at the kitchen counter, removing clean plates and silverware from the dishwasher, while Allison poured glasses of iced tea and Rose gathered the fixings for sandwiches.

Seated at the table, Sylvia pondered Zoe's question. "Hector's something of a recluse. He wasn't always that way. I remember back when his wife was still alive, he was just your average Joe. A little quiet, but in a shy kind of way. Not like now."

Zoe thought of her first visit to Curtis two days ago and the effect Hector had had on his crazy daughter, reining her in with a few words. "What do you mean? *Like now?*"

Sylvia appeared to consider her words carefully. "Well, now he seems a little...off. In the head. You know?"

Maybe Loco Lucy's insanity was inherited. "When they came into Curtis's room at the hospital, Lucy was the one who was 'off.' Hector stood back and watched. And then pretty much ordered her to behave. Which she did. I can't imagine anyone else being able to quiet her down with only a few words."

Allison carried a pair of glasses of iced tea to the table. Zoe noticed the dark scowl on the girl's face and thought of what she'd said about young Jason Dyer having had a relationship with Lucy.

"Do you think she's scared of him?" Rose asked. "Good heavens, you don't think he beats her, do you?"

Sylvia shook her head. "I don't think so."

"I don't either." Careful not to step on one of the two orange tabbies circling at her feet, Zoe set plates and forks at each of their places. "Lucy didn't seem scared or intimidated. She seemed to revert to a little kid being scolded."

Sylvia leaned back in her chair. "That sounds about right. Mind you, I rarely see Hector anymore, but I remember he adored his daughter when she was small. And then after his wife became ill and passed, Lucy was all he had left. It was the two of them against the world."

Rose moved the platter with baked ham, cheese, lettuce, and tomato to the center of the table. "Maybe I'm thinking of someone else, but I seem to recall Hector being on the fire department."

"Oh, yes." Sylvia came forward again, reaching for her glass of tea. "That's mostly how I knew him. He was several years older than Ted, but they were both on the Vance Township Fire Department."

"I didn't know. That must be why I had a feeling Wanda and Hector knew each other. They worked together back then." Zoe closed the dishwasher and moved toward her chair, but Jade let out a whole sentence of pitiful meows. "Oh, no. Mustn't forget to feed the kitties."

Allison jumped to the cabinet where they kept the cat food. "I'll get it."

"Thanks." Zoe slipped into her seat. "How long ago was that?"

"You mean Hector on the fire department?" Sylvia sipped her tea, her brow furrowed in thought. "Had to be eighteen...nineteen years ago. Ted was a junior firefighter, and I don't believe their time on the department overlapped more than a couple of years, if that. Hector quit when his wife passed. He pretty much dropped out of everything."

"Why all the questions about him?" Rose asked, while glowering in the direction of the dishwasher.

Zoe shared Curtis's interrupted story about the mysterious call to Oak Grove Road and his secretive reaction when Lucy burst in. "When the only accident report I could find named Hector as one of the victims, I got curious."

Allison poured fresh dry food into bowls already half full. Jade and Merlin dived in as though they'd been famished. "Maybe Lucy doesn't know about her dad being in the accident."

Zoe glanced at the teen, whose voice had been uncharacteristically low.

Rose continued to frown. "Or maybe she does know, and it's a sore subject."

Zoe ran a finger around the rim of her glass. "But what could any of it have to do with Barry and Yancy getting shot?"

"And Jason," Allison added.

And Curtis, Zoe thought.

Sylvia slowly straightened in her chair, like a balloon being filled with air, and her eyes shifted.

Before Zoe could ask what was wrong, Rose poked her arm. "You closed the dishwasher."

"Yeah?" Zoe asked, wondering what it had to do with the shootings.

"But you didn't unload all the clean dishes yet."

"No." Zoe had a feeling she'd given the wrong answer.

"You did that yesterday too."

This time Zoe didn't reply.

"And I didn't know the dishes in there had already been washed, so I loaded dirty ones with the clean."

From the look on Rose's face, Zoe gathered she'd broken some Bassi household law. A felony at that. The only response she could come up with was, "Sorry."

Rose shifted in her chair to face Zoe head-on. "I'm not the only one you owe an apology to. Patsy stopped by this morning looking for you."

The trail ride. Zoe let her head drop forward. "Crap. I completely forgot she said she'd pick me up."

"You need to be a little more responsible, don't you think?"

Rose's accusatory attitude reminded Zoe a little too much of her own mother. "I've been distracted. I have a few things on my mind that are more important than your stupid dishwasher."

"*Girls.*" Sylvia's sharp tone ended the exchange. "I know we're all on edge right now, but stop taking it out on each other."

Chastised, Zoe lowered her head. From the corner of her eye, she noticed Rose turn back toward her plate and sullenly start layering ham, cheese, and lettuce onto a slice of bread.

"Zoe," Sylvia said, her voice softer, "have you mentioned anything about Hector's accident to Pete?"

"I haven't talked to him yet today. Why?"

The older woman stared at her tea, but Zoe sensed she was seeing something entirely different. "Because if you're thinking of Hector as a possible suspect in these shootings, there's something Pete—and you—need to know. Hector's an avid hunter."

"So is at least half the population of Vance Township," Rose said.

Sylvia fixed her daughter-in-law with a hard stare. "Yes. But half the population hasn't won awards for sharp shooting."

The room fell quiet except for the crunching of the cats eating their lunch.

Zoe let the tidbit sink in as she reached for the loaf of bread. She definitely needed to share this information with Pete. But there was someone else she needed to talk to first.

*   *   *

Pete closed his office door and unbuttoned his drenched uniform shirt. The rain had ushered in a cold front, and if his jaw wasn't so tightly clenched from this case, his teeth would've been chattering. He peeled off the shirt and t-shirt underneath, dropping them in a heap behind his desk before retrieving a fresh uniform from the cramped closet.

Someone knocked on the door. "Chief?" Baronick's voice filtered through.

"Come in."

The detective bore no evidence of having been out in the deluge. "I personally delivered the casts of the tire tracks to the lab. They're short-staffed on a good day, but it's a weekend so..."

"Put a rush on it." Pete tugged on the dry t-shirt.

"Already did. We should hear something shortly."

Shortly. Pete hated that word. It could mean ten minutes, ten hours, or ten days.

Baronick picked up the coffee mug from Pete's desk—the one Zoe'd had made for Pete last Christmas—and squinted at the police chief emblem on the side. The detective glanced toward the half-full pot in the corner.

Pete snatched the mug from him and thunked it back in its spot. "Clean cups are in there." He motioned to the cabinet on which the coffeemaker sat.

"Feeling a little territorial, are we?" Baronick opened the cabinet door and came up with a mug bearing the Vance Township Volunteer Fire Department's logo.

The sight of it soured Pete's stomach. "Any word on Yancy?"

Baronick studied the design. "I was about to ask you the same thing." He set the cup down and reached for the pot.

Pete buttoned the clean, dry uniform shirt and made a mental note to call the hospital.

"So what do you think?" Baronick asked while pouring coffee. "Is Snake smarter than we give him credit for? Or are we completely back at square one?"

Pete tucked his shirttail into his trousers and headed into the hallway, letting the question follow him. He didn't like either option.

Baronick followed him into the conference room. "I know you've been saying Snake's too stupid to pull this off—"

"Yes, I have."

"I think you're wrong."

Pete spun on the detective. While they might disagree about a lot of things—procedure, methodology, Zoe—Wayne Baronick rarely called him out on his case assessment. "Why?"

Baronick waved an arm around, indicating the otherwise empty room. Or maybe the station. "Where is he? We haven't been able to catch him. Every police jurisdiction in three counties has BOLOs on this guy. He's smart enough to evade capture. Why shouldn't he be smart enough to mastermind these ambushes, plot his escape, *and* act dumb to throw us off his trail?"

Pete glared at the detective. He made a good argument. Except for one thing. "Have you ever *talked* to this guy?"

Baronick swallowed. "No."

Pete nodded. "When we catch him, you interrogate him. And then tell me about what a brilliant mastermind he is."

The bells on the front door jingled followed by an unfamiliar male voice calling, "Hello?"

Pete brushed past the detective into the hall. Two men stood at the doorway to the empty front office. The first wore a suit and tie and had his longish hair slicked back. Pete recognized him as Attorney Andrew McCoy. The lawyer blocked Pete's view of the second man.

"Chief Adams." McCoy flashed a mouthful of small but perfectly straight teeth and extended a hand. Oversized rings adorned three of his fingers. "I believe you've been looking for my client. We're here so he can turn himself in."

As the attorney stepped toward Pete to shake his hand, the other man, shoulders sagging, hung back.

Snake Sullivan.

Pete set a glass of water on the conference room table in front of the tattooed and pierced suspect and shot a glance at Baronick.

Now the detective would have his chance to experience "the mastermind" firsthand.

McCoy sat next to Snake, his briefcase, a legal pad, and a pen on the table in front of him. "I want the record to show that my client is here of his own volition."

"So noted." Pete eased into a chair across from them and studied the pair. One all slick and polished. Too polished. Too smooth. The other, sweaty and dirty and smelling like he hadn't bathed in days, looked like he wanted to crawl into a dark hole. "What were you doing out in the game lands last evening?"

Snake ignored the glass of water, choosing to keep his arms tightly crossed. "Just riding with friends."

"So why'd you run?"

"'Cause you cops was chasin' me."

"We were chasing you because you ran. Your buddies complied with Officer Williamson when he ordered them to stop. You didn't. Why?"

Snake glanced pleadingly at McCoy. "Do I have to answer him, Uncle Andy?"

The lawyer fixed Pete with a hard stare. "Let's cut to the chase. We are aware that you suspect my client—"

"Your nephew," Baronick said.

McCoy turned slowly to give the detective a withering look before bringing his gaze back to Pete. "You suspect my client of some rather heinous crimes."

"Murder," Baronick said. "Aggravated assault. Arson. Just to name a few."

The attorney's jaw clenched.

Realization hit Pete.

Baronick and McCoy knew each other. And not in a good way. "Yes," Pete said to McCoy. "We do."

"I didn't do none of that shit," Snake said, his voice trembling.

McCoy put a hand on the table in front of his nephew. "Quiet. Let me handle this." To Pete, he said, "We want to cut a deal."

"A deal? For what?"

"My client has information that you may find helpful. He's willing to give you a statement, but in exchange, you agree not to press charges against him for...certain minor crimes he might have to admit to in order to give you this helpful information."

"Minor crimes?" Baronick said. "Like possessing drugs with intent to sell?"

"I wasn't gonna sell none of it." Snake's voice had soared into falsetto range. "I planned on using it myself and sharing it with my friends."

Pete hid a smile behind his hand and lifted his gaze to meet Baronick's. Mastermind? Yeah. Right.

NINETEEN

Zoe paused in the doorway of Yancy's hospital room, debating whether to enter. He was alone, his eyes closed and his jaw slack. She knew from experience how difficult it was to get real rest in these places and considered walking away, leaving the patient to his nap.

On the other hand, she really needed to talk to him.

She crept into the room, wincing at the squeak of her shoes against the floor. Yancy didn't stir. She eased into the most comfortable-looking chair in the room.

Yancy appeared much as he had the previous day. Right arm bound to his torso. Oxygen flowed through tubing to a nasal cannula, which sat cockeyed under his nose. Two bags of fluids dripped into his arm from a pump attached to the IV pole. Zoe strained to read the labels on the bags.

One was dextrose—sugar water, a typical maintenance fluid to replace his lost blood volume. The smaller bag was an antibiotic to fight the potential for infection. Another pump contained morphine— the same stuff that made him loopy yesterday and was probably knocking him out today.

"Zoe?"

She flinched.

Yancy's eyes were open, although his lids appeared heavy. "When did you get here?"

"Just now. Sorry. I didn't mean to wake you."

"I wasn't sleeping." He shifted in the bed—a monumental task. "Goddamnit. Can you give me a hand here?"

She leapt to her feet. "What are you trying to do?"

"I keep slipping down in this damned bed and can't get back up with only one arm."

"Hold on a minute." Zoe pressed the button on the bed railing to lower the head. Then, ordering the fire chief to bend his knees and press with his feet while she tugged on his good shoulder, she managed to maneuver him in the preferred direction. "There." She pressed the button again, this time to raise his head.

"Who'd have thought sitting would be so hard?" Yancy grunted.

Zoe contemplated pointing out he was alive at least, but decided he already knew.

He fumbled with the sheets coming up with a button attached to a cable and pressed it. The morphine pump. "Weren't you and Pete just in here?"

"That was yesterday."

"Yesterday? Oh. I guess my days are running together a little."

She pointed at the IV. "Drugs will do that to you."

Yancy shrugged. His eyes hardened. "Did anything else happen last night?"

"The shooter staged another ambush, but the police showed up and scared him away."

"Anyone hurt?"

"Nope."

He gave a relieved sigh. "Good. Did they catch the son of a bitch?"

"No. He got away."

Yancy swore. "Did they at least figure out who he is?"

"Snake Sullivan's still at the top of the list."

The fire chief snorted. "That moron's lucky if he can tie his shoes."

Zoe pulled her chair closer and sat down. "I wanted to talk to you about something."

"About the shootings?"

"Maybe." She thought of Curtis in a similar room. Different hospital. Same gunman. "Do you know Hector Livingston?"

A look crossed Yancy's face that Zoe had never seen there before. Anger didn't quite cut it. Loathing was more like it. "That SOB? Hell yes. What about him?"

"Did you happen to be on call a few weeks ago at a traffic accident on Oak Grove Road?"

"Minor two-vehicle collision. Yeah, I was there. Hector was driving one of the cars."

The back of her neck tingled.

Hector, Yancy, Barry, and Curtis. All in one place. "What happened?"

The fire chief let his head drop back against the pillow. His gaze shifted to the ceiling tiles as if the answers lay there.

As Zoe watched, his eyes drifted shut, and for a moment, she feared he'd fallen asleep. But he took a deep breath and said, "The accident wasn't much of anything. The other guy—can't remember his name—swerved to miss a deer. Smacked into a tree. Wasn't hurt, but his car partially blocked the road. Hector was traveling the other direction. Came around a blind turn, saw the car, but couldn't stop in time. Clipped the back fender and ended up in a ditch."

As everyone had told her, the accident didn't sound serious. And yet she knew there was more. "What else?"

Yancy's eyes opened, but his gaze remained focused on something Zoe couldn't see. "No one was hurt, but the cars were both inoperable. Plus, the one that hit the tree was smoking, so we were called in."

"We?"

"Fire, ambulance, police."

She came forward in her chair, resting her arms on the bedrail. "Come on, Yancy. What aren't you telling me?"

He turned to meet her gaze, the same angry look in his eyes. "Hector used to be an okay guy, but that was ages ago. After he lost his wife, he went batshit crazy. Blamed everyone for his bad fortune. Did you know he used to be on the fire department?"

"Sylvia told me."

Yancy nodded. "He quit after his wife passed. Quit everything. Took their daughter and all but crawled into a cave. Got into that survivalist hooey."

"Survivalist? How do you mean?"

"Stockpiling shit. Canned foods. Bottled water. Guns. Gasoline for a monster generator. Hell, I'm surprised he didn't tape tinfoil to his windows to keep out aliens."

Zoe's grip tightened on the bedrail, her brain stuck on one thing Yancy had said. "Guns?"

"Lots of them." He tugged at the brace on his arm. "No one really cared. About him being into that survivalist stuff, I mean. He didn't bother anyone. In fact, he stayed completely to himself. What bothered me—and some others—was his daughter."

"Lucy."

Zoe wondered if Yancy knew her as Loco Lucy.

"Yeah. What the damned fool does to himself is one thing. But dragging that girl into it was a whole other matter."

"Dragged her into what?" Zoe couldn't picture the petite diva, crazy as she was, in camo, eating rations from a can.

As if reading Zoe's mind, Yancy gave a slow, knowing smile. "His paranoid world. He taught her to shoot when she was barely big enough to hold a damned gun. Took her hunting. She bagged a deer one year. I remember there being a question about legality. Oh, the deer was legal, all right. But we were all pretty sure she was too young for even a junior license."

The idea of Loco Lucy with a rifle turned Zoe's stomach. She forced her mind back to the present though. And the crash on Oak Grove Road. "I get the feeling something more happened at that two-car accident."

"Probably my own damned fault. Couldn't keep my trap shut."

Finally something that didn't surprise Zoe. Yancy was notorious for his lack of tact. "What'd you say?"

He fumbled with his morphine button, as if considering zapping himself into a coma rather than answering her questions. "I knew better. You don't badmouth a guy's kid."

"You said something about Lucy?"

"That girl goes through men the way most people go through loaves of bread." Yancy looked at Zoe askance. "I know she's got her hooks into your buddy Curtis right now."

Zoe decided to keep their breakup to herself for the moment.

"Well, a while back, she had a fling with Jason Dyer."

"I'd heard something about that."

"She was older than him. The damned kid thought he'd snagged himself the brass ring. He also thought he was in love and gonna marry her." Yancy's voice deepened into a menacing rumble. "Of course, he needed to graduate high school first."

Zoe imagined Rose's son, Logan, involved with a girl like Lucy, and mother-bear instincts kicked in.

"I don't know which pissed me off more. Hector's girl messing around with Jason or her dumping him and breaking his heart. Anyhow, that day at the wreck, Hector was being his usual *charming* self, so I made some crack about his daughter needing to be locked up for fooling around with an underage boy."

The comment hit too close to home for Zoe, bringing back a flash of memory from last winter—only with an underage girl and a grown man. She shook it off. "Was Jason there when you said it?"

"Hell no. I'd never have brought it up in front of the kid. He was devastated as it was." Yancy's expression changed from disgust to regret. "Probably shouldn't have said anything with Curtis standing right there though. I guess he didn't know. Looked like it knocked the pegs out from under him."

Zoe pictured the scene. Tried to imagine what went through Curtis's mind at the revelation. Was this the impetus behind their breakup? No doubt it was what he'd wanted to tell her and Earl. But not in Lucy's presence.

Yancy went on, interrupting her musings. "Hector went all postal. Cussed me out. Said my mouth was gonna get me in a world of hurt one day." His eyes widened. "Holy shit. Do you think...?"

Granted, it sounded bad. But some of the puzzle pieces didn't fit. "I doubt it. Barry and Curtis were the first victims. What reason would Hector have to harm them? Besides, whoever he is tried again last night."

Yancy didn't appear appeased. "That's not all though. Hector saw the look on Curtis's face. Must have figured the kid suddenly had second thoughts about Hector's little princess. Because he lit into Curtis right after he jumped all over me. Told him if he broke his daughter's heart, he'd have hell to pay. Poor Curtis looked terrified. Tried to assure Hector he'd never hurt the girl. But Hector kept ranting until Barry stepped in."

Zoe choked. "Barry?"

"And Seth Metzger. The two of them grabbed Hector and dragged him away. Metzger probably should've arrested him, but Hector finally cooled off and apologized."

Zoe sunk back in the chair, her mind swirling. Barry and Curtis. Yancy and Jason Dyer.

And Seth.

Fear bordering on panic sent an icy chill through her. "Yancy, I have to go." She climbed to her feet and reached over to give his good hand a squeeze. "You take care."

"You're gonna tell Pete?" Yancy knew her too well.

"Yeah," she said.

Before Seth became the next victim.

"Eli, shut up." Andrew McCoy appeared ready to slap his client.

"But—"

"Just..." The attorney tightened his fist and his jaw. "Shut up."

Snake complied, hunched in his chair like a sullen teenager.

Amused, Pete watched the family squabble in silence.

McCoy made a visible effort to regain his professional stature. "About that deal..."

Pete struggled to keep a straight face. "Seems like your client has already confessed to possession of drugs."

"For which I'd rather see him not charged. I promise you, he's not guilty of anything more egregious than possession." The attorney shot a fierce glare at his client. "With *no* intention to sell."

"Is criminal stupidity a chargeable offense?" Baronick muttered from his seat by the conference room door.

Pete cleared his throat to cover a laugh. At least the detective finally saw the light regarding Snake as an evil mastermind.

If McCoy heard Baronick's comment, which he surely had, he made a good show of ignoring it. "However, Mr. Sullivan does have certain information that might help you in your homicide investigation."

Pete grew serious. "Such as?"

"Do we have a deal?"

Pete turned to look at Baronick, who appeared noncommittal. To the attorney, Pete said, "No guarantees. But if your client has something we can use, and if he has nothing to do with the deaths of Barry Dickson and Jason Dyer, I can probably talk the DA into not pursuing drug charges."

Snake straightened, a smile on his lips.

"*If,*" Pete added, "he agrees to going into rehab."

Snake's smile faded.

McCoy gave a nod. "Agreed. Ask your questions."

Pete sat back and crossed an ankle over one knee. "Why'd you run when your buddies stopped?"

Snake slid farther down in his chair. "Because I didn't want to get busted."

"For possession," Pete offered.

"Well...yeah. I only had a little on me. Some crappy brick weed I'd brought from home. I was hoping to score a lot more though." Snake mashed his lips together and shook his head. "I knew something was off when that dude called me. But I didn't know for sure until I saw you cops."

"Didn't know what?"

"That I was being set up. Framed."

Pete picked up his pen. "Start at the beginning, Eli. What 'dude' called you?"

"My name's *Snake.*"

McCoy elbowed him. "Answer the man's questions, *Eli.*"

He huffed. "I don't know who he was. Some dude called me and said he'd heard I might be in the market for some good bud. Really high-grade stuff, you know? So I told him, yeah, sure. And he told me to meet him out there in the game lands—"

"Back up a second. He called you."

"Yeah."

"How?"

Snake rolled his eyes. "On my cell phone. How else?"

Pete heard Baronick shift in his chair. "Do you have your phone on you?"

"Sure. Why?"

"Give it to me."

Panicked, Snake looked to his uncle. "Do I have to?"

Pete held out one hand and snapped his fingers. "Do you want us to confirm your story or not?"

McCoy motioned to Pete. "Give it to him."

Snake dug in his pocket while mumbling something Pete couldn't hear.

But McCoy could. He turned sideways to fix his nephew with a fierce stare. "Watch your mouth, boy. I'm representing you as a favor to your mother, but I'll happily walk away and leave your ass to a public defender if you give me any more lip. You understand?"

"Yes, Uncle Andy." Snake slapped his phone into Pete's palm.

Pete handed it over his shoulder to Baronick, who snatched it and left the room.

"Do I get a receipt?" Snake asked.

"If we keep it," Pete said. "This 'dude' who called you. What can you tell me about him?"

"Not much. I didn't recognize his voice, and he didn't give me a name."

Stupid *and* trusting. Bad combination for someone determined to be a badass. Pete jotted a note. "So it was a male voice?"

"Yeah. A dude. I told you."

"Can you tell me anything about his voice? Did he have an accent? Anything distinctive about it?"

"No accent. But he sounded old."

"Old?"

"Yeah. He didn't talk like the guys I hang out with. He talked like you."

McCoy muffled an exasperated sigh.

Pete decided in this case to take "old" as a compliment. "Tell me, Snake, do you make a point of meeting total strangers in desolate locations to make drug buys?"

"Well, yeah...no. But he was offering me a really good deal."

McCoy covered his face and groaned.

"What about the ATV you were riding? You told us you sold it."

"I did. I sold mine. I borrowed that one from a buddy so I could get out there. Which reminds me. When can I get it back? He's gonna be plenty pissed when he finds out I ditched it."

"That might take a while. It's being held as evidence."

Snake swore under his breath.

"Why did you take your friends with you? To share the wealth?"

"Well, yeah. I told you I wasn't gonna sell it. Honest. And I didn't really trust that dude who called me. Especially when he told me to come alone."

"He told you to come alone?"

"Yeah. He made a big point of telling me twice—no, three times."

"Yet you ignored him?"

"Hell yeah. I'm not stupid, you know."

Pete managed to maintain a poker face, but noticed McCoy roll his eyes. Another scribble in his notebook caught his attention. "By the way, where were you between seven fifteen and eight thirty Thursday evening?"

Snake rubbed one of the studs piercing his brow. "Thursday? I already told you. I was at Rodeo's. Ask anyone."

"We did. Everyone agreed you were there. But we also learned you left at quarter after seven and didn't come back for forty-five minutes. Where were you?"

The kid's face flushed. He leaned over and whispered in his uncle's ear.

"You *what*?" the attorney asked.

Snake leaned toward him as if to whisper some more, but McCoy blocked him with a hand. "No. I heard you the first time." He gestured toward Pete, clearly exasperated. "Just tell him already."

Pete waited.

This should be good.

Snake shifted again. "One of my buddies offered to give me another piercing. So that's where I went."

"To get a piercing?"

McCoy closed his eyes and shook his head. "Do yourself a favor. Don't ask where and definitely don't ask to see it."

Oh.

Pete was saved from asking anything more about the new jewelry. Baronick stormed back into the room and motioned for him to step into the hall. Pete gratefully excused himself, gathered his notebook, and followed the detective.

Baronick pulled the door closed behind them. "The phone number's a match."

"To what?" Pete asked.

"The number in Snake's received calls list is a match to the burner phone used to call EOC last night to report the car fire. And that's not all. The tread marks from the ATV Snake abandoned don't match any of the tracks we've found. Not the ones from the hunting blind and not the ones from any of the crime scenes."

"Which supports Snake's story claiming he's been set up."

Baronick made a pained face. "Looks that way. And before you can say 'I told you so,' you were right. That kid isn't exactly the brightest bulb in the box."

"What about the rest of the tread marks? Do the ones from the hunting blind match the ones from the previous nights?"

"Afraid so."

Pete glanced at his watch. Almost three in the afternoon. Damn it. "Looks like we have another long night ahead."

TWENTY

Zoe parked Sylvia's Escort next to Wayne's unmarked black sedan in the Police Department's lot. Pete's personal vehicle sat in the next spot.

There was another car too. A dark Mercedes. She had no clue who it belonged to.

The bells on the door clanked and jangled when she entered. Pete and Wayne, who stood in the hallway outside the conference room door, looked up.

Pete spoke to the county detective in a voice too low for her to hear and aimed a thumb over his shoulder toward the room.

Wayne nodded and moved in that direction while Pete headed toward her.

"I need to talk to you," she said.

He must have picked up on her anxiety. "Come into my office."

As she entered, she eyed the coffeepot in the corner, but the last thing she needed was more jitters. Instead, she passed it and pulled one of the chairs closer to his desk.

Pete settled himself in his own chair. "What's going on?"

"I've been to see Yancy."

"Oh? Is he all right?" Pete winced. "I mean, I know he isn't all right, but—"

"He's about the same as when we saw him yesterday."

"Good. I've been intending to check on him." Pete let his voice trail off. He studied her, his eyes narrowing. "He told you something?"

"Yeah." Zoe started with her morning visit with Curtis, poured out the tale of Lucy's connection to young Jason Dyer and her volatile visit to the ambulance garage, told of Sylvia's revelation about Hector's shooting prowess, and concluded with everything Yancy had told her regarding the confrontation at the accident scene and Hector's survivalist background. Including the guns. And Seth's part in the confrontation.

Pete remained silent even after she'd finished.

"Did you know any of this?" she asked.

"Not nearly enough," he said, his voice a low growl.

She thought of the Mercedes parked out front and Wayne's retreat into the conference room. "Are you questioning someone?"

"Eli Sullivan turned himself in. He and Andrew McCoy are across the hall."

"Eli? Snake? How on earth can he afford an attorney like McCoy?"

"Family discount."

Zoe didn't make the connection.

"McCoy is Sullivan's uncle."

"Oh. What'd he have to say?"

Pete's mind appeared stuck on Zoe's disclosures. "He claims he was set up. Someone called and lured him out there with the promise of a drug buy."

"A *drug* buy? He told you that?"

"Indeed he did."

"Huh." Zoe leaned back in the chair. "And you believe him?"

Pete met her gaze. "Would you admit to scoring drugs for any reason other than avoiding homicide charges?"

She considered the possibilities. "Lesser of two evils?"

He shook his head. "If the kid was smart enough to stage three scenes to bait emergency responders, I think he'd be smart enough to come up with a better alibi." A pained look crossed his face. "And the more I get to know Sullivan, the less I think his name and 'smart' belong in the same sentence."

No argument there.

A spark glimmered in Pete's eyes. "I wonder if Hector owns an ATV."

Pete pulled into the Livingston's shady driveway half expecting to see a camo-clad Hector lurking behind one of the trees. Remembering how the man had slipped up on him during his last visit, Pete suspected he'd never see—or hear—Hector unless he *wanted* to be seen or heard.

The silver Hyundai was parked in front of the dilapidated garage, although not in the same spot as before. The dented blue Ram pickup was noticeably absent. Pete swung his Ford Edge around and backed in front of the Hyundai. This time the garage doors were closed.

He climbed out of the SUV and paused to survey the place. Last night's rain had scrubbed the air clean, creating a perfect early autumn afternoon. A few wispy clouds floated in a deep blue sky. Humidity had dropped well into the comfortable range. Nothing moved. Not a leaf. Not a squirrel or a bird in the maples. Perhaps the local wildlife knew the owner of this property was an avid hunter and had moved to more hospitable digs.

Staying alert, Pete strolled toward the house knowing he was being watched, provided anyone was home. At the back door, he knocked. Waited. Listened. There was no hint of footsteps, no rustling from inside. He knocked again. "Hello?" he called. "Miss Livingston? Hector? Vance Township Police. Anyone home?"

When Pete still received no answer, he ambled back down the porch steps. A pinpoint red light in a nearby tree drew his eye. A trail cam was aimed at the back of the house...and at him.

Pete stared into the lens with the same expression he'd use with a suspect, letting Hector know he was aware of the camera.

As Pete headed back toward his vehicle, he wondered if that was the only camera Hector had rigged up. Probably not. So much for clandestine snooping.

A bird yelped from behind the ramshackle garage. Pete stopped. A case could be made that the birdcall sounded almost human. Like someone calling for help. Sworn to protect and serve, Pete had a duty to investigate.

Yeah. That would work.

The flatbed trailer he'd almost tripped over on his last visit was gone, revealing a wide, previously concealed path next to the structure. The weeds had been flattened from frequent use, and Pete noticed the parallel set of grooves in the earth carved from a small vehicle. Riding mower?

Or ATV?

He picked his way to the rear of the garage, keeping vigilant for signs of movement and for hidden cameras.

Behind the building, a smaller lean-to had been pieced together from odd-sized sheets of T-111 siding, some of it painted, some of it blackened from weather exposure. Pete recalled similar scraps stashed inside the garage.

He followed the path to the rear of the lean-to where a pair of rickety plywood doors sagged open on warped hinges. He eased closer, his hand instinctively resting on his Glock.

The lean-to held an assortment of what appeared to be automotive parts. Belts and gizmos, which Pete didn't recognize, hung from nails pounded into the two-by-fours that framed the structure. Several red plastic gas cans sat in one corner. A snow plow, the kind he'd seen attached to the front of a garden tractor—or an ATV—perched on blocks in another corner.

The bulk of the space, however, was empty. A pair of oil spots on the floor suggested two small vehicles usually resided there.

As Pete's eyes grew accustomed to the shed's lack of light, he noticed a series of framed photographs hanging askew on the far wall. He edged closer.

The photographs were covered in a thick layer of dust, but not so thick he couldn't make out the subjects—Hector and Lucy Livingston posed proudly with a pair of trophy bucks and their high-powered hunting rifles—in front of a pair of ATVs.

"You don't have to be here, you know." Sylvia deposited her luggage-sized handbag into the front desk's bottom drawer. "I handled the phones and the radios here all by my lonesome for many years."

Zoe hung her own purse over the back of one of the chairs. "I know you don't need me. But I wouldn't be able to sleep anyway, so might as well do something useful."

"Don't tell me you're joining our insomniacs' club."

Zoe forced a smile. "Temporarily. Until they catch this guy."

Sylvia lowered into a chair with a grunt. "I understand. I know we can't really do anything to protect our boys." She raised an eyebrow at Zoe. "And girls. But I feel like I'm keeping watch over them from here."

"What do you mean, we can't do anything?" Zoe gave Sylvia a pat on her shoulder. "I think we can do a heckuva lot. You know the back roads better than anyone. Between the two of us, we can shave minutes off response times to these remote locations. That alone could save a life or two."

Sylvia sighed. "I hope so."

The police radio next to her elbow crackled to life. "Vance Base, this is Thirty."

Pete's voice held an edge that made Zoe's shoulders tighten.

Sylvia keyed the mic. "Go ahead, Thirty."

There was a pause. "Are you coming back to work full-time?"

"Yes, and since I'm also a township supervisor, I'm giving myself a raise." Sylvia released the button on the mic to add an editorial comment off the air. "Smartass." Keying it again, she asked, "What do you want?"

"I'm at Hector Livingston's place. No one's home, and there's evidence he and his daughter own quads. Put a BOLO out on him and his pickup. I'm going to sit here for a while in case he shows up, but I'm available if you need me."

"Copy that, Unit Thirty," Sylvia said.

After another pause, he asked, "Is Zoe there?"

Sylvia gestured to the mic and moved out of her way.

Zoe slid her chair closer to the radio and hit the button. "I'm here."

"Good. While Sylvia's handling the BOLO, I want you to contact the EOC, state and county police, the fire department, and your gang at the EMS. I want police response on all emergency calls again. Tell them same protocol as last night."

Zoe met Sylvia's gaze and swallowed. "Got it." She lowered her voice. "Hey, Pete?"

"Yeah?"

"Be careful."

She could almost hear his smile. "Copy that, Base. Unit Thirty out."

TWENTY-ONE

As the late afternoon sun filtered through the leafy canopy of Hector Livingston's yard, Pete stretched out in the Edge's front seat. Stakeouts in the country were damned boring. Thankfully, he didn't have to do them very often. But he had to admit, he wouldn't mind living in a place like this. He'd do a better job of upkeep, of course, but the soft whisper of the breeze through the leaves, the sense of privacy without losing the connection to nature—unlike that idiot who had built a fort-like fence around his place over in the new housing development—the cool shade in the heat of summer and the brilliant color of autumn...

Yeah, he could definitely see himself living here.

The pines growing next to the road softened the sounds of passing cars. Through his open window, Pete thought he heard a vehicle slowing down.

Hector's blue pickup turned into the driveway and chugged up the slight grade toward Pete, an empty flatbed trailer bouncing and clanking along behind.

Hector pulled into the empty spot next to Pete, cut the engine, and stepped out. Pete climbed out of his SUV as well.

Hector eyed the Edge. "What's the matter? Did the township muckety mucks take your police car away?"

"It's in the shop."

Hector grunted. "What're you doing here?"

Pete nodded toward the trailer. "Where are your ATVs?"

Hector lifted his chin, glaring down his nose at Pete. "What ATVs?"

Pete couldn't very well admit he'd seen the photo without confessing to prowling around Hector's property, something the man would likely figure out if he had another well-hidden trail cam back there. But for now, Pete preferred to play his cards close to his vest. "I've heard you and Lucy have a pair of quads."

Hector didn't even blink. "Can't imagine where you'd have heard that."

Pete decided to change directions. "Where's your daughter?"

Hector shook his head. "No idea. The girl's of legal age. I don't keep track of her."

Pete didn't buy that for a minute. He leaned back against the Edge, crossing one leg in front of the other, trying to look casual. "Must be hard. Having a beautiful daughter. Young guys must be lining up at your door wanting to take her out."

"Not so much as you'd think." Hector eyed Pete with the faintest hint of an amused smile.

From the man's tone, Pete wondered if Hector meant the girl's craziness kept the boys at bay, or if Hector and his gun collection scared all but the gutsiest away. "Still, you're her father. I'm sure you do your best to protect her."

All signs of amusement faded from Hector's face, replaced with disgust. Or boredom. Reading this guy was a challenge. "That what you're here for?" he asked. "To ask about my kid?"

Fine. So much for casual. Pete uncrossed his legs. "What I really want to know is where you were the last few nights."

The smug smile was back. "You got a warrant?"

"I just want to talk."

Hector shook his head and brushed past Pete and around the SUV. "No warrant, no talk." He stopped in front of Pete's vehicle and turned back to face him again. "And since you ain't got a thing on either me or my daughter, I know damned well you don't have a warrant. Get off my property."

Pete watched as the man turned on his heel and started toward the house. "I hear you were involved in a traffic accident out on Oak Grove Road," Pete called after him.

Hector froze.

Pete expected the man to face him. Expected a look that would tell Pete he had his man. Instead, Hector stood a little taller and continued ambling to his back door. His history with guns and the missing ATVs combined with his scuffle with several of the victims were cause enough to take him in. But Pete suspected Hector would gladly go to prison—even to his grave—to protect his daughter.

Pete slid behind the wheel and keyed the mic on his shoulder. "Vance Base, this is Unit Thirty."

Sylvia's voice came over the air. "Go, Unit Thirty."

"Cancel the BOLO on Hector Livingston." Pete glanced at the man climbing the back steps into the house. "And put one out on Lucy Livingston instead."

Zoe sat alone at the police department's front desk, having insisted that Sylvia go home two hours ago. The late nights were wearing on the older woman, and even though she argued, she eventually gave in.

The clock on the wall read a few minutes after one. Zoe stood and stretched, listening to a series of small pops in the shoulder she'd injured a couple of months ago.

Radio chatter was minimal at this hour, so she strolled down the hall and found Pete seated in the conference room, glaring at the whiteboard. He looked up when she entered, and she noticed the dark circles under his weary eyes.

"I thought you left with Sylvia," he said.

Zoe slid into the chair next to him. "Didn't we have this same conversation last night?"

A tired smile flickered across his face. "Anything new?"

"Nope. Wayne's sitting across the road from Hector's driveway. At last report, Hector hadn't left and Lucy hasn't returned. Nate's been keeping an eye on the Sullivan house. Snake's staying put like a good boy. No word on Lucy. And no ambushes. Don't suppose there will be now. He—or she—likes to strike at dusk."

Pete's eyebrows shrugged.

"What?" Zoe asked. "You think he's gonna change his MO?"

Pete chuckled. "I love it when you talk cop."

She gently swung a leg, kicking him under the table. "Why would you think he'd change now?"

"I just don't want someone else getting killed because I let my guard down."

She sensed there was more to it and held his gaze.

He sighed. "If Hector's as much into the survivalist culture as it seems, he could have military equipment. Like night-vision goggles. He knows we're being especially vigilant around dusk. And he knows we're on to him."

Zoe filled in the blanks and didn't like it. "You really think Hector's our guy?"

Pete pushed up from his chair and sauntered toward the whiteboard. "We've got him under surveillance and nothing has happened tonight. So far."

"What about Lucy?"

He stared at the notes on the board. "I definitely want to talk to that girl."

Zoe rose and moved to his side.

Part of the scrawl on the whiteboard was a timeline of events, locations, types of ambushes, and names of victims. Another part of the board listed Eli "Snake" Sullivan with notations about his connections to the victims. Then there was Hector and Lucy Livingston, and a list of names under them—*Jason Dyer, Rick Brown, Snake, Curtis Knox.* "Who's Rick Brown?"

Pete rubbed the stubble on his upper lip. "One of Lucy's ex-boyfriends."

"I figured that much. I knew about the others, but never heard of him. Is he from around here?"

"Not according to Hector. Apparently the kid died in a motorcycle crash out in Ohio about six months ago."

Zoe eyed Pete. "You don't sound so sure."

He shook his head. "Something about the name keeps bugging me. I swear I've heard it before, but I can't place where."

She rolled the name over in her mind. "Rick Brown. Doesn't ring a bell for me. It's kind of common though."

Pete choked out a short laugh. "That's what Hector said."

"Still..." She pressed a finger next to the name on the board. "If he died in a motorcycle wreck, fire and EMS would have responded. What if Lucy blamed them somehow for his death? Maybe a mistake was made, or maybe she believes there was."

Pete raised an eyebrow at Zoe. "But if it happened in Ohio, why take it out on our local guys?"

She fixed him with her best *duh* look. "She's crazy. *Loco* Lucy. Remember? She thinks I'm in love with Curtis. Why wouldn't she take out her grudge on any ol' emergency responder who was handy?"

Pete turned deliberately to face her and folded his arms. "She thinks you're in love with Curtis?"

Zoe's cheeks warmed. "I told you that earlier."

"No, you most certainly did not. You told me she came to the garage and pushed you around because she thought Curtis was in love with *you*, but not the other way around."

Zoe offered him a sheepish grin. "Yeah, well. She deserves the nickname Loco Lucy for a reason."

"Are you?"

"Am I what?"

"In love with Curtis." One side of Pete's mouth slanted upward.

Zoe slugged him in the arm. "No."

He made an exaggerated pained face and rubbed the spot. "Ow. Medic!"

"I didn't hit you that hard, you wimp." But she reached over to touch it anyway. "And Curtis isn't in love with me either. Everyone knows my heart is spoken for."

"Oh? Anyone I know?"

She made a fist again, and he lifted both hands in surrender, laughing. Closing the distance between them, she leaned against him, suddenly drained from the last four days. He wrapped her in both arms and pressed his cheek to her hair. Their closeness...the safety of his embrace...felt more right than anything she'd ever known. She opened her mouth, but the words—*I love you*—stuck.

"You might be on to something," he said. "About Lucy possibly blaming the rescue team in Ohio for Brown's death. I need to do some digging into that motorcycle crash."

Zoe eased free of the clinch. "But not tonight."

His hopeful look suggested he had something other than rest on his mind.

"You need to go home and get some sleep," she said.

"I'm not that tired."

"Are you kidding me? You're exhausted. So am I. And I have to be on duty tomorrow night." She realized the time. "I mean tonight."

"Tonight?" He frowned. "You aren't on duty again until Tuesday."

"We're pulling extra shifts so B crew can attend Barry's viewing and funeral. Earl and I are covering tomorrow—*tonight*."

A strange look crossed Pete's face. "You're right. I'll drop you off at Rose's." Lowering his voice, he added, "We both need to be on the top of our game."

Pete dragged back into the station well before his eight o'clock shift began. Sleep?

He might have dozed on and off for an hour. Tops. He'd be able to sleep when he cleared this case.

Zoe was on duty tonight.

Granted, he didn't want *anyone* else to fall victim to this shooter. Not another firefighter. Not another paramedic. Not another cop. Not a civilian either, although so far all the targets had worn uniforms. But the idea of Zoe being in the line of fire set his every nerve on edge.

He dumped an extra scoop of Maxwell House into his Mr. Coffee before hitting the power button and sinking into his office chair. Pulling out his cell phone he punched in Baronick's number.

The detective's "Morning, Pete" sounded drowsy.

"Did I wake you?"

"Ha. You'd like that, wouldn't you? Catching me sleeping on the job. Sorry to disappoint."

"Give me an update on Livingston."

"His truck hasn't moved. No one in. No one out."

Pete checked his watch. "I'll be out to relieve you within the hour."

"Bring coffee."

Pete ended the call and placed the next one to Nate, who reported Snake hadn't gone anywhere either.

Apparently all the township bad guys had gotten a good night's sleep even if the police chief had not.

Pete left his phone on his desk and rose.

After a stretch and a yawn, he shuffled back to the gurgling coffeemaker to pour a cup. Inhaling the steam, he returned to his desk and thumbed the computer's power button, sipping the hot brew while the machine booted up.

Hector Livingston knew he was under surveillance. Of that Pete had no doubt. The man had wisely opted to lay low all last evening and all night. Was it a coincidence that no ambush had been set yesterday?

Pete hated coincidences.

Snake hadn't been smart enough to arrange any of the recent incidents. But Hector? Hell yeah. Hector was smart—scary smart. He owned a quad. Two of them, as a matter of fact. He carried a grudge against all the victims. And he was an avid hunter known to be skilled with a high-powered rifle.

How had he known who would be on duty? Or did it matter? Was it sheer luck that all of his victims happened to be on the emergencies he'd set up and called in?

Lucy might have known.

As Curtis's fiancée—or ex-fiancée—Lucy would have been aware of his and Dickson's schedule. But she wouldn't have known which team on the crew would respond to the call.

Would she?

Pete jotted a note to look into the girl's connections with the county dispatchers. Hell, she'd probably dated one of them.

Pete's train of thought returned to his computer, which was taking too damned long to load.

Where was Lucy? If she was helping her father with this sick game of revenge, she might be out there somewhere, setting up the next fake accident scene. Maybe Hector had called her to warn her about the police being on to them—and sitting at the foot of his driveway. Maybe she was hiding out, waiting for the police to look the other way before springing the next trap.

Only there was no way on earth Pete was looking the other way.

The computer was finally ready. He typed in his password and logged on to the internet.

Ohio was a big state, and Pete had no idea where in it Rick Brown had lived or died. Hoping he'd get lucky, he typed Rick Brown and motorcycle into Google's search box, only to pull up an extensive list of sites about a man who was well known for restoring bikes. Not the man Pete was looking for.

He pulled up a people finder site and tried again. The number of Rick and Richard Browns it found was longer than even Pete had expected. And none of the ones listed in Ohio seemed right. Staring at the screen, he thought back to what Hector had said. The kid wasn't from around here and had died in a motorcycle crash in Ohio. And Hector hadn't claimed to be sure about even that much. Plus, simply because Brown died in Ohio didn't mean he'd lived there.

As Pete scrolled down the list of faces and locations, his phone vibrated on the desk. Baronick's name and number lit up the screen.

Pete hit the answer call button. "What is it?"

"Livingston just pulled out of his driveway in his truck, pulling a trailer." Baronick's voice was tight. "He's headed south on Route 15."

Pete logged off the computer as he leapt from his chair. "Stay with him. I'm on my way."

TWENTY-TWO

Zoe parked Rose's silver Ford Taurus in front of the Bassi house after a morning of barn chores and climbed out as Allison stepped onto the front porch lugging a backpack.

"Ready for your first day back at school?" Zoe asked, coming around the car.

"Absolutely." The tension on the girl's face belied the confidence in her voice.

Zoe longed to hug her, but a pair of teens were approaching from several houses down the street, heading for the same bus stop as Allison. Embarrassing her wouldn't be the best way to start the new school year. Instead, Zoe leaned closer as they passed on the sidewalk. "Remember what you told me. You're stronger now."

Allison grinned. "I am woman, hear me roar."

"Exactly."

She nodded in appreciation and strolled away, calling out to the other teens.

Zoe found Rose sitting over a cup of coffee in the kitchen. Tossing her friend's car keys onto the counter, Zoe grabbed a clean mug, filled it from the pot, and slid into the chair across from her. "You okay?"

Rose rolled her eyes. "Jet lag's a bitch."

"You've been back—what? Four days? Aren't you over it yet?"

"If you want to keep living in my house, you should shut up." Rose took a long hit from her mug. "Which reminds me. One of your cats threw up a hairball outside my bedroom door last night. Don't ask me how I found it."

Zoe winced. "Sorry."

Rose mumbled something Zoe couldn't make out and decided she shouldn't ask her to repeat it.

"How was Allison this morning?" Zoe asked.

The strain on Rose's face matched what Zoe had seen minutes earlier on the girl's. "She's putting up a brave front and insisting she'll be fine." Rose stared into her cup. "I'm not sure who she's trying to convince, me or herself."

Zoe rested a hand on her friend's arm.

"This thing with Jason isn't helping anything. Another loss of someone she cared about." Rose shook her head sadly. "It's almost too much to take."

Zoe thought about her late-night talk with Pete. "Did you know a guy by the name of Rick Brown?"

Rose braced an elbow on the table and rested her chin in her hand, one finger tapping her cheek. "Rick Brown? There are a lot of Browns living around Elm Creek. Is he one of those?"

"I doubt it. From what I heard, he's not local."

"Who is he?"

"Someone Lucy Livingston dated before Curtis."

Rose blew out a noisy breath. "That girl's dated just about every man and boy in Monongahela County. Guess she's sampled the goods elsewhere too."

It struck Zoe that she and Rose had dated and "sampled the goods" quite a bit in their wild youth too. She wondered how many times women had sat at a table and talked about them in the same manner as they were now discussing Lucy.

Except neither Rose nor Zoe had ever been suspected of killing someone.

"Do you think Allison might know who this guy is?"

Rose slammed a hand down on the table. "Do *not* bring this up with her."

Zoe flinched. "Why not?"

"I can't believe I have to explain it to you. This whole business with Lucy has threatened to push Allison back over the edge."

"Because of Jason?"

Rose stood, nearly tipping her chair over. "Yes, because of Jason. Allison had a huge crush on him."

"But I thought that was quite a while ago."

"She's not even sixteen."

True, Zoe thought. How long ago could it have been?

Rose took her cup to the sink, rinsed it out, and opened the dishwasher. "She's been *in love* twice." Rose said the words as if they tasted bitter on her tongue. "Once with Jason Dyer and then with..." She shook her head, unable or unwilling to speak the name of the man who had nearly destroyed her daughter.

"Pete thinks this Rick Brown guy might be the key to what's been going on." Zoe kept her voice soft. "If Allison knows something—"

"No." Rose spun and glared at Zoe. "Leave Allison out of it. If Pete thinks this man has something to do with his case, let Pete do the investigating to find him. But you're not going to use my child." The glare intensified. "Not *again*."

The reference to last winter's disaster stung more than a slap to her face. "I wouldn't—"

"And another thing." Rose jabbed a finger toward the appliance. "You did it again. Stop taking one thing out of the goddamned dishwasher and closing it again so I don't know if it's been run or not." She slammed her mug into the sink. Hard.

Zoe winced as it shattered. "I didn't." She spotted the blood on her friend's hand and jumped to her feet. "Oh my God, Rose. Let me get some bandages."

"No." Rose jerked her hand away. "Just leave me alone. Leave all of us alone."

She stormed out of the kitchen, leaving Zoe stunned, her mouth hanging open.

What on earth was going on in this house?

"He's pulling over." Baronick's words over the radio weren't what Pete had expected to hear.

"I didn't tell you to stop him," Pete snapped into his mic as he sped south on Route 15.

"Wasn't my intention," Baronick replied. "He must have made me." The location the detective reported was only about a mile from Hector's driveway.

"Don't stop. Wait up ahead in case he decides to keep going. I'll be there in two minutes."

Hector's truck and trailer sat at the edge of the road right where Baronick had said. Pete pulled his SUV up behind the rig, switched on his four-way flashers, and stepped out. All senses on high alert, Pete approached the driver's door, glancing at the empty trailer and hitch as he passed.

The truck's driver's window was open. Inside, Hector stared straight ahead, both hands on the steering wheel.

Pete gave the interior of the cab a quick inspection. No weapons in sight. In fact, the thing was cleaner than the interior of Pete's personal vehicle. "Hector? Is anything wrong?"

The man shot him a dark glance before returning his gaze to the front.

"Are you having car troubles? Do you want me to call for a tow?"

"Truck runs just fine."

"Are you waiting for someone?"

"Nope."

The man's monosyllabic responses were wearing on Pete's patience. "Mind telling me where you're going?"

Hector turned his head and fixed Pete with a level stare. "As long as you and your cop friends are in my rearview mirror, I'm not going anywhere."

Pete held his gaze for a moment and then smiled, which, from the puzzled look on Hector's face, wasn't what the man expected. "Oh, Hector, I'm afraid you are." He pulled out his cell phone and punched in Baronick's number. "Detective, I need you to call Bud Kramer and order a flatbed out here to transport a truck and small trailer. Then meet me at the station. I'm about to bring Hector Livingston in for questioning."

"Are you okay?" Earl asked as he pulled in front of Kramer's Garage.

Zoe realized she hadn't said a word since they'd left the funeral home. "Not really." She forced a tight smile. "I'll be fine."

She'd hated funeral homes since she was eight years old and had been told the man inside the closed casket was her dad. Only recently had she come to terms with not seeing the body—believing he really wasn't in there.

Barry's casket was open, and she couldn't get the image of him, in repose in his dress uniform, out of her mind. She closed her eyes and recalled the big, tough, loud, funny man she'd worked with instead.

"You don't look fine." Earl gestured toward Medic Two parked along the fence. "I guess she's ready."

Zoe's Chevy, however, was nowhere to be seen. She hoped that meant it was inside, being worked on. Begging rides was growing old. Besides, as snippy as Rose had been this morning, Zoe might need to bunk in her truck sooner rather than later.

The mingled odors of motor oil, paint, and tires greeted them the moment they stepped inside the garage.

Bud Kramer rolled over to the cashier's window, an invoice in hand and a stern look on his fleshy face. "Which one of you is paying for this?"

Earl wore a deer-in-headlights expression that had to match Zoe's.

Bud glanced at both of them and erupted into laughter. "You two should see your expressions." He waved the invoice. "I just need a signature. The bill goes to Mon County EMS."

Earl leaned on the counter. "You are an evil man, Kramer."

As the garage owner chortled at his own joke, Zoe left Earl to handle the paperwork and wandered into the work area. A red Toyota with heavy front-end damage occupied the first bay. A panel truck with the hood yawning open sat in the second. On the other side of it, she found her Chevy. None of the mechanics were crawling in, over, or under it, leading her to wonder if the work had been completed.

"We should get to it later today," said a voice behind her.

She spun to find Gabe Webber, the mechanic who'd offered to cut her a break on repairs had she only called *before* she needed a tow. "Oh. I was hoping it was already finished."

He shook his head. "We're waiting on parts."

"You haven't even started on it?"

"Sorry."

She heaved a disappointed sigh and rested a hand on the front fender, as if she could comfort the lonely beast.

"You should've called before wasting a trip in to check on your truck. Besides, the boss'll call *you* when she's done."

"I know. It's not a wasted trip though. Earl and I are picking up the ambulance. We're on duty tonight."

"Oh. Good. You won't need your truck today anyway."

Zoe hated to agree, fearing if Gabe didn't feel rushed he might push hers off until tomorrow. Or the next day. "I guess not. But I'd really like to pick it up first thing in the morning."

"No problem. First thing."

She watched him shuffle away and feared she might as well have told him, "*No rush. Next month will be fine.*"

She wandered back toward Earl and Bud. Once she rounded the panel truck, she could see the two of them with their heads bent together over the invoice. Opting against getting involved in any line item debates, she strolled toward the rear of the garage, studying the array of tools on the walls and workbenches. She had vague but happy memories of her dad's garage and of handing him wrenches and sockets while he puttered on his car.

A greasy tarp was draped over a large odd-shaped mound near a rear door. Her gaze slipped past it, but something drew her back. She studied the thing and noticed the tarp didn't quite reach the concrete floor in one spot, revealing a nubby tire.

Her breath caught. She glanced toward Earl and Bud. Both remained intent on the invoice. She crept toward the tarp. Looked around again.

No one appeared to notice her. She gingerly pinched a corner of the cover and lifted it, cringing at the rustle the movement created. But the sight of a plastic fender, a headlight, and handlebars whipped her pulse into high gear.

A gruff voice bellowing, "What the hell are you doing?" nearly stopped it.

Hector Livingston's gaze could almost scorch grooves in the interrogation room table. He slouched in a chair, his arms crossed defiantly across his barrel chest, his jaw clenched.

Pete studied him from the opposite chair. "Tell me about the accident on Oak Grove Road."

"I have the right to remain silent."

"You do. But if you have nothing to hide, why wouldn't you want to help us clear your name?"

Hector jutted his chin and looked away.

"All right. I'll do the talking then." Pete made a production of opening his notebook and thumbing through pages, settling on the one he wanted. "Three and a half weeks ago, you had a minor traffic accident on Oak Grove Road. Among those responding were Bruce Yancy, Curtis Knox, and Barry Williamson. Does it seem odd to you that those same three men have since been killed or wounded? Shot by a high-powered rifle?"

Hector's jaw worked ever so slightly, but he remained silent.

"The shooter eluded capture by escaping on an ATV."

As expected, Hector continued to stare at a spot on the wall.

"Hector," Pete said, acting as if he'd only now realized it, "you happen to have an ATV. And I've heard you're quite the hunter. I'll bet you own a high-powered rifle. Specifically, a thirty-ought-six."

Hector, wearing a smirk, brought his gaze back to Pete. "Yes, I do. So does most of the population of Monongahela County."

"That's true. In fact, so does your daughter."

The smirk melted away. "Leave Lucille out of this."

"Sorry. I can't do that." Pete shifted forward, resting his arms on the table. "You see, Hector, all of the motives we have for you also apply to her."

"She has nothing to do with those shootings. Nothing."

"Then where is she?"

Hector's shoulders hiked closer to his ears, but he pressed his mouth into a tight line and again looked away.

Pete sat back in his chair. "That's okay. I really don't need you to help me find her. Detective Baronick is on his way to see a judge right this minute. We're getting a warrant to ping her cell phone. The wonders of modern technology."

Hector growled like a defeated bear. "She has nothing to do with these shootings. I'm telling you the truth," he said, his voice softening.

Pete held his gaze and waited.

With a sigh, Hector said, "The girl's got a bug up her butt about competing in some sort of ATV cross-country race next month out near Harrisburg." His lip curled. "Total waste of time and gasoline, if you ask me. But she's my little girl, so if she wants to do it, I'll let her."

"That's next month. Where is she now?"

"I took her and both quads down to Greene County yesterday morning. She and a friend were going riding, but the friend's quad broke down so Lucille begged me to let the friend use mine."

"A friend," Pete said. "Male or female?"

Hector glared at him. "A *girlfriend*. You all like to make Lucille out to be some man-hungry floozy, but she's not."

Pete held up a finger and started counting. "Jason Dyer. Snake Sullivan. Rick Brown. Curtis Knox..."

Hector slammed both hands down on the table and leapt to his feet. "Shut the hell up."

Pete was on his feet too. "Sit down, Hector. Now."

He glanced at the door as if expecting an army to burst through at any moment, but he slowly lowered back into the chair.

As did Pete. "So you dropped your daughter and your ATVs off in Greene County yesterday morning?"

"Yeah. She was spending the night with this girl. I was supposed to pick her up this morning."

"That's where you were headed when you pulled over?"

Hector nodded. "I saw that unmarked car you had sitting by my place. Ain't nobody's business where I go. Or where Lucille spends her time."

"As long as you're both innocent of murder, that's true." Pete clicked his pen. "Give me an address."

"For what?"

"Lucy's girlfriend."

"No. I told you, it's—"

"Nobody's business. I know." Pete clicked his pen again. "And like I said, it doesn't matter. As soon as Detective Baronick gets that warrant, we'll be able to track her cell phone anyway. I just figured if you're both innocent as you claim, you'd want to cooperate."

Hector's gaze darkened. "Cooperate? Go to hell. Get your gawddamned warrant. We got nothing to hide."

Pete closed his notebook and rose. "We'll see." Because what he hadn't told Hector was the warrant to track Lucy's phone wasn't the only one Baronick was requesting.

He'd also filled out an affidavit for a warrant to search the Livingston property for a thirty-ought-six hunting rifle.

TWENTY-THREE

Zoe whirled toward the booming voice, dragging the tarp with her. Bud Kramer glared at her from the cashier's window. A startled Earl—and she imagined every mechanic in the place—stared at her too.

"What do you think you're doing?" Bud demanded again, speaking slowly as if she was dense.

"Um…" She glanced back at the tarp, one corner of which was still clenched in her fist. It continued to do a slow slide to the floor, revealing an ATV with cracked plastic fenders, but not a speck of dirt on it. Or its tires.

Someone came up behind her and gently tugged the tarp from her hand.

Gabe. "Don't mind him. The boss likes to keep his toy clean, and if we don't keep it covered, it gets coated in gook."

His toy? "Sorry," she said to the mechanic.

He gestured for her to rejoin Earl. A wise move.

Bud continued to glare at her as she approached. "I'm really sorry. I was looking for my truck and—"

"It's over *there*." Bud pointed.

"Yeah, I know. I found it, and Gabe said he hadn't started on it—"

"So you decided to go poking around my garage?"

Considering that was exactly what she'd been doing, she couldn't find a good excuse for it. So she apologized again.

Bud aimed a thumb at a sign tacked to a nearby post. "Can't you read?"

Authorized Personnel Only Beyond This Point.

Another apology seemed useless.

"I don't usually enforce it, but my liability insurance would skyrocket if anyone got hurt monkeying around with all the tools and machinery in here." He shook his finger at her. "Thanks to you, I may have to toughen my stance."

Chagrined, Zoe stared at her shoes. But the sight of the quad gnawed at her. "If you don't mind my asking, what are you doing with an ATV?"

"I do mind," Bud said. "I can't exactly take a hike in the woods like I used to. That little buggy gives me back some of my freedom."

Earl bumped her with his elbow and held out the keys to the ambulance. "We better get going."

Good ol' Earl, rescuing her from embarrassing herself any further. She snatched the keys and mumbled yet another apology to Bud.

Still, as she headed across the parking lot to Medic Two, she couldn't help wondering if Pete knew about Bud Kramer's "toy."

One of the county officers stood outside the Livingston house with Hector, who was snarling like a wounded grizzly, while Pete and Baronick stood in the middle of the dining room.

"I'm not impressed," Baronick said.

Pete took in the antique china cabinet filled with delicate plates and tiny cups. "What did you expect? Nazi posters on the wall?"

"Maybe. I don't know. But I expected something other than Grandma's house."

The detective had a point.

As far as survivalists' residences went, so far the Livingston house appeared remarkable in that it was totally *un*remarkable. "How long has Hector's wife been dead?" Pete wondered out loud.

"About sixteen years, I think." Baronick scavenged through the drawers in the cabinet searching for the burner phones listed along with the thirty-ought-six hunting rifles on their warrant. "Maybe seventeen. Why?"

Pete made a slow pivot, taking in the outdated wallpaper, the sun-faded curtains, the clean but scratched dining table, and the formerly plump cushions on the chair seats. "It looks like nothing's been updated since then."

Baronick turned away from the china cabinet and scanned the rest of the room. "You might be right."

Pete adjusted his gloves. "On the other hand, maybe even survivalists keep their weapons somewhere other than near the food."

"Speaking of..." Baronick gestured back toward the kitchen, where they'd found nothing more incriminating than a paring knife. "Was I the only one expecting to find MREs instead of Cheerios?"

"I suspect he'd save the packaged military grub for emergencies and keep it stashed in a bomb shelter under the house," Pete said, only half joking. "Let's keep going."

They moved together into the living room, which was as dated and as normal as the dining room and kitchen. Drawers and nooks in the end tables and curio cabinet revealed nothing of interest. A few discolored photographs showing a smiling family—a pretty young woman with a strong resemblance to Lucy, a grinning twentyish version of Hector, and a tiny dark-haired sprite of a girl with a button nose and a ponytail—decorated tabletops and a mantle.

A carpeted staircase led upward. Baronick opened a door under the stairs and looked down into the darkened cellar. "You wanna split up? I'll take the basement. You check upstairs."

Pete headed for the stairs to the second floor without responding.

The first room he encountered matched the style of the rest of the house. Double bed with a dingy chenille spread. Bureau. Chest of drawers. Two nightstands. And a closet. He started with a nightstand and was surprised to find the first one empty. The bureau was a combination of empty drawers and others containing women's clothing. Not modern like Lucy would wear. Pete was no expert in women's styles, but he guessed these to be at least twenty years old.

Hector's wife's things. Same with the chest of drawers. The second nightstand contained a few pieces of cheap jewelry, a couple bottles of lotions, and a hairbrush.

Pete opened the closet. Decades-old women's dresses, blouses, and slacks hung on one end of a pipe. The other end was empty. Shoeboxes were stacked neatly along one side. He knelt down and started going through them. Sandals. High heels. Sneakers. All women's styles. None modern.

Neither Hector nor Lucy had ever had the heart to toss these things. Nor had they hidden any prepaid phones among the vintage fashions.

Pete moved down the hall to the next closed door and pushed it open. Rumpled clothing, much of it camo, lay in piles on the floor and strewn on chairs. The bed wasn't made and didn't look like it had been in recent months. A muzzleloader was prominently displayed over a window with a shooting pouch and powder horn draped over the pegs supporting the rifle. Original or reproduction? Pete would look at it closer when he had a chance. It wasn't their murder weapon, so his curiosity had to wait.

Assorted boxes of ammunition sat on a dresser, some boxes closed, some open with shells scattered. Small caliber, probably used to shoot groundhogs around the house.

But the gadget, which at first glance might have appeared to be a walkie-talkie, perched atop a chest of drawers was what drew Pete's interest.

A handheld police scanner.

"Bingo," he said to the empty room.

A thorough search of Hector's room revealed nothing else of importance. No thirty-caliber ammo. No burner phones. No hunting rifle hidden under the mattress. Just the scanner, from which he could have tracked who was on duty and responding to calls.

A small bathroom in need of an update yielded nothing either. One room remained.

Pete opened the door to an assault of pink. And lace. Unlike her father's room, Lucy's was neat and tidy. The bed was made. All of her clothes had been hung up or folded in drawers. A corner shelving unit displaying framed photos and a number of trophies and ribbons. Pete crossed to it for a closer look.

The trophies—he counted fourteen of them—were topped with golden figures holding a rifle, similar figures with a handgun, or a sporting clay with a set of shotgun shells. Pete removed his reading glasses from his pocket and slipped them on his face. The small engraved plaques on the bases came into focus. Different shooting competitions, different dates. Same winner's name. Lucy Livingston.

Three of the trophies were for championship sharpshooter awards.

"Wow," Baronick said from behind him.

Pete flinched. Damn it. He hated when the detective sneaked up on him like that.

"I guess the girl can shoot."

"I already figured that much."

Baronick crooked a finger. "You might want to come downstairs and see what I found."

Pete followed him into the basement. Steel shelves lined the block walls and held dozens of jugs of water, what had to be several months' worth of assorted canned foods, and large tins with the lids popped open—probably the detective's doing—containing sacks of flour and sugar. Cardboard cases marked "Meal, Ready-To-Eat" filled another set of shelves.

Baronick pointed at them, grinning proudly. "I knew there would be MREs."

Seven five-gallon gasoline cans sat against the opposite wall. Pete had expected more. Maybe Hector had a buried gas tank somewhere on the property.

"This is what you wanted me to see?" Pete asked.

"Not quite." Baronick headed farther back into the cellar, ducking through a doorway. "Watch your head."

Pete followed the detective, avoiding the low clearance. Inside, a series of fluorescent light fixtures illuminated the room. The elaborate workbench and tool display forced Pete to tamp down a rush of jealousy. A deconstructed shotgun occupied a portion of the bench. Reloading supplies took up the remainder.

A trio of mammoth gun safes stood in formation against the wall opposite the work area. He blew a soft whistle of appreciation.

"What do you want to bet there's a thirty-ought-six in one of those?" Baronick asked.

Pete wasn't about to take that bet. "Have you found anything else?"

"Isn't this enough?"

Pete shot a look at the detective.

Baronick aimed a thumb at the storage cabinets over the workbench. "I haven't finished searching those yet."

"You keep looking." Pete turned to leave.

"Where are you going?"

"Outside to talk Hector Livingston into coughing up the combinations. Unless you plan on testing your safe-cracking skills."

As soon as Pete hit the top of the basement steps, his phone chimed. A check of the screen revealed he'd missed a call. Apparently there was no cell service in Hector's basement. Pete pulled up details of the missed call, hoping it was from the officers tracking down the Livingston girl. Instead, it was from Zoe. As much as he loved hearing her voice, right now he didn't have time. He needed to catch the shooter who was putting her in harm's way.

If he hadn't already.

He found Hector as he'd left him, standing in the shady backyard, his face ominous and still, like the sky just before the arrival of a storm. The Monongahela County uniformed officer assigned to keep watch over their suspect acknowledged Pete with a nod.

"Nice workbench you've got downstairs," Pete said.

Hector glared at him in silence.

Pete's phone chimed again.

Still hoping for word on Lucy, he checked it, but found a text from Zoe instead. He pocketed the phone without reading the message. "I need the combinations for your gun safes."

Hector responded with a disdainful suggestion that Pete do something which was physically impossible.

Pete studied the man. His eyes. His face. His stance. This was no cocky young thug. Nor was he a fool. No. This was a fiercely private man who believed in personal freedom. He was a father who loved his daughter, crazy or not, more than life.

But was he a killer?

"Look, Hector, I understand you hate having us here. To be honest, I'd rather not tear up your house and go through your stuff either. You could save us both a lot of grief by being straight with me."

A muscle in the man's jaw twitched. But he didn't tell Pete to go to hell.

"I *am* going to put an end to this killing with or without your help. If your daughter is involved in any way, I will stop her. No matter what." Pete let the full meaning of his words sink in before continuing. "If she's the one I'm after, and if you want to keep her alive, you need to help me stop her before it's too late."

Panic flickered in Hector's eyes. He looked away, his jaw tense. When he brought his gaze back to Pete, the mask was once again firmly in place. Yet the hostility seemed less intense. "Lucille didn't do this."

Pete folded his arms. "Did you?"

"No."

"Then prove it. Give me the combinations to your gun safes."

"You won't find anything to tie either of us to the shootings." Hector jutted his jaw. "Unless you plant it."

Pete suspected Hector was baiting him. "You'll have to take my word on that."

"Why should I?"

Pete leaned in a little closer. Lowered his voice. "Because deep down, I think we're on the same side. You used to be a firefighter. Life dealt you a damned lousy hand. In similar circumstances, I might have reacted the same as you. But you've been on the line of fire. You know what it takes to do the job. I don't think you could kill your own kind. And even if you could, I don't think you're coward enough to do it from a distance."

Pete wasn't sure he believed a word he was telling Hector. But he could tell the man was giving his words serious thought.

"If you didn't do this, and if your daughter didn't, then a killer is still out there ready to strike again, I'm wasting valuable time tearing your house apart, and another man or woman on the front line might die because of it."

Hector's gaze had shifted to one side. His lower lip pressed the upper one into an inverted U.

"The combinations," Pete said.

Hector deflated. Rheumy eyes met Pete's. "You got something to write on?"

Pete watched as a trio of county officers each carried two hunting rifles—thirty-ought-sixes—from the Livingston house. Hector had been moved to the backseat of one of the county cars. For once, Pete didn't give a damn about turning the case over to Baronick and his men. Their ballistics lab would make quick work of matching one of the half dozen weapons to the brass they had in evidence.

Or clearing them.

Let the county boys do the lab work. Pete intended to be the one to catch the killer.

Baronick appeared at the back door, spotted Pete, and jogged down the steps and across the yard to him. "We've got her," the detective said.

"Lucy?"

"Yep. Just got a call. She's in custody."

"Where'd they find her?"

"Greene County. At a friend's house."

Pete's phone rang. "So Hector was telling the truth," he said as he checked the screen, expecting to see Zoe's name. In all the hubbub, he'd forgotten to read her message. But this time the incoming call was from Chuck Delano. The guy was persistent. No doubt about it. Pete pressed the key to ignore the call.

"Yeah," Baronick said. "He told the truth about that much at least. I can't wait to hear what the girl has to say though. I've sent two of my men to bring her back to Monongahela County Police Headquarters."

"*County* Headquarters?" No. There was no damned way Pete would allow County to snatch this case from him now. "She comes back *here.*"

"Be reasonable, Pete. You're already stretched too thin. We have the facilities and the manpower. You don't. The only reason I've let you spearhead the investigation up until now is because this is where the action has been. But it makes no sense to bypass County and bring Lucy here for questioning."

Maybe not, but Pete wasn't letting go. He remembered Hector's words to him three days ago and echoed them to the detective. "Do you know how to tell when she's lying?"

"No. How?"

"I do," Pete said. *Her lips move,* he thought to himself, but he wasn't sharing the joke with the detective.

Baronick glared at Pete. Pete glared back. A game of who-blinks-first. They'd played it many times before.

"All right. We keep her at HQ, but you can sit in on the questioning," Baronick said.

"No deal." Pete wasn't about to leave his township when a killer might still be on the loose. And Baronick knew it. "You bring the girl here. After we both question her, County can have her."

The detective held eye contact, but took a deep breath. Pete refrained from smiling. He'd won this round.

"Fine. We'll play it your way. This time." Baronick pulled out his phone and walked away.

Pete keyed up Zoe's text message. He read it once. And then again. "*Hey,*" she wrote, "*did you know Bud Kramer has a quad hidden under a tarp in the back of his garage?*"

TWENTY-FOUR

Zoe and the rest of the A crew stood in front of the open bay door, gazing at Medic Two as if it were a wounded comrade newly out of the hospital. Earl fingered the metal where the bullet had pierced the fender.

"Does it pass your inspection?" Tony asked.

Earl tipped his head, squinting at the patch job. "Yeah. Gotta say, Kramer's guys do good work. I can't even see a dimple."

The crew seemed appeased. Their large orange and white team member had been pronounced fully recovered and ready for duty.

The mention of Bud Kramer set Zoe's nerves on edge. Had Pete received her message? Would he have time to check into the ATV hidden under the tarp? Or would he even bother when he was focused on the Livingstons?

She shook her head. Bud as a sniper was about as preposterous an idea as she'd ever come up with.

Besides, she was the one who had alerted Pete to Lucy as a potential suspect. He'd think she was nuts if she called him to check every single ATV in the county.

Tony clapped Zoe on the back. "So what's the latest?"

Had she missed something? "About what?"

He fixed her with a look. "What do you *think*? You're Chief Adams' girl. You have the inside scoop on the investigation."

Chief Adams' girl? That's how they saw her? "I'm not really his...I mean, we're not really..."

Tony further narrowed his eyes at her.

She glanced around and discovered the others giving her equally skeptical looks. "I haven't talked to him since this morning. They were watching Hector Livingston's house and trying to find Lucy."

"I heard they arrested Hector and were searching his house," Tracy Nicholls said. "And they captured Lucy down in Greene County and are bringing her back for questioning."

"Oh," Zoe said. Obviously she was out of the loop, Chief Adams' girl or not.

Tracy blushed when the other crewmembers all turned their attention to her. "I was talking to my friend at the newspaper a little while ago."

"So they've caught them." Tony sounded relieved. "Good."

Tony, Tracy, and the other two guys on the crew drifted into the office, talking about the case and whether Hector or Lucy...or both...was the killer.

Zoe ran the news through her head and wished it brought her the same sense of relief as the others felt.

"What's wrong?" Earl asked.

She blinked, realizing she'd been staring at, but not really seeing, him. "I was thinking."

"I know. About what? I thought you'd be happy to hear Lucy and her father were in custody."

"I thought so too. Maybe I would, if I'd heard it from Pete."

Earl crossed his arms. "He's probably busy."

"No matter how busy he is, if he believed I—*we* were safe, I think he'd let me know."

A trace of a grin crossed Earl's face. "A minute ago you were arguing about not being his girl."

She opened her mouth to throw the *we're just friends* line at him, but realized who she was talking to. Earl knew her too well. Instead, she said, "That's not the only thing bugging me."

"You're still hung up on Bud Kramer having a quad." It wasn't a question.

"Yeah. Maybe. No." Zoe laughed at her lack of conviction. "I know it's stupid. We're talking Bud. We've known him for years."

"Decades," Earl corrected.

"He has no motive to hurt any of us." That Zoe knew of. "Besides, he's in wheelchair. The shooter, whoever he is, may have used a quad to get in and out, but he had to climb off the thing to make his shots. Bud couldn't do that."

Earl fell silent, pensive.

The flicker of doubt in his eyes tightened a knot in her shoulders. "What?"

He fixed his gaze on Medic Two, but Zoe was pretty sure he wasn't seeing it any more than she'd been seeing him a moment earlier. He shook it off. "I remember hearing Bud used to be a wild man in his younger days. Hot tempered. Always goading guys into fights."

"That's still a long way from premeditated murder," Zoe reminded him. "Besides, he's in a *wheelchair*."

"Because of the pain when he stands."

"When he *stands*?"

"And walks. Bud Kramer isn't completely wheelchair bound. He can get around for short distances."

Short distances? Like the distance from a quad to a preselected vantage point for firing on unsuspecting fire and EMS personnel? Zoe shivered. "I have to call Pete again."

With Hector secured in Vance Township's holding cell under Kevin's scrutiny, and Lucy's ETA still about an hour out, Pete decided to take advantage of the lull in action to look into this quad Zoe had called him about. As Pete parked in front of Bud Kramer's Garage, his cell phone rang again. Zoe's name flashed on the screen.

"Hi," he said, wondering if she could hear him smile.

He definitely heard no smile in her voice, however. "Have you had a chance to check into Bud's ATV?"

"I'm just about to talk to him."

"Did you know he can walk?"

"What?"

"I guess that's a no. Earl told me Bud's not completely wheelchair bound."

This was news to Pete. He'd never seen the man on his feet. Whatever had put him in the chair had happened before Pete moved to Monongahela County.

When he didn't reply right away, Zoe added, "That means he could have walked from the quad to the spot where..."

Pete completed her sentence. "Where the killer fired the shots."

"Yeah."

"I'll look into it."

After a pause Zoe said, "I heard you caught Hector and Lucy?" There was a hopeful uptick at the end of the question.

"Yeah."

The silence on the line bore the weight of her unasked questions. Did they do it? Was it safe to go on calls?

Pete wished like hell he had answers for her. "I'm going to talk to Bud. I'll call you when I know anything."

Inside the garage, Bud was at his usual post, bent over a stack of papers. He looked up when Pete tapped the counter. "No, your cop car is not ready yet," he grumbled. "The thing's a mess. Gonna take us at least a week."

"That's not what I'm here about."

"Good." Bud glanced at his watch. "'Cause I'm about to call it a day. Quittin' time."

Pete took what he hoped appeared to be a casual look around the garage—with special attention to the area in the rear. The other mechanics must have already clocked out. The place was deserted.

"Whatcha looking for?" Bud asked.

Pete kept his voice level. "I hear you have an ATV."

Bud blinked. Nodded. And aimed a thumb toward the back of the first bay. "Hang on a minute. I'll be right out."

Bud spun his chair and wheeled toward the door leading to what Pete guessed was his office. A moment later, another door to Pete's right swung open, and Bud rolled through.

"What's with the interest in my ATV all of a sudden?"

That aspect of the crimes had been withheld from the public and the media. Bud's question seemed genuine. Unless he was covering his ass.

"We've had a rash of all-terrain vehicle thefts," Pete lied.

"You think mine's stolen?"

"I have to check, Bud. Just doing my job."

Bud performed another perfect spin in place before wheeling toward the rear of the bay. "If anyone claims I stole this one, they're lying. I bought it used, but legal." He continued to the back of the garage and stopped next to a tarp covering what had to be the quad in question. He grabbed the tarp and whipped it off, revealing a clean albeit battered Arctic Cat. Bud beamed at the ATV. "She ain't pretty, but she runs like a champ."

Pete strolled around it, taking in the details. For long hours, he'd stared at the photos of the tire tracks. These ones looked as close to a match as any he'd seen so far. The quad didn't have a speck of dust or mud on it. Either it hadn't been outside lately—or it had been washed recently. He eyed a gun rack mounted on the back fender to the left of the rider's seat. "What do you use it for?"

"So far I've only had it out once to putt around a bit. But I hope to do some deer hunting this fall. I used to go out with my dad when I was a kid and with my brothers after that." Bud slapped his leg. "Haven't been hunting in years though, for obvious reasons. Thought this buggy might give me back some freedom."

"How long have you owned it?"

"Not long. Couple weeks maybe."

Pete wished he'd agreed to upgrade to one of those phones with a camera that connected to the internet. He could take a photo of the tires and email it to the lab. "I'm going to get my camera from my vehicle and take some photos of it. If that's all right with you." He'd take the pictures anyway, but Bud's reaction might tell him what he needed to know.

"Sure. Whatever you want." The words were right, but Bud's eyes shifted as he spoke. He wasn't as happy to help as he let on.

Pete kept a wary eye on the garage while he walked out to his SUV. He wasn't sure what he expected. Bud to leap from his wheelchair onto the Arctic Cat and roar away? But he could see the man sitting in his chair in the shadows, waiting.

As Pete dug through the canvas bag that held his evidence collecting supplies, he placed a quick call to Baronick and learned the officer transporting Lucy was still about forty-five minutes away. Baronick chuckled when Pete asked if the officer had reported any trouble with the girl.

Back inside the garage, Pete adjusted the camera to take close-up shots and snapped photos of all four tires, making notes to label each frame. If the photos matched, he'd confiscate the quad and do more definitive testing. But his gut was at full alert.

"Tell me something," Pete said, keeping his tone conversational. "What happened to put you in that contraption?"

Bud chuckled. "You wouldn't believe me if I told you."

"Try me."

"I broke my back...boogie boarding."

Pete lowered the camera and turned to see if the man was joking. "*Boogie* boarding?"

Bud scratched his head. "I know, I know. Damned stupid thing for an old man to do. We were on vacation in Hawaii with the kids, and I got goaded into it. Gotta admit it was a blast. Right up until a wave got the better of me."

"I didn't know you had kids." Pete didn't know Bud had a wife either.

Bud's smile faded. "Two boys. Ain't seen them in years."

Pete waited for him to elaborate, but Bud lowered his head and rubbed one leg as if massaging a cramp. "So you haven't been able to walk since the accident?"

Bud straightened, but kept his gaze on the quad. "No."

Again, he didn't seem willing to explain further, and Pete decided pressing him—now—wouldn't accomplish much. Powering down the camera, Pete said, "That should do it. I'll let you know when we clear you." Or when they didn't.

Bud still avoided eye contact, but nodded. "You know your way out."

Pete slid behind the wheel of his Edge, setting the camera on the passenger seat. As he keyed Kevin's number into his phone, he watched the large garage door close.

"Where are you?" Pete asked when his officer picked up.

"Keeping an eye on Snake Sullivan."

"Is he doing anything?"

"Last time I cruised by, he was sitting on his porch with a six-pack. Only it's down to a three-pack."

Pete weighed the decision to pull Kevin off babysitting duties with Sullivan. It wasn't much of a choice. "Forget him. I need your eyes on Bud Kramer."

The call went silent for a moment before Kevin replied, "Bud Kramer? The paralyzed guy who owns the garage?"

"You know any other Bud Kramers?"

"Well, no."

It was Pete's turn to be silent. If Kevin came back with another stupid question, he'd have the young cop on desk duty. Including janitorial chores like scrubbing the toilet.

As if reading Pete's thoughts, Kevin said, "I'm on my way, Chief."

The call came in from county for a ninety-year-old female who was unresponsive, but still breathing. Nothing at all suspicious. Except for the location. A house on a lonely stretch of country road with no neighbors in close proximity.

"I hate being scared of doing our job," Tony grumbled. He and his partner were up for the call.

Zoe manned the radio and handed him the note on which she'd scrawled the address. "I'll call for police backup."

Tony waved her off. "I'm sure it'll be safe. If things look suspicious when we get there, I'll phone you and then you can call in the troops."

"If things look suspicious," she called after him as they headed out the door, "stay in the unit until the police get there."

Earl appeared in the doorway from the back. "I have to agree with him. I'm sick of being scared to do my job."

"They have both the Livingstons in custody, and Pete's checking on Bud Kramer. One of them has to be the shooter, so I think we're okay." She hoped.

"And yet you want to call for police backup for a routine medical emergency."

Zoe didn't reply. While it was true she hoped they were safe with the three main suspects under scrutiny, she wouldn't completely relax until Pete told her they had their man. Or girl.

"Control, this is Medic One, en route," Tracy's voice came over the radio.

"Ten four, Medic One," the EOC dispatcher responded and gave the time. "Eighteen twenty-six."

"I'm gonna call Pete," Zoe said.

Earl crossed to the bench in front of the window and flopped onto it. "If it'll put your mind at ease."

She keyed Pete's number on her cell phone. He answered on the second ring. "How's it going?" she asked.

"They're just pulling in with Lucy."

"Anything on Bud Kramer?"

"I sent photos of his tire treads to the county lab. Haven't heard back from them yet." He sounded busy. Which, of course, he was.

"The reason I'm calling—"

Before she could tell him about the unresponsive woman, the county dispatcher came on the radio. "Medic One, this is Control. Return to base. Repeat, return to base. Caller reports his mother has regained consciousness and refuses medical help."

Zoe blew out a relieved sigh.

"Hello?" Pete said over the phone. "Zoe?"

"Sorry. False alarm," she told him. "We're all a little jumpy around here."

He chuckled. "Roger that."

In the background, she could hear Lucy Livingston screeching at the top of her lungs. "I guess your suspect has arrived. I'll let you go."

"Thanks a lot," he said sarcastically.

The radio crackled. "Medic One returning to base."

As Zoe ended the call, Earl rose and patted her shoulder.

"Better safe than sorry," he said as he headed for the lounge.

She leaned back in her chair. Maybe she was just paranoid. Maybe the killer was in custody and the nightmare of the last few days was over.

Except Pete hadn't mentioned arresting Bud Kramer. Yet.

TWENTY-FIVE

"Get your hands off me, you moron!"

Lucy Livingston reminded Pete of a Chihuahua. All teeth and bark and no idea of how small she really was.

Or how much trouble she was in.

Two county uniforms each had one of her arms and "escorted" her into the Vance Township interrogation room, her feet barely touching the ground but flailing and back-pedaling the whole trip down the hallway.

From the holding cell farther back in the building, Hector bellowed, "She didn't do anything!"

"Daddy?" she cried out as the officers shoved her through the interrogation room door and closed it, cutting off her tirade.

Hector, however, continued to roar. "*Pete Adams. I want to talk to you.*"

Baronick had trailed in behind his officers and their suspect and stood at the front door, grinning like that damned Cheshire Cat. "I offered to keep her at County HQ along with the two quads we brought in. You insisted we bring her here."

"You can have her back when I'm done with her." Pete grabbed a folder from the desk in the front office, headed for the interrogation room, and called over his shoulder, "You coming?"

Baronick fell into step behind him. "Wouldn't miss this for the world."

"*Adams,*" Hector shouted from the back again. "Get your ass back here. I need to talk to you."

"Since you asked so nicely," Pete muttered to himself. He opened the door to the interrogation room and found the two county officers looming over a seated and subdued Lucy Livingston. He wondered what they'd done to shut her up, but whatever it was, she didn't appear physically injured. Nodding to the officers, he said, "Go tell her father I'll be there when I'm done speaking with his charming daughter."

Once Baronick and Pete were alone with the girl, she thumped her handcuffed fists on the table. "Oh, wonderful. I've traded one set of Neanderthals for another. Get these things off me."

Pete eased into the chair across from her, shaking his head. "I don't know. I hear you tried to kick out the windows in the back of the squad car."

Lucy held up her bound hands. "Because of these. If they hadn't put these on, I'd have pounded the windows out with my fists."

"You're not making much of a case for yourself."

She slumped back and blew a disgusted breath that made her dark bangs float up and settle again on her forehead.

Pete clicked on his recorder and read the Miranda rights to her. "Do you understand?" he asked.

"Of course I understand. I'm not an idiot."

Baronick snorted, but covered by coughing into his hand.

Lucy twisted toward him. "Don't you dare laugh at me. What's *your* IQ?" She thrust out her chest. "Mine's 168."

Pete had serious doubts. After all, her lips were moving. But he needed to get information from this girl and arguing with her wasn't the way to do it. "Impressive. Now if you'll promise to act civil, I'll take those cuffs off."

Her lower lip trembled, but she extended her arms toward him. "I promise."

He unlocked and removed the cuffs, and she massaged her wrists. She did not, however, thank him.

"All right," Pete said, opening the folder. "Let's get this over with so you can get out of here." He didn't mention *out of here* might mean into county lockup. "Where have you been the last few evenings?"

"I was at my friend's house down in Waynesburg last night. Just ask your storm troopers. They picked me up there."

"What about the three evenings before that? Thursday, Friday, and Saturday."

"I was at home."

"Really? As early as six o'clock?"

Her lips weren't moving, but her mind clearly was. After several long moments of silence, she crossed her arms. "I'm invoking my right to remain silent."

"Invoking," Baronick echoed. "Maybe she really does have an IQ of 158."

"One-*sixty*-eight," she snapped.

"Excuse me," Baronick said, doing vocal loopty-loops with the word *excuse*.

Pete glared at the detective. "Do I have to separate you two?"

"Please," Lucy said.

Baronick held up both hands in surrender, but he stayed in the room.

Pete removed a trio of photographs they'd taken in Lucy's bedroom and spread them in front of her. "You have a nice set of trophies there."

She glanced at the photos and then looked at Pete, her lips pressed into a tight thin line.

"I understand both you and your father are champion sharpshooters. Avid hunters too. So you know the area pretty well."

"I'm not talking to you." Lucy was definitely her father's daughter.

Pete withdrew another set of photos from the folder and set them in front of her one at a time. "Curtis Knox. He broke off your engagement well before you admitted to it. Now he's in the hospital." Pete laid down another photo, this one from Barry Dickson's autopsy.

Lucy winced and looked away.

"Barry Dickson. Curtis's partner. Did he just get in the way of your shot? Or were you angry because he helped convince Curtis to dump you?"

She swallowed hard and kept her gaze aimed at a corner of the ceiling.

Pete set down another autopsy photo. "Jason Dyer. Another ex-boyfriend of yours. Also shot from long distance. Imagine that."

A cell phone rang—not Pete's. Baronick dug his phone from his pocket and checked the caller ID. "Excuse me," he said, and ducked out of the room.

Pete tapped the photo of Jason. The girl *would* look at her handiwork whether she wanted to or not.

Lucy sniffed, but kept her eyes averted. Pete slammed his palm down on the table. She flinched. "Look at the damn picture, Lucy."

Trembling, she took a quick glimpse toward it and looked away again.

Pete leaned toward her. "What about Rick Brown?"

The name brought her gaze back to his, her eyes wide and damp.

"He's dead too. Did you have anything to do with that?"

"Snake," she said.

Snake? For a moment Pete wondered if she'd done something to him too. Or had Snake been responsible for Brown's death?

"I want to call Snake. His uncle's a lawyer, and I want him to represent me. I'm not talking to you any more without an attorney present."

The door swung open, and Baronick stepped inside, a strange look on his face. "I need to speak with you."

Pete gathered the photos and tucked them inside the folder. "Wait here," he told the girl. "I'll have someone bring you a phone."

In the hallway with the door again closed, Baronick asked, "Did she tell you anything?"

"Just that she wants Snake's uncle as her attorney."

Baronick nodded. "Figures. That was the lab on the phone."

"And?"

"Nothing from ballistics on the Livingstons' guns yet, but their ATVs definitely don't match our tire marks."

Not what Pete wanted to hear. "Damn it."

"That's not all. One of our detectives did a follow-up interview with the owner of the stolen Chevy Cavalier."

"Jack Utah," Pete said. The hoarder.

"Yeah. Turns out he had the car serviced recently." Baronick paused. "At Bud Kramer's Garage."

Pete's jaw tightened. "Did they run the photos of his ATV's tires I sent?"

"Yep. Perfect match. Looks like your mechanic is our killer."

Pete yanked his phone from his pocket and punched in Kevin's number.

"Who are you calling?" Baronick asked.

"Kevin Piacenza. I have him watching Bud's place."

"Good."

Except the phone rang several times and then went to voicemail. "Kevin, where the hell are you?"

Zoe sat reading a horse lover's magazine in one of the well-worn easy chairs in the crew lounge, her legs folded under her. The rest of the crew was taking turns shouting answers—or questions—at the TV, trying to best the *Jeopardy!* contestants. The sound of tones drifted back to them from the office.

Earl climbed to his feet. "That'll be for us."

"Maybe the old lady passed out again," Tracy said, "and the son needs us to transport her after all."

Zoe stuck one of the loose subscription cards between pages to mark her place and tossed the magazine onto the end table with the rest of the assorted reading material. "I hope not. It's been almost an hour. He darn well better have her in the ER by now." She uncurled her legs and stood to follow Earl.

He paused at the door to the office and gave her a playful nudge. "Got your life insurance paid up?"

"Not funny."

Tony waited for them, holding out the note with the address. "Guy called in complaining of severe chest pains. Male. Sixty-two years old. Says he was trying to drive himself to the hospital, but the pain got too bad and he's pulled over waiting for the ambulance."

Zoe snatched the note on her way past. "Ridge Road?"

Earl hesitated and met her gaze, his jaw tight. "Not much traffic out that way."

She hated this nagging fear. The dread of doing a job she loved.

"Should we call the police?" Earl asked.

"Let's go." She gave him a gentle push toward the ambulance. "If there's any question once we get there, then we'll call."

With Earl behind the wheel, they rolled onto Main Street. He flipped on the lights and sirens.

Zoe unclipped the mic. "Control, this is Medic Two en route to Ridge Road."

"Ten-four, Medic Two. Nineteen twenty-one."

* * *

"You got nothing on us. Let us go." Hector glowered at Pete through the bars of the holding cell.

Lucy hugged her knees close to her chest and pouted in the other cell.

Pete knew as soon as Andrew McCoy got there, he'd demand Pete cut them loose, but until the lab told him the rifles didn't match, he planned to keep both Livingstons on ice for as long as possible.

In the meantime, he had bigger concerns. Like why Kevin wasn't answering his phone or responding to the radio. Pete wanted nothing more than to charge out to Kramer's place himself, but he had Hector and Lucy to deal with. Instead, he'd called in Seth and Nate, and Baronick ordered his two officers, who had escorted Lucy, to meet them there.

"Are you listening to me?" Hector barked.

"I hear you." Pete checked his phone in case he'd missed Kevin's call. But he knew he hadn't.

"And?"

"You might as well sit back and relax, because until I get a report from ballistics, you aren't going anywhere."

"I'm telling you, they aren't gonna find anything because we didn't shoot anyone."

"Give it up, Daddy," Lucy said. "Snake's uncle will get us out."

Hector blew a raspberry. "Lawyers. They're as useless as tits on a bull."

The bells jangled on the front door, and voices drifted back to them. Pete recognized McCoy's as one of them. Moving away from the holding cells, Pete headed to the intersection of the T in the hallway where he could see two men, one in a suit and the other in oversized jeans, standing at the window to Nancy's office. "McCoy," he yelled. When the attorney looked Pete's way, he waved them back.

Pete met McCoy and Snake halfway and aimed a thumb over his shoulder. "Hector and Lucy are in the holding cells."

McCoy scowled. "I'd rather talk to them one at a time and in your conference room."

Which was where Baronick had set up a temporary office.

"You're probably only going to get one of them to talk anyway," Pete said. "I have business to attend to right now. If you want Lucy moved to the *interrogation* room, you'll have to wait until I check on the status of my men."

McCoy made a face as though he'd sucked on a lemon. "Fine. I'll talk to them back there. For now."

The attorney brushed past Pete. Snake started to follow, but Pete planted a hand on the kid's chest. "Not you."

"But—"

Pete grabbed Snake's shirt and spun him toward the front before giving him a firm shove. Slump-shouldered, the tough-guy wannabe lumbered down the hall ahead of Pete. When they reached Nancy's office, he held up a finger at the kid. "Stay."

Mumbling, Snake leaned against the wall, arms crossed.

"Any news?" Pete asked his secretary.

She shook her head. "Nate should be on scene any minute now. Seth said his ETA is five minutes. And the county officers should get there somewhere in between."

"Did you have any luck raising Bud Kramer on the phone?"

"None. No answer at the garage or at his home number. Detective Baronick is trying to track down his cell phone number."

Pete rubbed the space between his eyes where a tension headache brewed. "Come on, Nate," he said under his breath.

Nancy gave him a tight smile. "A watched radio never squawks."

He glanced at the closed conference room door and contemplated checking in on Baronick while he waited. But Nancy had said Nate should be at Kramer's any time now.

A perplexed look on Snake's face caught Pete's attention. "Do you need to use the restroom?"

Snake met Pete's gaze and shook his head. "No. What was that name you just mentioned?"

"Detective Baronick?"

"No, no, no. Bud. Bud...?"

"Kramer?"

Snake's eyes brightened. "Yeah. That's him. That's the name of the guy who bought my quad."

TWENTY-SIX

With no real address to go by, Earl eased around Ridge Road's blind curves and sped down the straight stretches, although the bumps and ruts of the tarred and chipped country road limited the definition of "speed."

"He's gotta be along here somewhere."

Zoe wasn't sure if Earl was talking to himself or to her. "Unless it's another false alarm." She glanced over at her partner whose jaw twitched. "False alarm" held a whole new cause for concern these days.

The woods with its branches stretching across the road overhead created the illusion of dusk with charcoal clouds preventing any sunlight to penetrate the patchwork green, gold, and orange leaves. The ambulance rounded another bend and broke into the open mown hayfields rolling away on either side.

"There," Earl said. Ahead, a familiar-looking brown Chevy pickup sat half on, half off the road facing them. He gunned the ambulance, closing the distance.

A knot of tension squeezed Zoe's chest. "That looks like my truck."

"I've seen at least four other trucks like yours in the area. Brown Chevys aren't exactly unique."

Which was true. Besides, this one had a load in the bed, covered with a tarp. And hers wouldn't start. She tamped down her fear and reached for the mic as Earl braked. "Medic Two to Control. Show us on scene."

"Ten-four, Medic Two. On scene at nineteen thirty-two."

Earl threw open his door, but Zoe caught his arm. "I have a bad feeling about this. Let me call Pete."

"Look." Earl pointed at the pickup. They could clearly see a gray-haired man slumped over the steering wheel.

"We have a patient who was complaining of chest pains," Earl said, "and it took us too darned long to get here already. Get the jump kit and let's try to save this guy." He jerked free of her grasp and bolted for the Chevy.

"Wait," she called after him. But he was already halfway to the truck. She leapt out, yanked open the side compartment door, and snatched the jump kit. With her free hand, she dug her cell phone from her pocket and pulled up Pete's number, ready to hit *send* if needed, as she jogged after her partner.

Earl had been right about there being a number of other brown Chevys in the area. And there may have been other two-toned ones like hers. And like this one. The knot of tension grew into a screaming banshee when she came up behind Earl, he opened the driver's side door, and she spotted the horse-head seat covers. *Her* horse-head seat covers.

"You expect me to believe you didn't know who Bud Kramer was?" Pete had long known Snake was an imbecile, but this was a new low, even for him.

Snake's eyebrows and shoulders both shrugged as if controlled by the same marionette string. "I never used his garage. My buddy's a mechanic and does all my work cheap."

"And you neglected to mention the guy just *happened* to be in a wheelchair?"

"He didn't have a wheelchair when I saw him." Snake's voice had slipped into the nasally whine realm. "I only saw him that one time, and the dude was sitting at one of the tables in the bar. He might've had a cane with him, but there wasn't a wheelchair."

"What about when he picked up the ATV? Or did you deliver it?"

"Neither one. He sent someone with a flatbed tow truck to get it."

Pete clenched his fists, fighting the urge to belt the kid. "I don't suppose the flatbed had a logo on it? Like Bud Kramer's Garage?"

Snake frowned in deep thought. After a moment he nodded. "Yeah. I think it did."

Pete's phone rang, distracting him from lunging at Snake's tattooed throat.

Before Pete could answer the call, Nate's tense voice came over the radio. "Vance Base, this is Unit Thirty-Five. I'm here. Kevin's car is parked across from Kramer's Garage, but he's not in it."

"Don't move," Pete told Snake. He let the call—yet another from Chuck Delano—go to voicemail, charged into Nancy's office, and snatched the mic from her hand. "Is there any sign of him?"

"None. No sign of a struggle either. Looks like he just left his vehicle."

"Backup's on their way. As soon as County and Seth get there, check out the garage."

"Roger that, Chief."

"What's going on?" Baronick asked from the doorway.

Pete's phone chimed indicating a message. Probably also from Delano. "We can't raise Kevin Piacenza on the phone or radio." Pete relayed Nate's report. "Do you have anything new?"

"Yeah. I've been talking to the lab. Not one of the guns we took from the Livingstons' house is our murder weapon. Basically, we have zilch on them."

"Good."

Baronick looked perplexed. "Good?"

"Nancy, get the keys to the holding cells and kick Hector and his darling daughter out of my station." Pete shouldered the detective out of his way. "You," he said to Baronick, "are driving me to Kramer's Garage."

Pete monitored the progress over the radio as Baronick jammed the accelerator to the floor. By the time they arrived, Nate's vehicle had been joined by the County officers' cruiser. Nancy reported state troopers were en route as well as more units from County.

Baronick wheeled into Kramer's lot, gravel flying, and stood on the brake. Pete leapt out before the car came to a complete stop and broke into a lope toward the building.

"Unit Thirty-Five, this is Unit Thirty on scene," he barked into his mic. "Status?"

"We're searching inside the garage, Chief," Nate responded. "No sign of him yet. And no sign of Kramer either."

Pete punched through the door to find Nate coming out of Bud's office.

"Clear," the officer reported.

"Where are the others?"

"One's checking out back. The other one's checking the stock room."

Pete dug his cell phone from his pocket. "Get them on the radio," he told Baronick, who had followed him into the garage, "and tell them to stop and listen for a minute."

Baronick looked puzzled, but then realized what Pete had in mind. "On it."

Pete keyed in Kevin's cell number. Waited for Baronick to inform his two county officers. And then clicked send. Inside, the garage remained silent except for the soft trill coming from Pete's phone.

"I hear something," one of the county officers shouted over the radio. "I'm behind the garage, and I hear something!"

Pete, Nate, Baronick, and the other county officer charged toward the garage's back door. By the time they joined the officer who had reported hearing Kevin's phone, the call had gone to voicemail.

"Which direction?" Pete demanded.

"I couldn't tell. The ringing stopped before I could home in on it."

Once again, Pete ordered quiet and redialed Kevin's number. Nearby, a muffled ringtone broke the silence.

"There." Nate pointed at one of the wrecked cars parked in the back lot.

The four men spread out and approached the mangled heap. Pete kept one hand on his sidearm and knew the others were equally prepared for whatever.

The car's windshield had been shattered and peeled away, probably by the fire department in order to extricate the occupants. The driver's door had been forced open at one point and was now jammed back into place, although not latched. The back door and window, however, were intact. Pete edged up to it and peered through the dirty glass. Inside, a man in uniform lay across the backseat, motionless.

"He's in there," Pete said and yanked the door handle. It snapped back out of his fingers without opening. Swearing, he reached through the missing driver's side window. Fumbled for the lock. On the other side of the car, Nate and one of the county officers were struggling to get either of the doors open. *Who the hell stuffs a body in a wrecked vehicle and then locks the damn doors?*

Pete found the lock, flipped it, and heaved the back door open. "*Kevin!*"

The young officer was on his side, his head toward the opposite door. He didn't budge. Pete leaned in, trying to find Kevin's wrist to check for a pulse, but his arms were bound behind him.

"Help me get him out of there," Pete said.

Nate and the other officer came around as Pete and Baronick grabbed arms and legs and handfuls of uniform, dragging Kevin out of the car and easing him onto the ground.

Pete flipped open his knife and cut through the zip-ties binding Kevin's wrists. Baronick pressed his fingers to the grove in Kevin's throat.

"He's alive," the detective said.

Pete grabbed the mic clipped to his shoulder. "Vance Base, this is Unit Thirty. We found him. Get EMS out to our location *now*."

He was vaguely aware of Nancy's confirmation as he patted Kevin's cheek. "Hey. Kevin. Hey. Wake up."

The young officer's eyelids fluttered, but remained closed.

Gravel crunched behind them. Pete glanced over his shoulder to see Seth approaching at a jog.

"What's going on?" Seth asked, his voice shaky, either from concern or from running.

Nate started to update him, but Pete interrupted. "Go find Bud Kramer. I want his ass in my jail." Pete looked at the two county officers. "You two go with him. I want every police officer and state trooper within a hundred miles out there looking for him. His ATV's not here, so he's probably on it or is hauling it. Put a BOLO out on his truck too."

Baronick already had his phone in his hand. "I'll call it in."

Nate cleared his throat. "Um..."

"What?" Pete snapped.

"Do you know if Zoe picked up her truck yet?"

Pete's nerves chilled. "No. She hasn't. Why?"

"Because the last time I was here it was parked inside, and now that bay is empty. I didn't see it out in front." Nate gestured to the collection of wrecked cars surrounding them. "And it's not back here."

Damn it. Zoe. Pete sent up a silent prayer that she and Earl would be the ones responding to his call for EMS.

Without waiting for Pete to tell him, Baronick said, "I'll put a BOLO out on it too." He moved away, the phone pressed to his ear.

As Seth and the county uniforms jogged toward the garage's back door, Kevin moaned.

Pete called his name and dug a knuckle into the young officer's sternum. If that didn't wake him up...

"Ow..." Kevin groaned.

"*Piacenza*," Pete ordered in the voice he'd been told could wake the dead. "Get up!"

Kevin clearly wasn't dead. "I'm up," he said, although he sounded like he'd tied one on the night before. His lids opened, revealing dazed eyes.

Pete couldn't help smiling in relief. "Good to see you. What the hell happened? Where's Bud Kramer?"

"Kramer?" Kevin reached up and grimaced in pain as he touched his head. "Ow. Where am I?"

"You were tied up in the back of a wrecked car behind Kramer's Garage. Do you remember how you got there?"

Kevin tried to sit up, but fell back with a groan. Pete slid an arm behind his officer's back and helped him into a seated position.

Nate dropped to his knees and helped brace him. "EMS is on its way."

"Good." Pete caught Kevin's chin when his head started to loll forward. "Stay with me, son."

Kevin's eyes fluttered open again. "Yes, sir."

"What do you remember?" Sirens whooped nearby. *Please let Zoe be in the responding ambulance.*

Kevin blinked. "I was...umm...parked in front of Bud Kramer's Garage. Right?"

"Right. Then what?"

The officer squinted in concentration. "I...don't know. That's the last thing I remember."

Damn it. Pete held his hand in front of Kevin's face. "How many fingers am I holding up?"

He listed to one side as he pondered the question. Pete and Nate hoisted him upright again. "I...umm...dunno."

The sirens grew close and then cut off.

Pete didn't need a medical degree to recognize a concussion. "That's okay, Kevin. Help's coming."

A voice from inside the garage floated out to them. "Hello?"

"Back here," Pete shouted.

A moment later, two paramedics—Mike and Tracy, although Pete couldn't recall their last names—trudged toward them lugging a gurney and a jump kit. He filled them in on what he knew of Kevin's condition as they started their assessment of him. Then Pete ordered Nate to stay with them.

"Roger that, Chief."

Pete climbed to his feet, wincing at the pain in his knees. "By the way. Where's Zoe?"

"She and Earl are out on a call," Mike said.

Not the answer he'd wanted to hear. "What kind of call?"

Mike shined a penlight in Kevin's eyes. Without looking up, he replied, "Suspected cardiac."

Pete blew out a breath. A medical emergency. Not a staged accident. And she'd know better than go into a situation where there was any doubt.

Which meant he had to catch Bud Kramer before the killer arranged his next ambush.

TWENTY-SEVEN

"This *is* my truck," Zoe said.

Earl supported the man's neck with one hand and pressed him back from his slumped-over-the-steering-wheel position with the other.

Zoe gasped.

Bud Kramer.

She barely had time to register the sickly blue tinge of his skin and the blood soaking the front of his shirt before a blast that sounded like a cannon shattered the glass in the driver's door window above her.

Earl's knees buckled. He dropped—straight down—with a soft cry.

Zoe hit the ground too, reacting on instinct well before her brain kicked into gear.

Earl's been shot.

Ignoring the safety-glass pellets that showered both her and her partner, she scrambled on her knees to hunch over him. "Earl?"

His eyes were wide, and his chest heaved. A deep red wet splotch spread from a gaping hole on his right shoulder just below his collarbone. "Son of a bitch," he groaned.

Zoe knew the fist-sized hole in his upper chest was the exit wound, and the bullet had entered from the back. She reached for the jump kit and her phone, both of which had hit the ground with her. The boom of a high-powered rifle and the almost simultaneous metallic plink of the bullet tearing through the open driver's door inches above her head sent her diving into the gravel next to Earl. Her phone sailed from her grasp, skittering down the road in pieces—the back, the battery, and the front scattered over several feet.

Zoe pushed up to her knees again. She fumbled with the jump kit's zippers, her fingers trembling. "Where's your cell phone?"

Earl's face contorted in pain. "In the ambulance." He drew his chin into his neck in an effort to see his injury. "I left it on the center console."

She managed to unzip the pocket holding the sterile dressings, pulled out a handful of sterile 4x4s, and clumsily ripped open the packages.

Boom. Plink.

Zoe clung to the bandaging as she huddled over Earl, shielding him from bits of beige fabric, plastic, and steel. She glanced back at the door—her door—which now bore two holes in addition to the shattered window.

"We need to move," Earl said through clenched teeth.

She had a feeling if this guy wanted them dead, they'd be dead. Instead, he was keeping them pinned down. The shots were coming from the woods they'd driven through moments earlier.

The ambulance stood between them and the gunman. To make a run for it would put her clearly in his sights. But she needed to call for help.

Zoe pressed the handful of gauze to Earl's shoulder, eliciting a stream of profanity from him.

"Sorry." She took his left hand and placed it over the wound. "Hold this."

He swore again, but obeyed.

She took a breath. *Think.* Up until now, she'd been reacting. Being the proverbial sitting duck wasn't gonna cut it. "Can you move?"

He looked at her as if she'd lost what was left of her mind. "*Where?*"

"Behind the truck." And closer to the scattered pieces of her cell phone. "If we move fast and stay low, we should be able to make it."

Earl twisted around, trying to calculate the distance. "My legs are fine, but the staying-low part? My arm doesn't work, which makes crawling a little tough."

Zoe grabbed the jump kit and slid it around them, stuffing it under that rear axle. Safe. Out of the way. And reachable from her intended new location. "I'll drag you if you can help push with your feet."

He made a face.

"Yeah," she said. "It's gonna hurt like hell. But another bullet will probably hurt a lot worse."

"You've got a point there." He released his hold on the bandages, which were soaked anyway. "Let's do this...before I go into shock and can't help."

"I didn't want to mention that, but since you brought it up..." Zoe winked at him.

Keeping close to the pickup, she scooted around, positioning herself at Earl's head. She slid both hands under his shoulders. Hoisted him into a half-sit...ignoring the moist, warm rush from the entrance wound she'd known she would find. She interlaced her fingers across his sternum. Holding him tight, she felt him shiver. He really was going into shock, even sooner than she'd expected.

"Bend your knees, put your feet flat on the ground, and—"

"*Push.*" He acted on the order at the same moment he voiced it.

The force nearly sent Zoe sprawling, but she dug in with her heels and dragged her partner toward the rear of her Chevy.

The moment Earl was completely sheltered—or so she hoped—by the pickup, she collapsed onto her backside, still holding him against her.

He moaned. "Son of a bitch, girl. You're rough on a guy."

"And you, my friend, need to drop a few pounds."

"Shut up and start an IV before I pass out."

She eased out from under him, lowering his torso gently to the ground. A slimy red trail indicated the path they'd just traveled. Her shirt clung to her skin, warm and damp. Forcing her eyes—and her mind—away from the blood and on to the task at hand, she reached under the truck's bed, grasped the jump kit, and hauled it close to her.

The phone. She needed to gather and reassemble her phone. Call for help. But Earl was right. First priority was getting pressure dressings on those wounds to stop or slow the blood loss. Second was getting some fluids running into him.

She tore open more sterile dressings, packing the gauze squares over the already saturated ones and adding more to the entry wound on Earl's back. Working quickly, she bound both bandages with Kling wrap and immobilized his entire arm in a triangular bandage.

"You still with me?" she asked.

He grunted, but met her gaze, an odd mixture of fear and trust in his eyes.

As Zoe opened another of the canvas bag's pockets and dug out the IV start kit, a cool breeze rustled the late summer grasses next to the road.

"It's gonna rain," Earl said.

Zoe looked up at the gun-metal gray clouds overhead. "They look like snow clouds."

He huffed. "I'm cold, but not that cold."

"I have a horse blanket behind the seat in the truck."

"I'll be fine." He didn't sound fine.

Willing her hands to be steady, she trusted muscle memory and years of experience to assemble the IV tubing and plug it into the bag of dextrose solution. She wished she had more than one bag with her, but the rest of their supply was stashed in the ambulance.

She straightened his free arm, wrapped the tourniquet below his elbow, and felt for a vein. It only took a couple of seconds to find a good one. She wiggled her hands into a pair of latex gloves and swabbed the vein with an alcohol prep. "You know," she said, "I'm glad you're not the one working on me."

A faint smile tugged at Earl's lips. "Are you insinuating that I suck at starting IVs?"

"I'm insinuating nothing. I'm saying it flat out."

"Hey, when you're right, you're right." He closed his eyes.

Zoe applied traction on the skin and slipped the needle in. Blood flashed back at the catheter hub. "Got it."

"Didn't feel a thing," Earl said.

In one smooth, practiced move, she advanced the catheter and removed the needle, dropping it into the jump kit's sharps container. A moment later and the IV was flowing. "How you doing?"

"I lied before. I really am that cold. Can I have that blanket now?"

"Right."

Fat raindrops started pelting them. "Crap." She rocked back on her heels and rose into a squat. Waiting for another bullet to whiz past her ear—or worse—she grabbed the tailgate with one hand and the release with the other, and gave a jerk. With a thunk, the heavy gate dropped, sending her sprawling into the gravel again.

"Are you okay?" Earl asked.

She peeled off the gloves, now embedded with dirt and stones, and inspected her hands. A few minor scrapes. Nothing a good handwashing wouldn't fix.

The rain quickly turned into a steady deluge, but the lowered tailgate sheltered Earl for the moment. Zoe's phone on the other hand...

She scrambled away from the truck, again anticipating a bullet in the back, scooped up the three pieces, and scurried back under the protection of the tailgate. It took a moment to clip the battery into the phone and snap on the back. Pushing the power button, she held her breath until the screen flashed to life.

"Here." She pressed the phone into Earl's left hand. "Hold this while it boots up. I'm gonna get that blanket for you."

"He hasn't shot at us in a while. Maybe he took off."

"Maybe." But Zoe wasn't putting money on it. She hadn't heard the getaway ATV. At the thought of the quad, she tipped her head to peer around the tailgate at the tarped load in the bed. She couldn't reach it without exposing herself to the shooter—if he was still there—but the size and shape? She'd bet good money her truck's cargo was the ATV from Bud's Garage.

"I wonder who he is," Earl said.

She'd been too busy to think about the shooter's identity. Obviously it wasn't Bud Kramer. Were Hector and Lucy still in custody? "Be right back," she told her partner.

Zoe edged around the driver's side of the pickup. Rain splattered her head, shoulders, and back as she bent low and crept toward the open door, complete with shattered window and two bullet holes.

He'd probably moved. The door might not provide even the small amount of protection it had before. *He's probably watching me through his scope right now.*

Swallowing her trepidation, she made it to the cab. Bud Kramer's dead body had tumbled forward over the steering wheel again, just as they'd found him. Poor old Bud. And she'd thought he was the killer. Had her suspicions contributed to his death?

She slipped a hand behind the bench seat and released the back. But even with the body slumped forward, his bulk kept her from tilting the seat far enough to reach for the blanket. The deafening rain pounded on the truck's roof. It soaked her back and her rear end, and the accompanying breeze chilled her. Temperatures were plummeting. She needed that blanket for Earl before he became hypothermic in addition to being shocky.

"Sorry, Bud," she said and muscled him over onto his side. Then she grabbed his top hip and rolled him away from the seat back. Just a little more. With one hand bracing the body forward, and the other one heaving on the seat, it tipped enough to allow her to reach the balled-up horse blanket.

As her fingers closed around the heavy duck fabric, a hand reached over her shoulder. Rammed the seat back, pinning her arm, sending hot needles shooting into her shoulder. But the muzzle of a gun barrel jammed against her chin made her forget the pain.

The breeze carried a chill and the smell of rain as Pete strode ahead of Baronick toward the detective's unmarked sedan. Their next stop—Bud Kramer's residence. Seth, the county officers, and probably a Pennsylvania State Police unit or two would already be there, but Pete wanted to at least be present when Kramer was put under arrest. Why the hell would a respected businessman and longtime area resident do such a thing?

Baronick jogged to catch up to Pete. "I suppose you're going to insist on bringing Kramer back to your station for interrogation too."

Pete considered it. "Honestly, no. You can have him. I don't want that bastard back in my township. Ever."

"No problem." The detective reached for the driver's door, but Pete's radio stopped him.

"Vance Base, Unit Thirty, this is Unit Thirty-Two."

"This is Unit Thirty. Go, Thirty-Two."

"We're at the residence in question. No sign of the suspect, the missing ATV, or the missing pickup," Seth said.

"Damn it." Pete ran a hand across his dry lips. "Leave the county guys there to watch the place. You get out on patrol. Check anywhere you think he might frequent. Vance Base, you there?"

"I'm here, Chief," Nancy replied.

"I'm here too," came Sylvia's voice over the air.

Good. He needed all hands on deck right now. "I'm heading in. Get the State Police helo in the air. I want every law enforcement agency within a fifty-mile radius looking for that truck and that ATV."

"On it," Nancy said. "Oh, and Chief?"

"Yeah?"

"Chuck Delano called. He said he's been trying to reach you."

The man simply would not give up. "I know. I'll talk to him later. It's about another job." Pete could almost hear Sylvia ranting all the way from Dillard.

"I don't think so," Nancy said. "He sounded worried. He said you need to look at your email. His exact words were, 'It's a matter of life and death.'"

After checking in with Nancy and Sylvia at the front desk, Pete left Baronick to coordinate the different departments' search efforts and headed to his office.

Chuck Delano might be as persistent as a bad cold, but he'd never been prone to histrionics. In the car, Pete had listened to the voice message Chuck left him, and Nancy was right. The man sounded frantic. "Check your gawddamned email," the recorded voice demanded. "You're in danger. Hell, we both are."

Pete slid into his chair and booted up his computer. While he waited, he placed a call of his own. To Zoe. Surely she'd be back from that cardiac run by now. Or at least be at the hospital. But the call went directly to voicemail. Why on earth would she have her phone turned off? "Call me. Now," he said after the beep and hung up.

He hit the icon for his email and waited for it to load. Sure enough, there was a message from Chuck. Pete clicked on it.

Read this and then call me.

Beneath the brief message was a link. Pete moused over it and clicked.

A new tab opened with a newspaper article. From Dayton, Ohio. About a motorcycle fatality.

Pete skimmed the story. The young man who'd died in the crash was one Richard Brown Junior. Rick Brown. Lucy Livingston's deceased boyfriend. The story, however, made no mention of her or Hector. So what was the connection?

Almost as soon as Pete asked himself the question, he came to the final paragraph. And then he knew.

Richard Brown was survived by his father, Richard Senior. Preceding him in death was a brother. Donald Moreno. *Donnie* Moreno. The boy who had crippled Chuck. The boy Pete had shot and killed.

TWENTY-EIGHT

So that was why the name Rick Brown kept nagging at Pete. Yes, it was common, but some part of his memory must have recalled the father's or the brother's name from all those years ago.

Pete reread the entire article, more carefully this time. There was nothing else of importance. Or at least nothing else he could see. He picked up his phone and made the call to Chuck in Hawaii.

"About time you got around to returning my phone call."

"I thought you were hounding me about that job."

"Hell no. You want to put up with low pay and cold winters all for the sake of a woman. I got it. Did you read the article?"

Pete squinted at the screen. "I did. In fact, I still have it in front of me. But there are some holes I need filled."

"I figured."

"For starters, why did you send this to me now?"

Chuck's anxious inhalation carried across the miles. "About three weeks ago I began receiving phone calls. Six...seven...eight a day. Hang ups. I thought it was an especially persistent telemarketer. Caller ID only showed a wireless number. So I blocked it. He must have switched to a different phone because the calls kept coming."

Burner phones.

"Then he started calling every blasted hour," Chuck said. "Twenty-four-seven. Yesterday, I picked up, expecting to get a robot, but planning to give the guy hell if a real person answered. Instead I got the most evil laugh I've ever heard. And he said, 'I hope you remember, because I do. And I'm gonna keep my promise.' He didn't tell me who he was. Didn't have to. I've never forgotten that voice."

Chuck had lost Pete. Completely. "What are you talking about? What promise?"

There was another pause. "How much do you remember from...back then?"

"Everything." Except the kid's father and brother's last name.

Chuck snorted over the phone. "I somehow doubt that. Do you remember Moreno's old man threatening to bring down the hounds of hell on both of us for taking his boy from him?"

"What?" This was news to Pete. "No. He did?"

Chuck grunted. "Come to think of it, I guess you weren't there at the time. The whack job came to my hospital room. Threatened to rip my IVs out and blow into them. Give me an air embolism. I believe he might have done it too, if an orderly hadn't walked in."

"Donnie Moreno's father did this?" Pete rubbed his forehead, struggling to conjure up an image of the man. "Richard Brown?"

"Senior. Yeah."

A mental picture formed. A dark-haired bearded man, mid-thirties. "That was—what? Ten years ago?"

"Eleven."

"That's a long time to carry all that hate," Pete mused out loud.

"I know. The way I figure it, he busied himself taking care of the other boy. Richard Junior."

"Rick."

"And when he lost him too, it stirred up the emotional shit that's been festering and eating him up inside for the last decade."

Pete struggled to bridge the leap in logic. And years.

"Once I realized who'd been calling me, I started doing some digging," Chuck said. "I wanted to know where Brown was and what he'd been up to. And what might have happened to wake the sleeping beast. I found that article. Since Dayton's only a few hours from Pittsburgh, I pulled up the *Post-Gazette* too and read about the shootings in your area. It's him, Petey. He's gunning for you. And I bet he already has a plane ticket for Hawaii to come after me next."

Pete wanted to believe his old partner was certifiable. But it all made a horrible kind of sense. Pete tried to age the picture of Moreno's father in his head. Tried to see details of the face beyond the beard. But all he kept seeing was a generic older man.

With a beard. Maybe it wasn't only the girl's lips that moved when lies were told.

"Hey, Chuck, did Richard Senior have any other kids? A daughter, perhaps?"

"Not that I'm aware of. But while I was digging around, I stumbled across one other thing you need to know. Richard Brown's not going by that name anymore."

Pete's brain chilled. "Hector Livingston." And he'd just kicked him free.

"Livingston?" Chuck sounded puzzled. "No. Webber. Gabriel Webber."

"Get in."

Zoe didn't move. Didn't dare to. The cold metal of the gun barrel was pressing into the soft flesh under her jaw. The big hand with nails stained black around the cuticles still palmed the seat back, pinning her arm. Bud Kramer's dead body sprawled inside her truck. She didn't dare turn to see who the hand belonged to. The voice was familiar though.

"I can't," she said, trying not to move her jaw. "You've got my arm stuck."

He removed his hand. Stepped back. But kept the gun fatally close to her face. "Get in," he repeated.

She slid her arm free. Swallowed. And turned to face the man who had shot Earl. And Curtis and Yancy. The man who had killed Barry Dickson and Jason Dyer. "Gabe?"

The mechanic smiled like the old friend she'd thought he was. "Hi, Zoe. Now don't make me say it again. Get in."

The bone-chilling rain soaked her shirt and her hair. The breeze didn't help. Gabe was drenched too, and shivering. Zoe forced her gaze from the rifle muzzle to his finger on the trigger. "You don't need to point that at me." She raised both hands to shoulder height, palms facing him. Then aimed one thumb toward the truck cab. "Bud's in there."

"You think I don't know? I put him there. Damned fool caught me borrowing his quad again." Gabe tipped his head toward the tarped load in the pickup's bed. "I didn't wanna kill him. He wasn't part of this. Drag him out. Won't hurt him none to get wet."

"Drag him?" Zoe risked looking away from Gabe to study the corpse. Bud had to weigh close to two hundred pounds. "I don't think I can."

"You muscle those horses around, don't you? You're strong."

She could argue, but rationalizing with a madman seemed counterproductive. Reaching into the cab, she grabbed Bud's belt and a handful of shirt. And heaved. Perhaps if she'd had leather seats, she might have been able to slide him, but her woven seat covers only provided more resistance. She tried again, grunting loudly for Gabe's benefit. Still nothing. She straightened and faced the rifle. "Maybe if you helped?"

"You mean put down the gun? I don't think so."

Somewhere in the distance, over the roar of the rain on the truck's roof and hood, another sound caught Zoe's ear. The low rumble of an engine. Not a car or truck. Perhaps a plane. No. A helicopter. She hoped Gabe didn't hear it too. Perhaps help was coming. Out in the open like this, they'd be spotted easily. "I'll try one more time," she said. Distract and delay.

But Gabe looked skyward. "Gawddamn cops. Probably out looking for you already." He gestured with the gun. "Get in. Just shove him out of the way to make room."

She glanced toward the rear of the truck. Earl. Right now he was being sheltered, somewhat at least, by the dropped tailgate. If she said nothing and let Gabe take her somewhere else, she'd be driving away Earl's protection. Not to mention leaving her partner alone on a desolate back road with a gunshot wound. Already shocky, the chill of the icy rain would kill him for sure.

"My partner's hurt." She left out the part about Gabe being responsible. "I was about to get a blanket for him from behind this seat. Let me run it back to him before we go."

Gabe's expression was unreadable. For a moment Zoe thought he might be considering her request. "I understand," he said. "You don't want your friend to suffer." He hefted the rifle. "I can put an end to that right now."

"No, no. That's okay. I'm sure he'll be fine." Besides, she'd left Earl her phone.

"Good." Gabe nudged her with the gun. "Ain't saying it again."

"Yeah. 'Get in.'" She grabbed the steering wheel and climbed inside. Gabe slammed the door closed, pinning her between it and Bud Kramer's ass. Never again would she complain about being crowded with three—or even four—*living* people in the truck with her.

Gabe kept the rifle aimed at her through the windshield as he crossed in front of the truck. Too late she thought she should have started it, shifted into drive, and gunned the thing. But that reminded her...

When Gabe opened the passenger door and started wrestling with Bud's torso, Zoe said, "I didn't think my truck would start. You said you hadn't gotten around to fixing it yet."

Gabe tugged and heaved, leveraging the corpse into a limp seated position before climbing in. "I lied." He pulled the door closed, braced Bud upright with one shoulder, and nestled the rifle, still pointing the business end at Zoe, in his lap. "Let's take it for a test drive."

The engine turned over on the first try. Zoe decided thanks for a job well done was not in order.

Gabe reached across the dead man's legs and forced the transfer case shifter into four-wheel drive. "Go around the ambulance and then follow the road into the woods," he ordered, stealing a glance out the window.

Zoe did too, hoping to see a helicopter sailing over the trees toward them. But all she could make out through the rain-streaked windshield were leaden gray clouds sagging closer and closer to the ground.

She dropped the gearshift into drive and eased forward, saying a prayer that Earl would be able to forgive her for leaving him. And that he would live long enough to hate her for it.

"Do you mean to tell me," Baronick asked as he wheeled into Webber's driveway, "you've seen this guy at Kramer's place and never made the connection?"

Pete gripped the passenger door handle, ready to dive out the moment the car came to a stop. "He doesn't look the same. He used to have a beard and a full head of dark hair. Now he's clean shaven, and what hair he has is white." But Baronick's question gnawed at him.

Pete *should* have recognized the man whose son he'd killed. "Besides, now that I think about it, he always managed to find a good reason to excuse himself when I showed up."

"You have that effect on a lot of people."

Smartass. "Let's go."

Baronick caught his arm. "Backup will be here in two minutes with a search warrant."

Pete jerked free. "Then you stay here and wait for them." He bailed from the unmarked County car, tugging his ball cup lower over his eyes, shielding them from the steady rain. With one deft move, he released his Glock from the holster. Behind him, the detective grumbled as he stepped out.

Grime coated the garage windows. Pete squinted and could tell the garage held no vehicle, but an impressive array of tools and red tool chests lined the perimeter.

"You take the back," he said.

"Bullshit. We should wait for backup. Not to mention the warrant."

"I'm not letting this guy get away again."

"So you're gonna bust in there illegally and lose him later on a technicality?"

Baronick's words stopped Pete. Damn it. He hated when the young detective was right.

"Besides." Baronick rapped a knuckle on the dirty window. "Doesn't look like he's home anyhow."

"Fine. We wait."

Baronick studied Pete for a moment. "I suppose you mean wait right here. As opposed to inside my vehicle. Where it's dry."

The detective had traded in his slicker for a trench coat, which made him look more like a mobster than a county cop, but the matching fedora's small brim provided little protection from the deluge. "You want to wait in the car," Pete told him, "go right ahead."

Baronick sighed and flattened against the garage door, seeking the minuscule shelter of the door frame. "That's okay. I'm good."

Pete took in the house—small and boxy with no landscaping, unless you counted the overgrown weeds sprouting around the cinderblock foundation.

Sided in yellow aluminum bearing patches of mold, the place clearly hadn't been lavished with upkeep.

"I still feel like I'm missing something," Baronick said. "I get that this guy wants your blood. But is he the same one who's been ambushing the others? Or are these two separate cases?"

Pete had been trying to figure it out too. He wasn't buying the option of Gabe Webber not being connected to the shootings. "They're tied together. Somehow."

The wail of approaching sirens sliced through the slushy roar of the rain. Baronick tugged his trench coat's collar closer around his neck. "Lucy Livingston dated Gabe Webber's son. There's a connection for you. Do you think Hector and Gabe joined forces to wipe out all their perceived enemies in one big murder spree?"

"Murder spree?"

Baronick shrugged. "Murder spree. Shooting rampage. Call it what you will. Wearing a uniform has gotten to be friggin' dangerous around here. Glad I'm in plainclothes."

Which brought Pete back to a subject he'd been afraid to think about. Zoe. She had yet to call him back.

He pulled out his phone. No missed calls, messages, or texts. Before he could call her number, a parade of squealing police vehicles appeared around the bend in the road.

Baronick slapped Pete's back. "She'll be fine."

He eyed the detective and knew from his creased brow Baronick was trying to convince himself as much as Pete.

Zoe kept an eye on the rearview mirror as she pulled forward. Earl was sprawled flat in the middle of the road. No protection from the cold rain or the swirling winds. Bleeding, shocky, and holding on to one lone bag of IV fluids.

And her phone. Please, God, let him be able to call for help on the phone.

Gabe nudged her leg with the rifle muzzle. "If you're so worried about your partner suffering, we can go back and I'll put an end to it."

She considered calling his bluff. Hoping the helicopter they'd heard put in an appearance. Except she knew it was no bluff.

Barry, Curtis, Yancy, and Jason were evidence the man wasn't playing games. No, as much as she hated abandoning Earl, the best she could do for him was to take this killer far away.

The Chevy rocked and bounced as she drove off the road and around Medic Two. The ambulance's emergency lights continued to flash. EOC would be trying to contact her and Earl, wondering why they hadn't reported in. With everything that had happened in recent days, the dispatcher wouldn't wait long to send help.

Earl would be okay. He had to be okay.

In fact, Pete and every other law enforcement officer in the tri-state area might be bearing down on them right now.

She just had to stay alive long enough for help to arrive.

The Chevy lurched again as she steered it back onto the road. Bud Kramer's body, still not in rigor, moved like a two-hundred-pound water balloon and shifted, pinning her against the door. Her foot slipped from the gas pedal and, for a moment, the pickup slowed to a near stop.

Gabe swore, grabbed a handful of Bud's collar, and dragged the corpse off her.

If anyone had told Zoe she'd spend an evening driving around in her pickup with a killer and a dead guy, she'd have told them they were nuts. Now she didn't know whether to laugh, cry, or scream over the absurdity of it.

"You ever seen that movie?" Gabe asked.

"Movie?" Absurdity appeared to be reaching an even higher—or lower—level. Now they were going to discuss cinema? "What movie?"

"The one where these guys are dragging their dead boss all over the place, acting like he's still alive." Gabe snapped his fingers. "*Weekend at Bernie's*. That's it."

"Sorry. Can't say that I've seen it."

Gabe grunted. "Too bad. It's funny. This really reminds me of it." He patted Bud's back. "Right, Boss?" Leaning forward, Gabe looked at Zoe. "I'd tell you to look it up on Netflix, but you ain't gonna be around long enough."

Her shoulders tightened.

The woods engulfed them in shadows and she reached for the light switch.

"Leave 'em off. For now."

"Do you want me to drive into a tree?"

"You can see good enough to stay on the road. I'll let you know when you can turn 'em on."

Zoe brought both hands back to the wheel. "Where are we going?"

"Just drive. I'll tell you when you need to turn."

She continued down the narrow country road, hoping she'd meet another car coming the other way. But what would that accomplish? If she tried anything to attract attention, she'd be putting an innocent stranger's life in danger.

"Why are you doing this?" she asked. "What have any of us done to you?"

"Nothing," he said simply.

"Then why?"

She felt his gaze on her, but he didn't speak for several long moments. Finally, he said, "This has been a long time coming. I've thought about it and dreamed about it for over ten years now."

"Ten years?"

"More like eleven. That's how long my boy's been gone."

Zoe struggled to think back eleven years. What had happened eleven years ago?

Gabe must have guessed what she was wondering. "Oh, you had nothing to do with it."

"One of the others then? Barry? Yancy?"

Gabe blew a disgusted burst of air through his lips. "Hell no. They was just part of my plan."

Something he'd mentioned earlier leapt to her mind. "You said before that Bud wasn't part of this. What did you mean?"

In the dim twilight, she sensed more than saw Gabe shaking his head. "He wasn't supposed to be part of it. My plan. And the others?" He chuckled, a low vicious laugh that chilled every nerve in Zoe's body. "I guess you could call them necessary collateral damage. If everyone thought random firemen and ambulance attendants and such was being killed, they'd never figure out who I was when I kill the man I'm really after."

Zoe glanced across Bud at Gabe and was met with a smile as evil as the laugh. "I still don't understand."

"Good. Then my plan is working. Now keep your eyes on the road. I need you alive. For now. But—" He nudged her again with the gun. "You can be injured and still be bait."

TWENTY-NINE

Pete sat at a rickety desk in Gabriel Webber's living room, staring at a collection of news clippings when Baronick called out, "I found something."

"So did I," Pete said, more to himself than to the detective or the other officers crawling through the house.

"Do you want to see this?" Baronick asked from the bedroom.

Pete read one of the articles, trying to tamp down the urge to toss his dinner. "What is it?"

The detective appeared in the doorway, a triumphant grin on his face. "Burner phones. Three of them, still in their packaging. What have you got there?"

Pete didn't reply, but held one of the yellowed clippings up between his gloved fingers.

Baronick took it and read it out loud, although Pete already knew what it said. "Vance Township hires new chief of police. Township board of supervisors voted unanimously Monday night to hire Sergeant Peter Adams of the Pittsburgh Bureau of Police to replace the retiring Chief Warren Froats." The detective looked up from the article and met Pete's gaze. "Holy shit."

Pete shuffled through the collection. "And that's not the oldest one. This is." He handed over a clipping he couldn't stomach reading. The news brief from the *Pittsburgh Post-Gazette* told of a nighttime shooting in the Mexican War Streets.

Officers Adams and Delano faced down two armed drug suspects. Delano had been taken to Allegheny General. Both drug suspects had been killed in the gunfight.

One of them was Donald Moreno, son of Richard Brown.

Who now called himself Gabriel Webber.

Baronick wisely read the entire account in silence. When he finished, he handed it back to Pete. "What about the rest of those?"

Pete let the stack drop from his fingers onto the desk. "He must have saved every single thing written about me in the last eleven years. Every arrest. Every commendation. Every interview. Every goddamned thing."

One of the county officers appeared at the entrance to a hallway. "Excuse me. Sir?"

"What?" both Pete and Baronick said at once.

The wide-eyed officer looked from one to the other as if afraid to speak to either of them.

"What is it?" Pete demanded.

"We found a gun case under the bed in the spare bedroom. One of those hard-shelled jobs with the foam egg-carton interior? It's empty, but from the shape of the cut-out, it could very likely have contained a thirty-ought-six with a scope."

Pete's cell phone rang before he could comment on the find. Caller ID showed his station's number. "Yeah, Nancy, what is it?"

"It's me, Pete," Sylvia replied.

He didn't like the strained sound of her voice one bit. "Okay."

He could hear the moist intake of Sylvia's breath. "EOC just contacted me. They've been trying to reach Medic Two with no luck and were about to request backup when they received a phone call from Earl Kolter. He's been shot. And Gabe Webber has Zoe."

The nagging fear that had been gnawing at Pete's gut detonated inside his head. "Where? How long ago? How bad is Earl hurt?" The questions poured from him. All but the one he really wanted to ask. *Was Zoe okay?*

"They're Life Flighting Earl to Pittsburgh right now. Reports are sketchy, but he's lost a lot of blood and is suffering hypothermia on top of shock. As I understand it, Webber lured them into another of his ambush scenarios, shot Earl, and forced Zoe to drive him—Webber, I mean—out of there. In her truck. And Pete...there's more."

Pete closed his eyes. "Great. What?"

"Bud Kramer's dead."

Pete's eyes flew open, and he met Baronick's questioning gaze. "Kramer's dead?"

"Webber used Bud's body to lure Earl and Zoe out of the ambulance."

"Did Earl give any indication of where Webber was taking her?"

"He reported that the last he saw they were headed north on Ridge Road. The State Police helo is already searching the area, but now that it's dark out, he could be holed up with her anywhere."

Pete was on his feet. Baronick already stood at the front door, once again wearing his trench coat and holding Pete's slicker and ball cap. "I'm heading in that direction. I don't care what hole he's dragged Zoe into. I'm going to flush them out."

"Pete." Sylvia's plaintive voice kept him from hanging up. "I'm afraid that's exactly what he wants you to do."

He paused. "If I'm what that bastard wants, he can have me." He ended the call, shoved the phone in his pocket, and snatched his rain slicker from Baronick on his way past. "What he *can't* have," Pete said under his breath, "is my girl."

As a kid, Zoe had heard tales about the little coal mining town of Reed's Grove, situated at the intersection of two lightly traveled country roads. Even in its heyday, the village had only boasted a dozen houses, a company store, and a one-room schoolhouse. The houses and store had vanished before Zoe was born. She vaguely remembered someone turning the school into an antique shop, but the short-lived venture failed after a year or two. Nature had done its best to reclaim the structure, cocooning it in ivy and brambles as the paint peeled off, leaving gray wood bare to the elements.

Until this night, Zoe had thought the schoolhouse no longer stood. She rarely drove either of the roads, and even when she did, the building had become invisible unless you looked hard enough.

Apparently Gabe had.

He ordered her to pull the truck off the road against her protests about not being able to see and not wanting to get stuck in mud. He assured her the ground would hold the Chevy.

As she cut the wheel in the direction he indicated, her headlights revealed a path chopped through the thicket, wide enough for a smaller vehicle. Vines and branches screeched against the paint, slapped the windshield, and reached for her through the shattered driver's window.

Gabe forced the passenger door open. The dome light illuminated Bud's corpse and the blue tint to his skin. It also shined on the rifle still clutched in Gabe's hands.

He motioned with it. "Get out."

Saplings and underbrush attempted to hold her captive. She managed to muscle the door open just enough to slide out. Gabe clearly wasn't worried that she would bolt.

Other than the truck's interior light, there wasn't as much as a star to show her a potential escape route. The wind had died down—or perhaps it couldn't cut through the dense growth—but the cold autumn rain pattered on the leaves around and above her. Those same wet leaves slapped her face and her arms—already cold and soaked from driving with a broken window—when she moved toward the back of the truck and slammed the door.

With the dome light doused, the total darkness startled over her, and she froze in place. She patted her leg, feeling for the penlight in her cargo pants pocket, but a larger beam of light appeared from behind the pickup.

Gabe shone the flashlight directly in Zoe's face, blinding her. She turned away and raised a hand to shield her eyes.

"This way," he said. "Move."

Still blinking at spots even after he aimed the light away from her, she slid along the wet truck bed. Rain-soaked brambles clawed her cheek, and she held up both arms, swatting away the grabby undergrowth.

He waited for her behind the truck and swung the light toward a spot in the vines. Closer inspection revealed a gap. He waved her toward it. "You first."

He shone the light on the path ahead of her, and she could see where the bushes and vines had been cut, clearing the way. Someone—Gabe—had been out here before and had prepared this escape plan.

Just like he'd planned the ambushes and his previous getaways. For a moment, Zoe imagined being shot here and left to die. No one would find her. She'd rot away to bones.

Nature would reclaim her DNA the way it had reclaimed the village of Reed's Grove and its buildings.

No. Earl would have called for help by now. Or the EOC would have sent someone to find them when they didn't radio in. Pete was looking for her. Every cop within a hundred miles was looking for her.

The path ended at the front door of the old schoolhouse.

"Go on. It's not locked."

She grasped the pitted latch. It grated and released. The door swung open with a minimal groan and scrape.

"Go on," he repeated, ramming the rifle into her back. "Get inside."

She staggered into the dark building, hoping the floorboards would hold her. In the blackness above her head, something fluttered. Pigeons? Or bats?

Pigeons, she lied to herself. Definitely pigeons.

"Stop. Don't move." Gabe clomped past her. The beam of his flashlight revealed a table with what appeared to be a lamp of some sort.

Drenched and shivering, Zoe sneaked a glance back at the door. She could lunge for it. Into the rain and the dark and the jungle-like brush. If she was very lucky, she might make it back to her truck without having a bramble snag an ankle and trip her.

If she wasn't lucky, Gabe would blow a hole in her before she crossed the threshold.

Stay alive. Give Pete a chance to find you.

One-handed, Gabe struck a match and set the flame to the mantle of a kerosene camp lantern. As the lamp flickered and the room brightened, Zoe could see his other hand holding firm to the rifle aimed at her.

No, this was definitely not the time to make a run for it.

Gabe fumbled with a small black box lying next to the lamp. It clicked and then produced a familiar burst of static. A handheld police radio. "Just a little easy listening to pass the time."

She rubbed her arms, trying to coax some warmth into them. Her clothes clung to her, leaching away body heat. She pinched the front of her shirt, peeling it away, but the air that rushed in was colder still.

In the flickering lantern light, she scanned the space, hoping to spot a potbellied stove like the one she'd seen in a restored one-room schoolhouse at a local historic village. But whoever had converted this building into an antique shop had removed the primitive heat source, replacing it with a now useless electric version.

Gabe dragged a single chair from the shadows. "You might as well sit down. We're gonna be here a while."

For a fleeting moment, Zoe thought he was offering the chair to her, but the rifle aimed her way contradicted such an invitation. She looked around for another seat but could only make out grimy shelves edging the room.

Gabe chuckled. "Pull up a piece of floor. You can sit or lay down and take a nap. I really don't care."

The wood beneath her feet was strewn with dirt, bird droppings, and a few feathers. Lie down and take a nap? Not a chance. Moving slowly and deliberately to avoid any mistaken notion she was trying to escape, she eased over to one wall and used her boot to scrape a spot clear of debris. Figuring that was as good as it was gonna get, she sunk onto the floor, using the wall as a backrest.

"Don't suppose you have a blanket around here," she said through chattering teeth.

"If I did, I'd use it myself." Gabe tucked the rifle into the crook of his elbow, extracted something from his pocket, and approached her. Kneeling, he rammed her ankles together and bound them with what she now saw was a zip tie. "Hold out your wrists."

She hesitated.

He poked her shoulder with the rifle. "Either give me your wrists or I'll come up with another way to immobilize your arms."

In an instant, she visualized knocking the gun aside. He was close enough. She could do it.

The imagined scenario continued with him slamming her across the face with the gun's butt and shooting her anyway.

She extended her arms, hands clasped. He slipped another zip tie around her wrists and yanked it tight. She winced as the thin nylon band bit into her flesh. "I still don't know why I'm here. What is it you want from me?"

He stood and ambled back to the chair. "Nothing." Straddling it, he used the back to support his arms and the rifle. "Or at least nothing more than I've already got."

"I don't understand."

"You don't have to." He shifted his weight to one hip and dug in his pants' back pocket.

Zoe drew her knees in. Clearly Gabe wasn't going to volunteer any more information. But he'd already given her some. His plan. Eleven years since his son had died. "You said Yancy and Barry and the rest were necessary..."

"Collateral damage. Necessary collateral damage." Gabe sounded pleased with the phrase he'd substituted for murder.

She tried to fight off the chill and to remember his exact words. "They were supposed to appear random, part of your plan, so no one would suspect it was you when you killed the man you were after."

He didn't reply, but withdrew a small item from his pocket. With the lantern behind him, she couldn't see what he held. Nor could she see his face.

She closed her eyes, replaying the events of the last few days—and last few hours—over again in her mind. And then it clicked. Bait. They had all been bait. Gabe had said she too was *bait*.

For one man.

She opened her eyes again, trying to pierce the darkness to make out Gabe's expression. "Oh my God," she said. "You're after Pete."

Gabe grunted. "I figured Adams would show up at one of those calls sooner than he did."

The rifle never wavered. And while Zoe was soaked to the bone and freezing, her mouth was as dry as the Mojave Desert.

"But I had to get outta there quick so I never got a shot at him like I'd hoped. I knew eventually though..." Gabe shouldered the gun and mimed firing it at the door, complete with sound effects. Then he lowered it to the back of the chair with the muzzle aimed again at Zoe. "It was getting tough. Too many cops crawling all over the place. But then—" He snapped his fingers. "You came into the garage this afternoon to pick up the ambulance. And you said you were on duty tonight. And I knew. This was my one big chance. If I got *you*, I knew I'd get Adams."

"But why? What did Pete ever do to you for you to want to...?" She couldn't say the words.

For a long moment, Gabe didn't speak. And in the darkness, she couldn't read his face.

Finally, he said, "Do you have any idea what it's like to lose a child?"

Now it was Zoe's turn to fall silent. She thought of nearly losing Allison last winter, but as close as she felt to Rose's daughter, Allison wasn't Zoe's child.

"Well, do you?"

"No."

His heavy breathing carried across the space between them. "Adams took what was dearest to me in all this world. Now I have nothing. I intend to leave him with nothing too."

Zoe lowered her head, blocking out the glow of the lantern...the flame glinting off the gun barrel. If only she could as easily block out the thoughts roaring through her mind. She'd spent the last—how many?—hours praying for Pete to find her. Come charging to her rescue. Only now she knew that was precisely what Gabe wanted. This abandoned one-room schoolhouse in this graveyard of a town wasn't meant to be a shelter from the rain.

It was meant to be a trap. She needed to somehow warn Pete to stay away.

"Hey," Gabe called to her. "Heads up."

She looked up in time to see him toss something to her. Instinctively, she reached out and caught it in her bound hands. A cheap flip phone. That's what he'd dug from his pocket.

"Adams' number is the only one saved on there. Call it. Tell him where you are. And tell him to come alone. I'll know if he doesn't." He tipped his head toward the police radio on the table. "But you mention one word about who I am and I'll shoot."

Zoe stared at the phone. Gabe wanted her to lure Pete in so he could murder him. "You kill me and you'll *never* get him here."

"Oh, I won't kill you. But a well-placed bullet would make you pray for death. I'm a pretty good shot, in case you haven't noticed. From this distance, I could blow your fingers off, one at a time. No sweat."

She considered his words and knew he'd do it too. She opened the phone.

"No tricks. You try anything clever and he'll find you in pieces when he does get here."

Zoe didn't much care. Gabe wouldn't leave her alive afterwards anyway. Not if he was delusional enough to believe he could still get away. But she might be able to do something—she had no clue what— to help Pete when he showed up. If she hoped to save him, she'd need to be in one piece.

"Make the call."

She swallowed hard. Not needing to pull up the phone's lone saved contact, she keyed in Pete's number from memory.

THIRTY

The hilltop along Ridge Road was ablaze with emergency lighting. The earlier downpour had settled into a steady drizzle as the temperatures continued to drop. Pete watched a flatbed tow truck—not one of Kramer's this time—winch Medic Two up its steep incline. They'd blocked off the road until the crime scene techs could go over every square foot, but Pete knew they wouldn't find squat. Not with this weather. And not with someone as meticulous as Gabe Webber.

Or Richard Brown.

Baronick in his gangster trench coat and fedora ambled over after speaking with one of the State Troopers. "This would be the perfect night for some asshole to hold up a bank. As long as the heist took place anywhere else but Monongahela County. I think every cop within a hundred miles is crawling the streets and back roads of Vance Township right now."

And it wasn't enough.

Pete tipped his face toward the night sky and let the rain pelt him. He wanted to bellow, but instead he growled it through clenched teeth. "You want me? Well, here I am."

His cell phone rang. He snatched it, hoping somehow his wish had been answered. But the screen lit up with *Station*.

"I thought you'd want to know." Sylvia's voice was somber. "They're trying to stabilize Earl before sending him into surgery. It doesn't look good."

"Anything from Zoe?"

"If there was, I'd have called you."

Pete knew that. But he had to ask. Had to hope.

A man who wanted him dead had Zoe. A man who had already killed at least three times. Why? If Webber—or Brown or whatever the hell his name was—wanted Pete, why kill a paramedic and a junior firefighter?

A hand closed around his wrist. He flinched.

"Easy, big fella." Baronick took Pete's phone from him. A phone he'd forgotten he was holding and was about to drop into the wet grass at their feet. The detective moved in closer and in a low, determined voice said, "We're going to get her back. And we're going to nail this asshole."

In the off-color glow of emergency lighting, Pete met Baronick's steely eyes. "You're damned right we are."

The phone, still in Baronick's hand, rang again. They looked down at the detective's open palm.

The number on the screen wasn't a familiar one. Baronick shoved the phone at Pete, while pulling his own from his coat pocket. "I'll trace it."

Pete gave a nod and answered.

"Pete?" Zoe's voice was deeper than usual.

Relief weakened his knees. "Are you okay?"

"I'm not hurt."

Pete read the unspoken "yet" between her words. "Are you with Gabe Webber?"

Her breath resonated in his ear. "Yeah. Listen. I'm in the old schoolhouse in Reed's Grove. Do you know it?"

"Yes."

"Come alone. Completely alone. If you bring anyone else with you..." She trailed off and for a moment, Pete thought he'd dropped the call.

"Zoe?"

"He'll know if you have anyone with you." Her voice had risen an octave.

"I understand."

Pete heard a man's voice in the background—Webber saying something to Zoe. Then she relayed the orders. "And he says keep the helicopter away. If you try anything..." The voice barked something else to her. A ragged inhalation. "He says for every inkling he gets that you're bringing in other cops, he'll put a bullet into me."

This time Pete could make out Webber's words. *"Now hang up."*

Before Zoe did as ordered, she managed a soft, high-pitched, "I love you."

"I love you too." But the line had gone dead. "Zoe? *Zoe?*" He glared at the screen. Cranked his arm back to hurl the damned phone into the night.

Baronick caught his wrist and rescued the thing a second time. "I have a pretty good idea where they are."

"I *know* where they are. The Reed's Grove School."

Baronick again reached for his phone. "I'll have an army there in two minutes."

"No. She said no one else but me."

"Of course she did. He told her to say that. They never want backup. Don't you watch television?"

Baronick's humor failed to hit its mark. "She said he'd know. He's been at least one step ahead of us the entire time. He wants *me*. This is between the two of us and no one else. But..." Pete might not watch cop TV shows, but he *was* a fan of old movies, and a line from a classic came to him. "When it's done, if I'm dead, kill him."

It took a moment to register, but a smile crept across the detective's face. "Love to...*Butch.*"

Any other night, the soft hiss of rain on the roof and the steady *splat, splat* on the floor beneath a half dozen leaks would have lulled Zoe asleep. She had no idea what time it was, but the radio had grown quiet, with only occasional bursts of static or transmissions from different departments around Monongahela and surrounding counties. The lack of on-air activity meant nothing. Pete would know they were being monitored. Police communications regarding this case would have been transferred to a frequency not available on commercially purchased scanners. Or they'd use cell phones.

Gabe would likely know that.

Zoe's wet clothes clung to her skin like a sheen of ice. She'd lived all of her life in Pennsylvania and had worked outdoors through every brutal winter, but she couldn't remember ever being this cold before.

Forcing her mind to focus on something—anything—besides the falling temperatures and desperately wanting a warm blanket or coat to wrap up in, she looked around the dilapidated building for something she might be able to use once Pete showed up. She leaned her cheek against her bound hands, appearing, she hoped, to be simply resting. In truth, she shielded her eyes from the lantern and allowed her pupils to adjust to the darkness.

About all she could make out was the shadowed outline of a display case near the front door. The windows had been boarded up, but glass shards glinted on the floor beneath them. One useless ceiling light dangled precariously from a patch of plaster, which appeared ready to drop at any moment.

"What's taking him so long?" Gabe asked.

Zoe turned toward his voice and squinted into the lantern's light. "Maybe he got stuck in the mud." What she hoped was Pete had every cop in Pennsylvania, West Virginia, and Ohio surrounding the place. *Come alone.* Surely he wouldn't give into that foolish demand.

Most folks drove through Reed's Grove without realizing a town had once existed. It had been long gone before Pete moved to Vance Township, and his only knowledge of the place was anecdotal. He and Baronick had tried to locate intel on the property, but the address drew a blank on GPS, and Google Maps produced only a pin on a stretch of country road. Google Earth showed a photo of woods. County was working on digging up information from the assessor's office and from the power company, but he—and Zoe—didn't have time to wait on a detailed report.

Had any of Pete's men been in his situation, he'd have insisted on calling in SERT, Monongahela County's Special Emergency Response Team with all their robots and surveillance equipment. Baronick had taken his best shot at convincing him to put out the call. However, this wasn't one of Pete's men walking into a trap. He knew what he was doing was foolhardy. But Richard Brown—Gabe Webber—had Zoe, and her words kept ringing in Pete's ears.

"For every inkling he gets that you're bringing in other cops, he'll put a bullet into me."

No. In spite of Baronick's insistence that Pete go in with a TAC team, he would face the beast alone.

However, Pete *had* accepted Baronick's offer of a few of County's toys.

Pete slowed. The last thing he wanted to do was drive past the school, alerting Brown to his arrival. Bad enough he was already expecting him. Pete's element of surprise was minimal at best. Preferring to err on the side of caution, he pulled off the road, shut off his lights, and parked well shy of where he recalled the schoolhouse to be.

Once he cut the engine, the only sound was the steady rush of rain on the roof and windshield. Darkness enveloped him. No streetlights. No moon or stars. No nearby houses.

He stepped out into the weeds edging the road and lifted the borrowed FLIR thermal vision scope to his eye. Scanning the underbrush in case Brown planned an ambush, Pete spotted a bright image deep in the thicket. Not a man. A deer.

Damn. He needed to get one of these things. Provided he survived the night.

No two-legged hot-spots appeared in the area. Pete tucked the device into a pocket, zipped his rain jacket, and pulled the hood over his ball cap.

For a moment he considered the risks of being spotted if he used his flashlight. Then he considered the likelihood of falling if he stumbled around in the dark. He'd be a sitting duck and no help to Zoe if he had a broken leg.

His cell phone vibrated in his pocket. Baronick's name lit up the screen. Pete answered with a biting, "What?"

"That button cam doesn't do a damned bit of good if you have it covered by your coat."

"It won't do any good if it shorts out in the rain either."

"It isn't gonna short out."

Pete tugged his cap lower over his eyes. "No, but *I* might. I'll unzip my jacket once I get there." He hit "end" and started slogging down the road.

With the light aimed at the ground, he was careful to avoid the deep potholes in the unmaintained asphalt. At the same time, he kept watch on the wall of weeds and saplings to his left, hoping to spot a clue to indicate he was getting close.

Fifteen minutes later, he feared he'd badly misjudged his location and that of the old village. Had he passed the schoolhouse, either walking or in his vehicle, without seeing it? Or had he stopped miles too soon?

He was debating turning back when his flashlight reflected off something other than a discarded beer can. He raised the beam. A Pennsylvania license plate. Attached to a pickup. A Chevy.

Zoe's Chevy.

Pete clicked off the light and let the *eureka* rush of having found the place ebb into the necessity to be calm. Focused. Determined.

He extricated the FLIR scope and ran a hand over his chest, fingering his body armor, the button cam, and a few other surprises. Raising the thermal imaging device to his eye, he did a slow canvass.

There. Ahead of him, two large heat signatures and not wildlife this time. Brown and Zoe.

"I'm here," Pete whispered, mostly to himself. "Let's do this."

THIRTY-ONE

The nylon bands binding Zoe's wrists sliced into her skin the more she tried to work them...stretch them. There was no give. She remained as tightly trussed as the first moment Gabe had put the zip ties on her.

Her captor hadn't budged or spoken in what felt like a long time. Without her phone, she had no idea how long it had actually been. Had he fallen asleep?

She wasn't putting money on that.

Outside the wind kicked up, whistling through the gaps in the schoolhouse's walls.

Branches and leaves scraped against the outside of the building, tapping and knocking. The police radio offered nothing in the way of information.

Where was Pete?

Zoe imagined she heard a twig snap. A footstep? Impossible to tell with the noises provided by the weather.

But Gabe must have heard, or thought he heard, something too. Keeping the gun aimed at the door, he reached back and extinguished the lantern's flame.

She'd only thought it was dark before. Now she couldn't even make out the shapes of the counter, the ceiling fixture, or Gabe and his rifle.

The cell phone she'd used to call Pete rang, startling her. She'd forgotten she'd let it drop at her side. Now it glowed, a bright beacon in the blackness.

"Answer it," Gabe said.

She had to twist to reach for the phone. Her fingers were so numb with cold she struggled to hold on to it and thumb it open. "Hello?"

"Are you all right?" Pete said.

Hell no, I'm not all right. I'm freezing and terrified and tied up with a madman in a pigeon- and bat-infested dump that's ready to collapse on my head, she thought. Instead, she replied, "I'm fine."

"Good." For a moment, Pete was quiet. Then, in a low voice, he said, "Put him on."

She extended the phone into the darkness. "He wants to talk to you."

"Uh-uh."

Zoe heard the chair creak. A scrape against the floor.

"Tell him if he wants to talk, he needs to come in here."

She put the phone back to her ear. "He says—"

"I heard him. Put me on speaker."

Crap. Did this cheap phone even have the speaker feature? She looked at it. Pushed a button. Then another. Found it. "Okay."

"Brown?" Pete's voice boomed. "I know that's you. And I know what this is all about."

Who on earth was *Brown*? Pete had asked her if it was Gabe Webber who held her, and she'd told him yes.

Gabe swore. Footsteps on the creaking floor told Zoe he was moving across the room. Away from her.

"If you know, I gather your friends all know too," Gabe said.

"They do."

"Doesn't really matter anymore." Glass crunched underfoot. He was near the display case. "You still need to come in here if you want your girl."

"That's not how this works." Pete's voice was steady, but deadly. "You send her out first. Then I come in."

"Ha. You think I'm an idiot? No way. You come in, and maybe I'll let her go."

"No!" The word burst from Zoe before she could think.

"Shut up," Gabe snarled.

"Don't come in. It's a trap!" He was going to shoot her anyway. She might be able to save Pete if Gabe did it now.

She sensed more than saw movement from the area she knew Gabe to be. "I told you to shut up."

Instinctively, she dived to her right.

And the air around her exploded.

* * *

Standing next to a tree in front of the structure, Pete had the FLIR scope to his eye when Brown moved, swinging what had to be a rifle toward Zoe's seated form.

Pete dropped the scope and yanked his Glock from his holster. He pounded toward the door.

Inside, the crack of a rifle shattered the near-silence.

Pete lowered his head and led with his shoulder, throwing everything he had dead center. The rotted wood splintered, yielded with less resistance than he'd expected. But the hinge and latch held. His momentum carried him through the hole in the door. But the surviving boards tripped him. He slammed to the floor. The impact sent a searing jolt of pain through his shoulder. And jarred the Glock from his hand. The weapon hit the floor with a thunk and skated away in the dark.

From somewhere very close, Zoe screamed. Glass crashed. Movement. A shadow closing in. Fast. Pete rolled, but it felt like trying to turn over while encased in sludge. He sensed something coming down at his head. Tried to raise an arm. The glancing blow discharged a burst of fireworks inside his head. Followed by...nothing.

Pete had no idea if he'd been unconscious for a minute or a day. But when he opened his eyes—or thought he was opening his eyes—the darkness had been replaced by faint, flickering light.

"Pete!" Zoe's hysterical cry echoed inside his skull, sending icy sharp slivers into his brain.

He groaned. Flopped over onto his back. A move he instantly regretted. His head wasn't the only body part that hurt like hell. He blinked and the fog in front of his eyes cleared. A little. Above him, an ancient glass globe swam into view. He blinked again. It was a light fixture, dirty and gray. Beyond, a beadboard ceiling with gaping black holes.

A shadow passed over him. He shifted his gaze to the form looming in front of a Coleman lantern.

The form grunted. "Guess I didn't hit you hard enough."

The voice brought Pete's mind back in focus even if his eyes were still blurry. "Screwed up again, didn't you, Brown?"

Richard Brown, a.k.a. Gabe Webber, chuckled. "From where I stand, you're the one who screwed up."

Pete rolled onto one side—the side that didn't hurt. Except that meant pushing up with his bad arm. He gritted his teeth and did it anyway. Nothing broken.

He ran one hand through his hair, fingering the start of a goose egg. He slid his other hand down one leg, hoping Brown wouldn't notice or would think Pete was rubbing another sore spot.

"If you're looking for your backup weapon, it's right here."

Pete raised his eyes. Brown stood a few feet away, leaning on his rifle as though it were a cane and holding up Pete's revolver like a trophy. The Glock had gone flying. Where was it? Pete shot a furtive glance around the floor. Glass, dirt, plaster, bird shit and feathers, and some other kind of droppings too. But no sign of a gun. Did Brown have it?

Pete shifted and turned his head. Zoe sat on the floor, her back to the wall, her eyes wide with terror. Her white uniform shirt was smeared with blood. Hopefully not hers. Her hair looked matted and pasted to her head. Even in his brain fog, he could see she was trembling. And she was tied.

But she was alive. He gave her what he hoped was an encouraging smile.

She didn't appear the least bit encouraged by it.

"So now what?" Pete asked Brown.

"Now I finally get to watch you die. Like you watched my son die eleven years ago."

"Your son was a thug. A drug-dealing punk. He shot my partner." Pete touched his chest. Acted as if he were rubbing it. Maybe Brown would think he was having chest pains. In truth, he was taking inventory. Brown had checked his ankles and taken the revolver he kept there. But he'd left the Kevlar vest. Probably figured on a head shot at close range.

"Donnie was a good boy. He was going through a rough patch. But he'd have gotten himself straightened around if you cops had given him half a chance."

"If I'd given him half a chance, he'd have killed my partner and then me."

"I don't believe that for a minute. You were out gunning for kids who just happened to be on the street at night."

Pete unzipped his raincoat and again touched his chest. The button cam was still in place. But it must not be working. If he'd been unconscious as long as he had to have been for Brown to light the Coleman and search him for the revolver, Baronick and every officer within fifty miles would be blasting through that door by now. However, he felt a few lumps still hidden in his shirt. Brown hadn't discovered all of his borrowed "toys."

"What's wrong with you?" the gunman asked.

Pete made a face. "Pain. In my chest. It's nothing."

"Oh no you don't. You aren't gonna croak from some heart attack before I get a chance to get my justice."

"Justice?" Pete snorted. "You don't know the meaning of the word. You killed two good men. Brave men who put their lives on the line to save others every single day. How is that justice?"

"None of them was there to save my boys. Either one. As if losing Donnie wasn't enough, I had to go and lose Rick too."

"That was an accident. Horrible, yes. But there wasn't a thing anyone could have done for him."

"You don't know anything about it." Brown's voice cracked. "After Donnie, Rick was all I had in this world. If those so-called medics had gotten there sooner...done something more...he'd still be alive. Now I got no one." He swiped an arm across his nose. "But at least I'll have my justice."

Pete sensed the man was getting ready to make a move. For Zoe's sake, Pete couldn't let that happen. "And what good will that do? You're not getting away this time. I saw you had the quad in the back of the pickup. Every law enforcement officer out there knows who you are and what you've done. There's no place you can hide. Not anymore."

Brown lifted the revolver. Studied it. "That's unfortunate. I set this up originally to look like a random killing. You would have been just another unlucky sap taken out by an unknown assailant. Then the killings would have just stopped. Eventually, the case would be filed away. Unsolved."

"That's not going to happen now."

"I know." His voice trailed off into the dark. "Doesn't really matter though. I have nothing to live for. My boys are both gone. I'll let your friends take me out too, and then I'll be with my kids again. But—" Brown brought the revolver up. "Not before I have the pleasure of watching you die."

THIRTY-TWO

Zoe's heart pounded on the inside of her sternum. She watched the interaction between Pete and Gabe, trying to piece it together. But the *why* didn't concern her as much as the *what*. What was Gabe going to do? What kind of plan—if any—did Pete have? And what was going on with his chest pains?

The chill of the dropping temperatures combined with her sodden clothes was making her loopy. Her bound hands and feet had lost all feeling.

Neither Pete nor Gabe appeared to notice when she shifted to one hip and drew her knees in. She wiggled around until her right shoulder supported her against the wall. A little more and she wrapped numb fingers around the Glock at her side.

In the moment when Gabe had fired at her and she dove to the floor, showered in splinters from the bullet piercing the wall above her, Pete had crashed through the door and sprawled on the floor with a hard thud.

Something heavy and cold had struck her in the dark. She'd touched it, realized what it was, and had scooped it close to her. Gabe had been too busy relighting the lamp and searching Pete to bother looking for the gun. Especially after he located Pete's ankle holster and revolver.

Gabe's voice rose in a crescendo. He lifted the revolver, its muzzle aimed at Pete.

It was now or never.

She rolled onto knees she could barely feel and brought the Glock up. "Drop the gun. *Now.*"

Gabe turned his head to look at her with crazed eyes. But the revolver didn't budge.

Neither did the Glock, in spite of her bound wrists forcing her to clutch it with something other than the proper grip she'd learned at Citizen's Police Academy. Zoe fought a smirk. She could do this.

To save Pete, she could definitely do this. Her voice had been strong and firm.

In one move—smooth and fast as a big cat—Gabe stepped toward Pete and dropped behind him. The rifle hit the floor. But Gabe had Pete around the neck and had the handgun jammed into Pete's jaw. Same as he'd shoved the rifle muzzle into hers back on Ridge Road.

"You put the gun down," Gabe said. "Or so help me, I'll blow his brains out right here and now."

Zoe met Pete's gaze. *What do I do now?*

Pete's eyes didn't waver. "Shoot him."

"What?" The mortified question popped straight from her thoughts and out her mouth.

"Shoot him."

Gabe's hand trembled. He rammed the gun into Pete's jaw harder, and he winced.

Shoot him, he'd said. Had he gone mad? Gabe was using Pete as a human shield. Zoe could see maybe half of Gabe's face. None of his body. A target that small...she'd stand a much better chance of hitting the wrong man.

"Zoe. *Shoot him.*" Pete clawed at his chest. Maybe he was having a heart attack.

Maybe he figured he was dead either way and wanted her to—

No. The gun felt heavy and awkward with her wrists strapped together. She couldn't take the chance.

"Zoe," Pete said again, his voice dropping lower in timbre. "Zoe...Oo-*rah.*"

That night...not even a week ago...the same shot...but in a simulator. She'd made it then. But—

She caught a glimpse of something shiny against Pete's chest. And she squeezed the trigger.

The rain had finally stopped, but dawn was still a couple of hours away. Zoe sat in the passenger side of Baronick's black unmarked car, wrapped in two blankets, with the heater blasting on high. And she was still cold.

The driver's door swung open, and Pete slid behind the wheel. He reached across the center console to put an arm around her and pulled her toward him, pressing a kiss to her forehead. "How are you doing?"

"I don't think I'll ever be warm again."

"A hot bath and a bowl of soup will help."

She thought for a moment about inviting him to join her in the hot bath, but decided now was not the time. "Is Gabe...?"

"He's alive. Lost a lot of blood, but he'll probably make it." Pete nodded toward the ambulance backed close to the schoolhouse door. "They're about ready to transport him."

Zoe knew Tony and his partner would take good care of the man who had killed or tried to kill several of their own. "Any word on Earl?"

"Still in surgery." Pete gave her a squeeze. "He's tough. And leaving him your phone no doubt saved his life."

Zoe leaned into Pete's shoulder, not caring about the console digging into her side. "I wish I knew what you had planned in there. I mean, what if I'd really taken the shot the way I did at Citizen's Academy? I'd have killed you."

Pete laughed softly. "I trusted you to know the difference between real and simulated. And I trusted you didn't really want to risk putting a bullet into me."

If only he knew how befuddled she'd been thanks to the cold, he might not have been so trusting.

"The shot you took over our heads was just the distraction I needed." Pete patted his chest.

Zoe hadn't been able to tell earlier that the shirt he had on was not his usual uniform blouse. Now she knew it was borrowed from county's TAC team—courtesy of Wayne—and contained several hidden pockets, which held a knife and another small pistol. Pete's feigned chest pains allowed him to work open the Velcro closures without Gabe hearing the *rip*. When Zoe fired high—*way* high—Pete pulled the knife and buried it into the killer's upper right chest.

A rap on the driver's window drew their attention. Pete released Zoe and powered down the window. Wayne leaned inside. "Break it up, you two. You're fogging up my windows." He winked at her.

"Get lost," Pete told him, only a hint of humor in his voice.

Wayne ignored him. "How are you feeling?" he asked Zoe.

"Cold."

"DeLuca said to tell you the other ambulance is on the way, and you're both to go with them to the hospital."

Pete and Zoe rebelled in unison.

Wayne held up a hand, silencing them. "I'm only passing the information along. But Pete lost consciousness and needs to be checked for a concussion—"

"I'm fine," Pete said.

Paramedic mode kicked in, and Zoe looked at Pete. "Wayne's right." She turned to the detective. "But I don't need to go to the hospital. They'll wrap me in heated blankets, draw a bunch of blood to find out I'm still alive, and then they'll send me home with a big ER bill."

Pete's suggested soup and hot bath sounded more appealing as well as more effective.

He closed his fingers over her hand. "Tell you what. I'll go if you go."

She considered arguing, but decided she'd rather ride in the ambulance with Pete, both of them relatively unscathed, than face being escorted back to Rose's house by Wayne or one of the other officers. "Okay."

"Good. That's settled," Wayne said. He looked at Pete. "And for the record, if you were one of my men, I'd have suspended you. What the hell was that busting-down-the-door thing you pulled?"

Pete shrugged. "It's a good thing I'm not one of your men. I did what I had to do." He gently nudged Zoe. "And I'd do it again. No regrets."

The smile he gave her warmed her more than the blankets or the car's heater.

He turned back to Wayne. "Thanks, by the way, for the use of County's gadgets. I need to talk the township supervisors into buying me one of those night vision scopes." Pete touched his chest. "Maybe a couple of these shirts with the secret pockets too."

Wayne stuck his hand in front of Pete palm up and wiggled his fingers. "Speaking of...Hand over the button cam."

Pete looked down and tugged the front of his shirt. "Doesn't work anyhow."

"It works just fine."

"You mean you knew what was going on in there and didn't send in backup?"

Wayne grinned. "You had it all under control. We were in place and ready to breach the whole time."

Pete clenched a fist. Wayne didn't appear eager to stick around and find out exactly how pissed Pete really was, so he snatched the button cam and ducked away.

Once Pete had powered the window back up, he looped his arm over Zoe's shoulders again. She gazed through the windshield as Tony wheeled the yellow Stryker gurney through the shattered schoolhouse door and into the back of Medic One. From where she sat, she couldn't see her truck, which she assumed was still parked next to the building. She unwrapped the blankets enough to look at the front of her uniform shirt and the palms of her hands, still covered in a mix of Bud Kramer's and Earl's dried blood. "I may take your advice and sell my truck."

Pete eyed the red smears for a moment before bundling her back up. "Good idea. After we release it from evidence."

"And after I get it detailed. And the driver's door replaced."

"Yeah." He straightened and reached for his seat belt. "Buckle up."

"But—the ambulance. We're supposed to—"

"We will. I'll drive us to the Med Express in the morning."

"What if—you know—Wayne or somebody needs to question us?"

"He knows where I live." Pete dropped the gearshift into drive. "And you'll be in police custody."

Blessed warmth made its way to her cheeks. "Police custody?"

He shot her a crooked grin. "Yeah. In my bathtub."

THIRTY-THREE

Nearly a week had passed since that bitter rainy night at the schoolhouse. Zoe sat astride Windstar, her face upturned to the glorious autumn sun.

"Beautiful day for a ride." Pete patted her leg.

She looked down at him standing next to her. "You should come along."

He laughed. "Me? Ride a horse? I don't think so."

"I could give you lessons."

"Definitely not. If I'm going to make an ass of myself, it's not going to be in front of my girl."

My girl. She liked the sound of that.

Behind her, a joyous whoop followed by cackling laughter drew her attention. She turned in the saddle to see Patsy aboard Jazzel, who was galloping and kicking up her heels, while a beaming Allison loped along behind on a lazy bay borrowed from one of the boarders.

Everyone was enjoying the gorgeous weather.

Zoe faced forward once again and gazed down the slope at the newly constructed modular home on the site where the Krolls' farmhouse once stood. Three men worked on the finishing touches to a large deck from which the older couple would be able to look out over Route 15 and the rest of the valley.

"You miss living here," Pete said. It wasn't a question.

"Yeah. I do."

"Move in with me."

She met his earnest icy blues and realized this time he wasn't joking. Her heart lurched in her chest. "Rose and I have been best friends almost all my life, and she couldn't put up with me for more than a week." Stupid dishwasher. "I don't want to wear out my welcome with you too."

"You won't."

She wasn't so sure. "I'm not the easiest person to live with."

"Neither am I. We'll make it work."

She looked at the distant hillside dotted with Angus cattle. The idea of sharing Pete's life—his house, his bed—appealed to her. In theory. But in reality? "I'm not ready."

He lowered his face. "But you're moving out of Rose's."

"I have to if we're going to keep on being best friends. We had a long heart-to-heart the other night. It wasn't just the kids who were affected by everything that happened last winter. Rose is having problems finding a new normal too. The dishwasher and my cats made an easy target. The truth is, she's just not ready to share her space with anyone else right now. Including me."

"Where will you stay?"

"With Earl and Olivia and their kids. For a while. He's being released from the hospital tomorrow. I can help take care of him while she's at work. And they all love animals. An occasional fur ball won't upset anyone."

"But you can't stay there forever."

"No." Zoe felt Pete's gaze on her and met it. "Maybe by the time I've worn out my welcome there too, I might be ready for..." She couldn't bring herself to say it.

"For me?"

She smiled.

"Hey!" Patsy galloped up beside them. Jazzel was feeling full of herself, throwing her head and jogging in place as Patsy attempted to rein her in. "You ready to ride or are you gonna just sit on that fat old gelding all afternoon?"

"I'm ready."

Allison rode up at an easy lope, as relaxed as Zoe had ever seen her.

"You sure I can't entice you to come along?" Zoe asked Pete.

"Positive." He patted Windstar's neck. "Have fun. And whenever you're ready, I'll be waiting for you."

She laid the rein alongside the gelding's neck and touched a heel to his girth. She knew Pete didn't just mean this afternoon.

And she had a feeling she might be ready sooner than he realized.

ANNETTE DASHOFY

USA Today bestselling author Annette Dashofy has spent her entire life in rural Pennsylvania surrounded by cattle and horses. When she wasn't roaming the family's farm or playing in the barn, she could be found reading or writing. After high school, she spent five years as an EMT on the local ambulance service, dealing with everything from drunks passing out on the sidewalk to mangled bodies in car accidents. These days, she, her husband, and their spoiled cat, Kensi, live on property that was once part of her grandfather's dairy.

Her Agatha-nominated Zoe Chambers mystery series includes *Circle of Influence, Lost Legacy, Bridges Burned* and *With a Vengeance*.

**Books in the Zoe Chambers Mystery Series
by Annette Dashofy**

CIRCLE OF INFLUENCE (#1)
LOST LEGACY (#2)
BRIDGES BURNED (#3)
WITH A VENGEANCE (#4)
NO WAY HOME (#5)
UNEASY PREY (#6)
CRY WOLF (#7)

Henery Press Mystery Books

And finally, before you go...
Here are a few other mysteries
you might enjoy:

A MUDDIED MURDER

Wendy Tyson

A Greenhouse Mystery (#1)

When Megan Sawyer gives up her big-city law career to care for her grandmother and run the family's organic farm and café, she expects to find peace and tranquility in her scenic hometown of Winsome, Pennsylvania. Instead, her goat goes missing, rain muddies her fields, the town denies her business permits, and her family's Colonial-era farm sucks up the remains of her savings.

Just when she thinks she's reached the bottom of the rain barrel, Megan and the town's hunky veterinarian discover the local zoning commissioner's battered body in her barn. Now Megan's thrust into the middle of a murder investigation—and she's the chief suspect. Can Megan dig through small-town secrets, local politics, and old grievances in time to find a killer before that killer strikes again?

Available at booksellers nationwide and online

Visit www.henerypress.com for details

MACDEATH

Cindy Brown

An Ivy Meadows Mystery (#1)

Like every actor, Ivy Meadows knows that *Macbeth* is cursed. But she's finally scored her big break, cast as an acrobatic witch in a circus-themed production of *Macbeth* in Phoenix, Arizona. And though it may not be Broadway, nothing can dampen her enthusiasm—not her flying cauldron, too-tight leotard, or carrot-wielding dictator of a director.

But when one of the cast dies on opening night, Ivy is sure the seeming accident is "murder most foul" and that she's the perfect person to solve the crime (after all, she does work part-time in her uncle's detective agency). Undeterred by a poisoned Big Gulp, the threat of being blackballed, and the suddenly too-real curse, Ivy pursues the truth at the risk of her hard-won career—and her life.

Available at booksellers nationwide and online

Visit www.henerypress.com for details

LOWCOUNTRY BOIL

Susan M. Boyer

A Liz Talbot Mystery (#1)

Private Investigator Liz Talbot is a modern Southern belle: she blesses hearts and takes names. She carries her Sig 9 in her Kate Spade handbag, and her golden retriever, Rhett, rides shotgun in her hybrid Escape. When her grandmother is murdered, Liz high-tails it back to her South Carolina island home to find the killer.

She's fit to be tied when her police-chief brother shuts her out of the investigation, so she opens her own. Then her long-dead best friend pops in and things really get complicated. When more folks turn up dead in this small seaside town, Liz must use more than just her wits and charm to keep her family safe, chase down clues from the hereafter, and catch a psychopath before he catches her.

Available at booksellers nationwide and online

Visit www.henerypress.com for details

Made in the USA
Middletown, DE
18 January 2020

83308330R00155